CHARMED, I'M SURE

THE DEVIL YOU KNOW: BOOK 2

CHRISTINE POPE

CHARMED, I'M SURE

Published by Dark Valentine Press

Cover design by Lou Harper

Formatting by Indie Author Services

PROLOGUE

ALLAN D'ALESSANDRO—KNOWN IN A FORMER life as Asmodeus, left-hand man to the Devil himself—scowled at the screen of his laptop and shut it with the kind of force definitely not intended by the manufacturers at Apple. A slight crunching noise told him that he'd probably just cracked the screen, but right then, he didn't really care. He had far more important issues to worry about.

Still frowning, he got up from the couch in his living room and walked over to the sliding glass door so he could let himself out into the backyard. Usually, standing there and taking in the expansive vista his home in the Hollywood Hills offered was enough to allow him to relax, to remind him of how good these past ten months here on Earth had been, but in that particular moment, he could only see the blazing headline on the entertainment website he'd just visited.

Hot Rising Star Inks a 3-Movie Deal...and Finds New Romance!

The "hot rising star" in question was Nina Nomura, five feet ten of exquisite Irish/Japanese/African-American lusciousness. She'd also been the only woman in his life...up until six weeks earlier, when she'd informed him out of the blue that hey, it had been fun, but it was time to move on.

"I'll always be grateful to you, Allan," she'd said, her hypnotic green eyes shimmering with emotion. Exactly which emotion, he still wasn't quite sure, although he was certain she'd practiced that expression in the mirror to make sure it vibrated with the correct amount of intensity. "But we always knew this thing between us wasn't going to last. Actually, this is probably the longest I've ever been in a relationship with someone."

Had that comment been intended to make him feel better? If so, she'd woefully underestimated him.

Then again, it wasn't as though Nina had really known who she was dealing with. He'd never told her the truth about his identity. Revealing that he was a fallen angel who'd spent the last several millennia helping Lucifer run Hell hadn't been a stipulation of the agreement that had allowed him to remain topside all these months, living the life of a successful Hollywood agent, right down to the house in the Hills and the fancy cars in his garage, and he'd figured it was probably better to let the status quo remain in place for the time being. *One day,* he'd always promised himself whenever he began to waver and think it was time to come clean. *One day, I'll tell her the truth.*

Except she'd bailed on him, and now he could only be relieved that he hadn't revealed any of his secrets to her after all. Not that she would have believed him to begin with. Like his master Lucifer, Asmodeus was very good at blending in with humankind, and he knew the façade he presented to the world was nearly flawless.

A fresh breeze was blowing in from the ocean, bringing with it a faint scent of salt air. The cool touch of the wind reminded him that the summer and autumn had come and gone, and the end of the year loomed depressingly close.

Two weeks. He had two weeks to truly lose his heart to someone, and to have her love him in return. Otherwise, it was back to Hell, and he could kiss this house and the Tesla roadster and the parties and all the trappings of this glamorous life he loved so much goodbye.

And if the prospect of losing this lovely exis- tence wasn't bad enough, he'd also have to deal with Beelzebub's gloating. The other demon was still in Hell, running things now that Lucifer had found true love and become mortal himself. Unlike his other two compatriots, Beelzebub had absolutely no desire to be anywhere except precisely where he was, acting as lord and master of the underworld. He might not be particularly thrilled to have Asmodeus back, although it was pretty much a given that he'd still take advantage of the opportunity to torment his fellow demon over his failure any chance he got.

Asmodeus told himself that he didn't begrudge Nina her current success. From the moment he spied her at that film festival at the ArcLight Cinemas in Hollywood this past February, he'd known she had a face destined for stardom. But did she have to embark on a torrid affair with her new agent without even attempting to hide their romance?

Something that sounded like a growl escaped his throat, and Asmodeus shoved his hands in his pockets, telling himself to get over it, since Nina so obviously had. And really, he wasn't even sure if he'd ever been truly in love with her, since he'd never spent so much time with a woman before and didn't know for sure what being in love even felt like. Madly in lust, certainly…easy enough to do when you were dealing with a woman who looked like Nina Nomura. But those three special words had never escaped his lips, although they'd crossed his mind once or twice. For some reason, though, he'd hesitated, had decided to remain silent.

Now he knew why. Because he'd realized that there was no way Nina would have ever offered them to him in return.

"Bad day?" came a man's voice, one that Asmodeus knew well enough. Talk about the last person he wanted to see today.

He turned away from looking at the view and spied an elderly gentleman in a tweed jacket standing on the far side of the swimming pool that dominated the backyard. The man was regarding him with something that looked like sympathy in His dark eyes, and yet Asmodeus knew better than to trust even that small sign of compassion. After all, it was God's fault that he was in this position in the first place.

"No, it's a great day," he said, making sure he sounded casual and breezy, as though he didn't have a care in the world. No doubt God would see right through the bravado, but Asmodeus still felt better for responding in such a manner. "I mean, look at that view."

"It is quite splendid," God agreed. He came around the deep end of the pool and paused a few feet away from the spot where His fallen angel now stood. "So, I can suppose that what just happened to your laptop screen was simply an accident?"

Asmodeus ran a hand through his hair. Since it had been precisely cut to fall in an artfully messy manner whenever he made a gesture like that, he knew it still looked just fine. "Human artifacts can sometimes be quite…fragile."

"True enough," God said, giving a thoughtful nod. "I just thought I should come and check on you, see how you were doing."

As if that was necessary. By His very nature, God knew everything that was going on in Asmodeus' life, just as He was able to see everything in the lives of all His creations. No, this little visit was the Creator's way of letting His fallen angel know that the clock was ticking…and ticking a bit more loudly with each passing day.

"I'm fine," he rasped. So much for sounding suave. Asmodeus cleared his throat. "Just enjoying my Saturday."

"Hmm." God took one more glance at the view, then glanced up at Asmodeus. "Christmas isn't all that far off."

Subtle. "It's still a week away. And two weeks until the end of the year."

That painfully obvious comment earned him a smile. "Yes, I know, my boy. I am able to count."

"Yes, of course," Asmodeus said quickly, even

as he told himself, *Maybe it would be better if you just shut up....*

However, he knew he had to ask, even if he guessed his request would be immediately shot down. "I don't suppose you'd be interested in giving me an extension...say, another six months?"

That appeal only earned him the mildest of frowns. "The bargain was until the end of the year. When I first offered it, you seemed happy enough with the conditions of our agreement."

"That was before I knew I was going to waste almost ten months with Nina," Asmodeus snapped, then wished he'd taken the effort to moderate his tone. Getting tetchy with one's Creator was generally not considered a good idea.

God lifted an eyebrow. "You shouldn't look on it as wasted time. You enjoyed yourself while you were with her, didn't you?"

Of course, Asmodeus had. The sex had been varied and abundant, and Nina had such boundless energy for hedonistic pursuits that even a demon might have found himself a bit worn out by her nonstop partying. Maybe that was part of the problem; the days had passed in such a whirl of activity that he honestly hadn't paid much attention to the weeks and months slipping right by him. When she'd brought him back to reality with a screeching halt, it was much later than he'd thought.

"I did," he responded, since to say otherwise would be a lie...and God could spot a lie before it even left someone's lips.

"Well, then." The Creator picked a piece of lint off the sleeve of His tweed jacket and let it drift on the wind. "Perhaps you learned something about yourself in the process."

If his relationship with Nina was supposed to have taught him a lesson, Asmodeus couldn't think of what it had been. Not to put all his eggs in one basket, he supposed; he probably should have tried to line up a few other prospects, just in case things with her went sour. Unfortunately, even though he possessed many otherworldly powers, turning back time so he could return to the past and fix the things he'd screwed up was not an option.

"No, I'm afraid the deal will have to stand as is," God went on. "I'm sorry things didn't work out with you and Nina, although I rather doubted they would. She's simply not your type."

Asmodeus wished it was permissible to give the Creator a good shake. However, since he knew better, he did his best to keep his tone mild as he inquired, "And what exactly is my 'type'?"

The question only elicited another smile. Despite His otherwise aged appearance, God did have very good teeth. "Well, I suppose you'll have to discover that for yourself, won't you?"

About all Asmodeus could do was shrug. He didn't trust himself to do anything else.

"Well, then," God said. "I'll leave you to it. Have a good day."

And then He disappeared.

Since Asmodeus could come and go in much the same way, he didn't even blink at the way his Creator had removed himself from the backyard. Instead, he crossed his arms and stared down at the streets of Los Angeles, many hundreds of feet below the spot where he stood. Somewhere down there was the woman who could ensure his continued existence here, who would make it so he would never have to leave this place and dwell once again in the dreary confines of Hell, where the air was cold and dank and smelled of decay, where the winds carried the unceasing moans of the dying and creature comforts such as Netflix and Uber Eats were in short supply.

However, after Nina had cast him aside like a used tissue, he'd realized it was time to start making some contingency plans, although he'd allowed himself far more time to brood over her desertion than was wise. The past few days, though, he'd been thinking back over the women he'd met over the past several months, trying to recall if there was anyone in particular who'd stood out for him. Actually, he'd seen a very likely prospect at Lucifer—that is, Luke Nicolini—and Christa Simms' wedding, just a few weeks before Nina had so heinously dumped him. At the time, Asmodeus had noticed the woman in question simply because he was in the habit of noticing pretty women, even if he'd considered himself happily attached. Now, though, he found himself thinking of her again.

It shouldn't be that difficult to have his path cross hers. He wouldn't even have to waste any time finding out exactly who she was, because Nina, as Christa's maid of honor, had mentioned the young woman's name several times. Belinda Carson, Christa's wedding planner.

Good thing he'd always been a sucker for redheads....

CHAPTER ONE

THIS WAS ALWAYS THE TIME DURING A wedding when I could start to relax just the tiniest bit—the bride and groom were safely married, the pictures taken, the food served and the cake cut. All I had to do at this point was make sure that no one threw up in the chocolate fountain or harassed the band to play "Fat-Bottom Girls" or something else that might upset either the mother of the bride or one of the bridesmaids, depending on who was feeling more sensitive on any particular topic, and I should be home free.

But, as I'd learned the hard way a long time before, it wasn't over until it was over. Relaxing was for when I got home, not while I was still on duty.

I stood off to one side of the reception hall, watching as the various 325 guests at the Richman-Lowell nuptials danced or chatted or availed themselves of the open bar once more. Eyes narrowed, I noticed how one particular tall, blond guy in his early thirties was in fact staggering toward the bar yet again. Lewis Lowell, the bride's cousin, and obviously someone who'd attended mostly so he could get drunk on someone else's dime.

"You want me to do something about that?" asked Dee Rodriguez, my assistant. She'd just come back from fetching me another bottled water from my car while I continued to keep an eye on things; I liked to bring my own supply rather than drink from the water provided for the guests. A fine point, but doing so made me feel a bit more professional, someone separate from the assembled reception-goers.

I shook my head as I took the bottle of water from her, along with the key fob to my car. After slipping the key into my pocket—I wouldn't buy a work dress that didn't have pockets—I said, "Not yet. I mean, the guy's obviously had a few too many, but he's not being obnoxious or anything. With any luck, he'll pass out behind the cookie bar."

Dee grinned. As usual, her dark magenta-dyed hair was styled into perfect 1930s-style finger waves, and her red lipstick and cat-eye liner were on point. I admired the work she put into her appearance, even though I knew I myself would never do anything that would make me stand out so much from the crowd. A wedding planner should be unobtrusive, polished, but not overly done. Or at least, that was how I convinced myself that I didn't need to put too much effort into my looks.

After all, the last thing I wanted was to attract attention…particularly male attention.

"Okay," Dee said. "I'm pretty sure I can convince some of the groomsmen to haul him away, though, if he gets out of hand."

"Noted," I replied. "Is the top layer of the cake safely stored?"

"Yep. And the matron of honor and best man have promised me that it'll go home with them, so I don't think we have much to worry about."

That was one handy thing about this particular wedding—the best man and matron of honor were husband and wife, and so they could be counted on to be helpful partners rather than bickering rivals the way those individuals had been at some of the other nuptials I'd planned. Of course, there was always the chance that the top layer of the cake might get absconded with by someone on the wait staff, as had happened at one of my previous weddings, but the odds of that happening again were, I hoped, fairly low.

And even if someone decided to walk off with

that layer of red velvet cake with amaretto-laced cream cheese frosting, it wouldn't be the end of the world. I could always have the bakery make another, and substitute it without the bride and groom even noticing. After all, they were going to be jetting off for Aruba the next morning, and the cake was going to sit in their friends' freezer until they got back. No harm, no foul.

"Then I think our work is pretty much done," I told Dee. "You can go on home—it looks like smooth sailing from here."

Dee's perfectly lacquered lips pursed for a second or two. This wouldn't be the first time I'd sent her home before the reception was officially over, but she always felt compelled to protest. "I don't mind hanging around."

I knew she didn't, but there was no reason for her to stay. Part of the reason people hired me was that my weddings almost always ran smoothly, with a minimum of drama. Or rather, any nuptial drama was caused solely by the members of the wedding party or their family, and not by me. An event planned by Carson Creations would have good weather, caterers who showed up on time, a flawless kitchen, and flowers that never wilted.

Magic?

As a matter of fact, yes. While I knew better than to divulge the truth about myself to any of my clients—or anyone at all; even Dee didn't know anything about the supernatural side of my personality—the fact of the matter was that I just happened to be a witch from a long line of witches. I couldn't do anything truly earth-shattering, but a few little charms to make things run smoothly, a snap of the fingers to get a red wine stain out of a wedding gown or to make sure that champagne uncorked too early didn't go flat, could definitely go a long way toward ensuring a successful event.

"It's fine," I told Dee. "Anyway, it's almost midnight, and things are winding down. Go home. We've got our hands full with finalizing the Blankenship wedding next week anyway."

That reminder made Dee roll her big brown eyes. "No kidding. I can't wait for that one to be over."

To tell the truth, neither could I. While I really tried not to judge any of the brides I worked with, and always reminded myself that they were dealing with their own particular set of stressors, Melissa Blankenship was a real piece of work. A transplant from Texas—and a former Miss Rodeo Something-or-other—she wanted everything to be bigger, more expensive, more flamboyant. And since her fiancé played second base for the Dodgers, they had money to throw around. Although it was often fun to work on a wedding where the budget wasn't really an issue, in this case, the apparently bottomless coffers involved only made my life more difficult, since every time I thought Melissa had finally settled on something, she'd change her mind once again as soon as something new and shiny crossed her path.

"Seven more days," I said lightly. Seven more days, and then we could take a break. The Holloway/Blankenship wedding was scheduled for December twenty-second, and I didn't have any more events planned until after the first of the year. My company handled both weddings and big corporate parties and events, but I'd turned down several New Year's gigs just because I knew the Blankenship wedding was going to wipe me out.

"Feels like seven years, but yeah." Dee scanned the crowd, but everyone seemed to be behaving—in fact, I could tell the party was tapering off, people quietly gathering their coats and other belongings and slipping away—and it was pretty obvious that there was no real need for her to stay. "Then I'll see you Monday."

I smiled at her. "Have a good rest of your weekend."

She nodded and headed for the exit. I pulled my phone out of the pocket unoccupied by my Mercedes' key fob and checked the time. Eleven forty-seven. We had the room until one o'clock, and I hoped the attrition I'd already noticed would begin to accelerate the closer the hour got to midnight; the hotel staff was contracted to do the actual clean-up, but I had to stay until everyone was gone and gather any purses, wraps, lost earrings, or other abandoned personal items I might find in the room. If I were lucky, I'd make it home to Santa Monica by one-thirty. If not, my head probably wouldn't hit the pillow until after two.

Thank God I didn't work on Sundays. Well, all right, I worked, in that I checked personal emails and read industry blogs and put together vision boards for upcoming events, but I kept my work cell phone turned off and also wouldn't allow myself to look at work emails until Monday morning. That was part of the reason why I always stayed until the bitter end at any events I was managing; better to be out until the wee hours than get called back in on a Sunday morning to handle something I'd left undone. I actually always gave the manager at any venue that was hosting one of my weddings or parties my personal cell phone number in case of dire emergency, but I knew they wouldn't abuse that privilege. However, I'd learned the hard way that if actual clients thought you were accessible 24/7, then they'd be calling in the middle of the night or first thing in the morning on a weekend, and I had to have some boundaries. Not many, but a few.

"Hey, pretty lady," a slurred voice said from behind me, and I turned to see the drunk cousin standing there, looking definitely the worse for wear.

Great. Obviously, I'd sent Dee home a little too early.

But I reminded myself that I could certainly handle a guy who'd had one too many martinis… or whatever it was that he'd been drinking all night. And no, not by putting a hex on him or something; I didn't practice that sort of magic. But because of the curse I labored under—a curse put on the entire line of Carson witches long before I was even born—I was used to deflecting male attention.

"Hi, Lewis," I said, my tone casual. It always helped to address these types by their names, which was why I made a habit of learning the names of as many of the guests as I possibly could…especially the ones who seemed as if they might cause problems somewhere down the line. And since I'd heard Tanya, one of the brides-maids, talk about what a jerk Lewis was, I knew I had to keep an eye out for him. "Are you looking for your table? I can walk you back over there—"

"No," he cut in, bleary eyes fixed on my face. Or at least, I hoped that was where he was looking. I wore a simply cut sheath dress in a muted beige, the sort of thing calculated not to attract any kind of attention, but right then, I got the impression that it wouldn't have mattered if I was wearing a potato sack. "Let's dance."

It actually sounded more like "lesh dance," but I got the point. Pasting the phoniest of smiles on my face, I said, "I don't dance, Lewis. But thanks for the offer. Why don't you go sit down for a bit?"

Stubbornly, he shook his head. "No. Wanna dance. C'mere."

And he reached out to slip his arm around my waist.

Oh, hell no. I did my best to evade his grasp, but he had the luck of the drunk and managed to catch me in the crook of his elbow. And, like a lot of drunks, he was exerting way more force than he needed to. I found myself smashed up against his chest, even as I pushed against him with my free hand—I was still holding the bottled water Dee had brought me—and protested, "Lewis, I don't want to dance. I'm working."

"Working at a wedding?" he scoffed, and began to drag me toward the dance floor.

I stumbled along, doing what I could to pry myself from his grasp. The last thing I wanted was to cause a scene, but clearly, my more subtle efforts to get away weren't working. Probably a stiletto to the balls would have stopped him in his tracks, although I had a feeling if I took that kind of drastic action, I'd have to spend the next six months repairing my reputation and doing my best to assure any prospective clients that I didn't generally have a habit of kicking people's wedding guests in the nuts.

Lewis tried to pull me closer to him, even as he swayed along to "You Are the Reason." I gritted my teeth and resisted as best I could, grinding my heels into the carpet rather than into his groin the way I would have preferred. "Really, I *am* working tonight. I'm the wedding planner."

"Wedding's over."

Well, that was true, but—

A stranger's voice at my ear. "Is this man bothering you?"

I craned my head as best I could and saw an attractive man in a very expensive suit standing about a foot behind my right shoulder. He had sandy blond hair and actually looked halfway familiar, although I couldn't say for sure where I'd seen him before. Most likely, an event I'd planned in the recent past, even if I couldn't remember which one.

"Back off, buddy," Lewis said. "She's with me."

The stranger lifted an eyebrow. His eyes, which I thought were blue, met mine. "Are you?"

"No," I said at once. "I'm afraid Lewis here has had a little too much to drink—"

"Have not," he cut in, tightening his grasp on my waist. I couldn't help wincing a little.

Obviously, the stranger noticed, because his mouth compressed in distaste. However, his voice remained smooth as he said, "Oh, I think she's right, friend. I think you need to go someplace to sleep it off."

As he spoke, he lowered a hand to Lewis's shoulder. Almost at once, the drunk man blinked, got as far as saying, "Wha…?", and then promptly collapsed in a heap on the floor.

I let out a startled gasp and backed away, even as the stranger bent toward me and murmured, "Best to let someone else handle this, I think."

Sure enough, two of the groomsmen converged on Lewis's limp form, slipped their hands under his arms, and raised him from the floor so they could drag him over to a chair and lower him onto it. Almost immediately, he began to sag sideways, but, as the luck of only the very drunk would have it, he toppled over on the table instead of back onto the floor. Since the groomsmen had had the sense to deposit him at an unoccupied table, he didn't seem to be bothering anyone there.

"I should really see if there's someone who can

drive him home—" I began, but the stranger shook his head.

"Not to worry," he said. "The groomsmen will handle it."

I stared at him in consternation. He seemed very assured, although I couldn't guess why. It wasn't as though he was a member of the family, or of the wedding party, or I would have known who he was.

A smile, and he said, "Look."

I glanced back over at Lewis. The two men who had carted him over to the table were now talking with a third. Apparently, they reached some sort of agreement, because all three of them hoisted him again and took him out through one of the exits.

"There," the stranger said. "All taken care of." A flash of a smile, showing extremely white teeth. He was very good-looking, although not really my type, since I tended to go for dark-haired men.

Right. Like I had a type. Mostly, I did whatever I could to make myself as unavailable as possible.

"I'm Allan," he went on. "Allan D'Alessandro."

The name sounded familiar. I did a hasty mental flip through the Rolodex I carried in my brain and then remembered where I'd heard it before. "You were at Luke and Christa Nicolini's wedding."

He looked pleased. "Right. Not a member of the wedding party, but Luke and I are old friends."

Something about the way he said "old" made me think there was some subtext to his words that I really hadn't caught, even if I couldn't begin to guess what it was. Allan looked to be in his mid-thirties, maybe seven or eight years older than my own twenty-seven, and Luke was probably a couple of years older than he, although I'd never asked.

Maybe they'd known each other in New York. At least, I assumed they must have met there, since that was where Christa told me Luke had moved from. He hadn't lived in Los Angeles for even a year, and yet he'd already made a pretty big splash, attending lots of charity functions, setting up his own foundation to support a variety of local nonprofit organizations. From what I could remember, Allan was some sort of entertainment-industry agent....

It clicked into place suddenly. He'd been dating Nina Nomura, the actress who'd come out of nowhere to a starring role in an HBO limited series and now was moving on to feature films. I spent a lot more time reading celebrity gossip than I would have otherwise cared to, mostly because it never hurt to get wind of engagements before other people did. So far, I hadn't done any A-list weddings, but I figured it was only a matter of time.

Anyway, I couldn't help but feel a little sorry for the man who stood before me, now that I knew who he was. From what I'd been able to tell, he'd done a lot to get Nina's career started, and then she'd dropped him like a rock once she was established enough that she didn't need him anymore. And also, I had to be grateful to him for rescuing me from Lewis Lowell. I supposed I would have extricated myself eventually, but whether I would have been able to do so in a way that didn't make a scene was an entirely different story.

I held out a hand. "Belinda Carson."

"You did a wonderful job on Luke and Christa's wedding," Allan said.

"Thank you," I replied, hoping against hope that the compliment hadn't made me blush. Luckily, the lighting in the reception hall was dim enough that maybe he wouldn't be able to notice. "They're lovely people—very easy to work with."

For some reason, Allan's mouth quirked. "Yes, I suppose they would be." He paused for a second, then said, "I know it's late, but would you be interested in getting a cup of coffee after this?"

Damn. He was friendly and attractive and

seemed kind, all qualities that should have made him a great prospect for sharing a cup of coffee… except I didn't dare do such a thing. The last thing I wanted was to like him…or, even worse, have him like me.

"I'd like to," I said, then went on, knowing I needed to quash the hopeful expression on his face, "but I really can't. I have to stay after the reception is over and help with the clean-up. I won't be out of here for at least another hour, probably more."

"Pity," he responded. "But I understand. Have a good evening, Belinda."

Then he sent me another of those megawatt smiles and headed off toward the exit, pausing for a moment to exchange a few words with one of the wedding guests. After that, though, he was gone, and I allowed myself a melancholy sigh.

Maybe at some point, I'd get used to letting men walk right out of my life.

CHAPTER TWO

I OPENED MY EYES AND STARED AT THE ceiling of my bedroom, at the white-painted beams and the little crystal chandelier that hung from the center of the space. Usually, when I woke up the day after a big event, I always had a sense of well-being, even if I was tired from being out so late the night before. Still, weariness could never take away the satisfaction of knowing that I'd steered yet another wedding to a successful completion, or the realization that I had an entire day to myself before I had to hop back on the merry-go-round to take another ride.

That particular Sunday morning, though, I mostly felt irritated…and I knew exactly why. Despite my best efforts, I kept seeing the flash of Allan D'Alessandro's smile, hearing the warmth of his voice, which hovered somewhere between tenor and baritone and was strangely reassuring. Or maybe I'd only found it reassuring because he'd been the one to intercede with Lewis Lowell on my behalf. Either way, I couldn't seem to get Allan out of my mind, which annoyed me no end.

This goddamn curse would be a lot easier to deal with if my hormones would just cooperate.

I sat up in bed and pulled off the scrunchie I always wore to sleep to keep my long hair from tangling overnight. It fell against my shoulders, dull copper in the soft light slipping past the bedroom curtains. Maybe it was my imagination, but I could have sworn I'd noticed Allan giving my hair an admiring glance the night before.

Still, it didn't matter if he admired my hair, or whether he thought I was this generation's answer to Helen of Troy. I absolutely couldn't see him.

All right, that wasn't exactly the truth. Sure, I could see him. I could even sleep with him if I wanted to. The one thing I absolutely could *not* do was allow him to have any real feelings for me.

Well, if I was going to start brooding about the curse for the millionth time, I definitely needed some coffee first.

I slid out of bed and went over to the closet so I could put on yoga pants, a pair of Uggs, and a sweatshirt. Thus attired for my morning, I headed out to the kitchen.

Not a moment too soon, as Mr. Mittens, my

cat, appeared in the hallway and gave a loud meow to let me know what he thought of my sluggish behavior this morning.

"Like you're not used to it by now," I remarked as I got out a can of Blue Buffalo chicken paté and then dumped it into his bowl. "Wedding last night, remember?"

Of course, he didn't respond, because he already had his head in his bowl and was chowing down. I had to say that for my feline friend—unlike a lot of cats, he ate pretty much whatever was put in front of him, although I was careful about what he ate, since I wanted him to stick around for as long as possible. Noting that it looked a little low, I refilled his water fountain setup and put it back down on the floor next to his food dish.

The cat taken care of, I could now attend to my own needs. I got out a K-cup of French roast and stuck it in my Keurig, then pressed the button to get the brew cycle going. Almost at once, the warm scent of coffee began to fill my small kitchen, and I pulled in a breath, savoring the aroma.

Unfortunately, thinking about coffee led my thoughts back to Allan. He hadn't seemed that disappointed by my rejection the night before. Maybe he'd asked someone else out for coffee after I turned him down, although it had looked to me as though he left the reception almost immediately afterward. I hadn't really been able to check for sure, since then it was time to wind things down, to have the band play the last dance and for the partygoers who still remained to say good night to the bride and groom before the couple headed upstairs to their suite. And once that custom had been followed, I was busy helping to get the site tidied up, switching into flats once the guests were gone so I could get some actual work done.

All through the routine, though, I'd kept thinking about Allan D'Alessandro—and during the drive from downtown to my house in Santa Monica as well, although by that point, I was tired enough that the only thing I really should have been concentrating on was getting home safely. That sort of behavior was very unlike me. My business brought me into contact with quite a few men, actually, whether they were vendors or relatives of the bride and groom or managers at the various event spaces I utilized. I would never say I didn't notice some of them, because that would be a lie. However, I'd gotten pretty good at noting a man's good looks and then moving on, and making damn sure I had a repertoire of believable excuses in case any of them showed the slightest sign of interest in me.

True, I'd done that with Allan D'Alessandro at

the reception, turning him down as soon as he made the request. What I hadn't done, though, was file him away and move on. No, I'd kept thinking about him, which was definitely not a good sign.

The Keurig machine beeped, and I went to get a mug from the cupboard and fill it with my morning dose of caffeine. I always allowed myself one cup, but after that, I drank green tea all day—my work usually kept me wired up enough that there was no need for me to do much more than maintain a very mild caffeine buzz during the rest of my waking hours. Sleeping was hard enough without being completely juiced when I finally went to bed each night.

To my big, empty bed.

"Stop it," I said aloud, and Mr. Mittens gave me a semi-curious glance from his big amber eyes before he stalked over to the back door, the one that opened on the yard, and gave a peremptory meow. He had a litter box, but he much preferred to go outside. Since he'd never shown any interest in exploring beyond the backyard—which was fairly large by Santa Monica standards—I went ahead and let him out.

My cat's commands obeyed, I could finally allow myself a sip of coffee. Strong and black, exactly what I needed after getting barely six hours of sleep. During the week, I forced myself to go to bed by eleven, just so I could try to get around seven hours, but it was tough. There was always one more email to read, one more website I needed to visit, something else I needed to add to my to-do list for the next day.

Not that I needed to do any of those things this particular Sunday. No, while there were a few chores I needed to manage and errands I should run, there probably wasn't enough on the schedule to prevent my thoughts from straying back to Allan. As far as I'd been able to tell from reading the gossip sites, he'd been lying low ever since his relationship with Nina Nomura flamed out, but I wasn't sure whether that was because he'd been nursing his wounds for the past month —or however long it had been—or because TMZ and that lot really had no reason to be following the romantic exploits of a Hollywood agent, no matter how successful he might be. It was Nina the gossip-mongers were interested in, not Allan.

Was I the first person he'd approached since being dumped? I hated to think about how I'd shot him down when he was probably still stinging from Nina's rejection, but I really didn't have much of a choice. The last thing I wanted was to lead him on. And that was all having coffee with him would have been. A relationship with me was doomed to failure before it ever got started…all thanks to my great-great-great-to-the-umpteenth-power-grandmother.

According to my mother, Carson women had been witches going back into the hazy mists of time. Our powers weren't strong enough to make us really stand out from ordinary women, but we'd always had a little something extra. My ancestors had always been able to fly under the radar, though…until Harriet Carson came along.

Family legend said she was a beauty with flaming red hair. I had to take that on faith, though, because no portraits of her had survived. At any rate, sometime around 1720 in Massachusetts, she'd fallen seriously in lust with a man named Thomas Sinclair, who just happened to be married to a rival witch.

As you can imagine, Thomas and Harriet's affair didn't turn out well for anyone involved.

When Thomas's wife Jane found out he'd been doing the horizontal mambo with Harriet, she flew into a fury. Unfortunately for Harriet, all that fury was directed at her, and not at Jane's own wandering husband. Drawing on all her anger, Jane fashioned a curse strong enough that it had dogged the Carson witches through all their succeeding generations.

Aye, Harriet Carson, you and all the daughters of your line will never know the love of a man or the security of a husband. You will be cursed with only daughters, and calamity will fall upon any man foolish enough to care for you and your own.

As curses went, it was a sticky one. My mother had never gone into detail about exactly *what* had befallen those men who'd lost their hearts to Carson witches from there on out, but my grandmother had let slip one particularly gruesome tale where the unfortunate soul had been thrown from his horse onto a frozen pond, where the ice promptly cracked under his weight, submerging him in the icy water beneath. No one even knew what had happened to him until the ice on the pond melted the following spring. Anyway, thanks to incidents like that, for three hundred years, my female ancestors had to struggle to survive on their own, each Carson witch having exactly one daughter to carry on the line, and no more.

Of course, my mother had a fairly neat solution to the problem—she was gay, and had been happily with the same woman for more than thirty years. In fact, the house I lived in actually belonged to my second mom, Faye. Even twenty years ago, she and my mother had realized the property was too valuable to sell, so they'd rented it out until I was old enough to move in and live on my own. Otherwise, even though I made a comfortable amount with my business, I never could have afforded the place, not when even a modest two-bedroom house like the one I occupied was going for nearly two million in Santa Monica's crazy real estate market.

I never knew anything about my father, except that he'd been the sperm bank donor who appealed the most to Faye and my mother. All right, I also knew he'd been twenty-four at the time he donated his sperm, and that he'd been tall and had red hair and a degree in biology.

"And that's all you need to know," my mother had told me in junior high, when I was feeling restless and wanted to find out more about the man who'd contributed to half my genetic makeup. "They're very careful to keep those donors anonymous. Faye and I are your parents, and that's the important thing."

While even at thirteen I understood intellectually what she'd been saying, I still wished there had been a way to learn a bit more than the bare facts that my father's donor profile had contained. Had I gotten my face shape—slightly narrower and with more of a pointed chin—from my father? What about the hint of green in my blue eyes? I had a pretty singing voice, when my mother couldn't carry a tune. Had that come from my father as well, or was my musical talent... undeveloped as it might be...something that was just the luck of the draw?

I'd never gotten the answer to any of those

questions, and most of the time, I didn't let the mystery of my father's identity bother me too much. In another part of the country, being raised by two women who were obviously romantic partners might have raised a few eyebrows, but even twenty years ago, no one in Santa Monica had batted an eye. My childhood had been a happy one, and Faye was so much a part of my life that most of the time, I forgot we weren't related biologically.

The only real blot on that idyllic childhood had been the Carson curse. My mother had explained it to me as soon as I was old enough to understand its ramifications, around about the same time when I really started to notice boys... and they started to notice me. She'd let me know in no uncertain terms that I couldn't encourage male attention. In fact, she'd even hinted that I would lead a much happier life if I could follow the same path she had.

If only it had been that easy. I was pretty much hardwired to be attracted to men...even if they were forbidden fruit.

All right, not completely forbidden. I could have sex, I could do the same thing that all those great-great-etc. grandmothers of mine had done and had a child without benefit of a husband or any kind of man in my life. But I didn't want that. Although I hadn't been able to say such a thing to my mother—or my grandmother, who'd had a fling with a handsome lawyer back in the day to conceive my mom—I told myself that the Carson line would die with me. Kids were fun, in an abstract way, but my life was busy enough that I didn't even want to contemplate raising one, especially not on my own.

At least, that was the excuse I gave myself.

Mr. Mittens meowed at the back door, and I let him in. He must have sensed something of my edgy mood, because he came up to me and rubbed against my legs, a show of affection usually reserved for the times when he was trying to wheedle a piece of chicken or fish from my dinner. I set down my coffee mug so I could bend over and scratch him behind the ears, feeling him push against me, letting myself take some solace from the sensation of his thick, velvety fur beneath my fingertips. After a minute, though, he'd had his measure of affection for the day and stalked off toward the living room, where he no doubt planned to curl up on the couch and get in his morning three-hour beauty nap.

Going back to bed sounded like a great idea, but I knew I'd never allow myself to escape in such a way. I'd finish my coffee, have some fruit and yogurt, then get out my planner and decide which of the umpteen tasks I'd jotted down for my day off absolutely had to be handled today, and which could be pushed back for a spare moment later in the week.

Spare moment. There was a joke.

I'd just dished up some yogurt and cut some strawberries on top when my cell phone rang. Annoyed, I glanced at the clock on the stove. Just barely past nine o'clock, and definitely not a time anyone should have been calling me on a Sunday morning.

Or rather, not the time that any considerate human being should be calling. However, in my line of work, people tended to forget that event planners needed downtime just like everyone else.

The thing was, that was my personal cell ringing, not my work phone, which I'd left in my tote bag and dumped in my office after I'd come home the night before. That hadn't been an oversight; I made sure to keep the work phone in my office on Sundays, since I'd be less inclined to look at it that way.

I could feel a frown crease my brow as I set down my bowl of yogurt and reached for my purse. I'd left it in the kitchen when I came home, figuring I wouldn't need anything in it until the next morning anyway.

The number displayed on the screen was from the 310 area code, but it definitely wasn't my mother's number, or Faye's, either. Dee's phone had a 323 area code, and anyway, she wouldn't have called me at that hour on a Sunday unless there was a dire emergency.

Answer the call, or allow it to go to voicemail and figure it out later?

I hesitated, then decided the hell with it. For all I knew, my mother had gotten a new cell phone or something, although usually she would have informed me of any big life changes like that. Besides, I couldn't see her changing her number unless she'd been a victim of identity theft or something equally traumatic, and I knew for certain she would have told me about anything so important.

"Belinda Carson," I said, using my brisk phone voice, the one that—I hoped—made me sound as though I was fully dressed and properly made up, and not sitting in my kitchen in a sweatshirt, faded yoga pants, and a pair of beige Uggs with coffee stains on them.

A man's voice, one I thought I should have recognized but didn't. Maybe the caffeine from my French roast hadn't fully kicked in yet. "Hello, Belinda. I'm sorry to call so early. This is Allan D'Alessandro. We met last night at the Richman wedding."

I blinked. What the hell? How had he even gotten this number? The number for my work phone was listed on the Carson Creations website, but my personal cell information was a closely guarded secret. Had I been so rattled by Lewis Lowell's assault that I'd given Allan my number while in some sort of fugue state?

I didn't think so, but I couldn't come up with any other scenario where I would have been crazy enough to give him my personal contact information.

He must have gleaned something of the reason for my shocked silence, because he went on, "I bumped into your assistant—Dee?"

"Yes, Dee Rodriguez," I said, figuring I need to make some sort of reply.

"Of course. Anyway," he went on, "I bumped into her in the parking garage and told her I was interested in working with you on an upcoming event, but that I didn't want to bother you while you were trying to wrap things up at the reception. She said I should give you a call today."

I mentally thought of about five or ten pointed things I needed to say to Dee when I saw her at the office the next day. Yes, she'd been tired, too, but that didn't mean she should have been so out of it as to give a perfect stranger my cell phone number. And all right, maybe Allan wasn't a perfect stranger, since he had rescued me from Lewis Lowell and we'd had a brief conversation afterward. However, Dee couldn't have known any of that, since she'd already left the reception before Lewis started manhandling me.

"Well, Mr. D'Alessandro—" I began in my briskest voice.

"Allan, please."

"Well, Allan." I paused, then went on, "I'd be more than happy to meet you at my office sometime tomorrow to discuss your event."

"I was hoping you could meet me this evening."

Pushy bastard, wasn't he? I supposed he had to be, in his line of work, but if he thought he was going to try to bulldoze me like some producer he was squeezing to get another five percent for one of his clients, he had another thing coming. I didn't bulldoze.

"I'm afraid I don't work on Sundays—"

"Completely understandable, but time is of the essence. You see, I've decided to leave Hart Hathaway and strike out on my own, and I want to have a launch party at my home to kick things off."

Great. Good for him, but I still didn't see why this couldn't be handled on a weekday. But, since I was already on the phone, I figured I might as well find out exactly what he wanted. "And time is of the essence because…?"

"It's going to be a New Year's party. As you know, that only gives us two weeks."

Nice how he said "us" even though I hadn't agreed to anything yet. "Allan, I don't think that's nearly enough time. I generally need at least a three-month timeframe to work with. Two weeks? Not possible."

Now his tone lowered a bit, silky and persuasive. "Everyone says you're a miracle-worker, though."

Yes, but there were miracles, and then there were miracles. I held back a sigh, wondering how best to politely tell him it just wasn't possible.

Before I could speak, he asked, "What's your usual rate?"

Well, that was blunt. But since he'd asked…. "It depends on how much I'm expected to handle. Sometimes people want me to do everything, and some only need me to show up the day of their event to wrangle the caterers and the event staff."

"I'd want you to do everything."

For some reason, my mind went, *Oh, I'd like you to do everything.* And then I told it to shut up, because this was definitely not the time for my brain to go places it had no business going.

"Then my standard fee is fifteen percent of the overall cost of the event." And while fifteen percent didn't necessarily sound like a lot, when you were dealing with a wedding with a budget in the quarter-mil range, it could add up to a very nice payout.

"I'll pay you thirty."

I blinked again. "Excuse me?"

"I'll pay you double your regular percentage," Allan said, apparently in case I wasn't up to mental arithmetic that early in the morning. "It's only fair, since I'm asking you to do this in such a short amount of time."

After being in this business for almost seven years, I hadn't thought I'd be surprised by much. But I stood there, cell phone pressed to my ear, and actually found myself at a loss for words. Although I doubted his party would cost as much as a high-end wedding, thirty percent on an overall budget of even fifty grand or so would definitely make it worth my while.

"Well…."

"Can you come over to my house this evening?" he asked, then added, "I want to hold the party there. I figured that would make things easier, since I'm sure the prime event venues are already booked for New Year's."

He was right about that, although a lot depended on his house and its suitability for a swanky New Year's Eve party. That is, I assumed he wanted it to be swanky, and not luau-themed or something similarly kitschy.

And also assuming that this wasn't a ploy to get me alone in his house. Normally, I would have gotten around that particular concern by inviting Dee along, but I didn't feel comfortable asking her to do something business-related on a Sunday night…even if it was partly her fault that I was in this predicament in the first place.

Besides, I always carried pepper spray in my purse. Mr. D'Alessandro would be in for a nasty surprise if he tried anything funny. Unfortunately, my witchy talents weren't much good for self-defense.

"Sure," I said, hoping he hadn't noticed the way I hesitated and fairly certain that he had. "What time?"

"Six o'clock?"

Full dark at this time of year, but definitely not the middle of the night. I supposed it could be worse. "Address?"

"Fourteen hundred Carlton Crest Drive."

I thought that was somewhere in the Hollywood Hills, but I'd know for sure when I entered the address in my car's nav system. "Got it," I told him. "I'll see you then."

"I'm looking forward to it. Have a good day."

He hung up, and I set my phone down on the kitchen counter and stared at it for a long moment.

I probably should have told him I couldn't do it. In general, I tried to avoid turning down events unless they conflicted with something I already had on my schedule, just because it was never a good idea to alienate people, especially in a town like Los Angeles, where the bride you refused one year could reappear somewhere down the line with a new fiancé and a new set of plans. But this? Two weeks to plan a high-end New Year's party, one that just happened to be hosted by someone I clearly found all too distracting? When all the florists and caterers and valet parking services were already booked?

This could turn into a very big problem....

CHAPTER THREE

ALLAN'S HOUSE TOOK SOME FINDING, THAT was for sure, even with the nav system in my little Mercedes GLA sport-utility guiding me along the twisty roads that wound around the outskirts of Runyon Canyon in the Hollywood Hills. I turned off Franklin just a block before I got to the land-mark Magic Castle, then followed Outpost Drive farther up into the hills, winding around until at last I reached Carlton Crest. My destination was located at nearly the end of the street, meaning the property faced out toward downtown...and that it probably had a spectacular view. As I'd driven over here from Santa Monica, I'd found myself wondering whether the house would really be suitable for hosting the kind of party he prob-ably wanted, but as I pulled into the driveway and looked up at that sleek, modern edifice of gray concrete and exposed wood, I realized I didn't have anything to worry about.

My hand hadn't even touched the buzzer before the front door opened and Allan looked out at me. This evening, he was more casual, in a dark shirt and jeans, but everything fit just as perfectly as the bespoke suit he'd been wearing at the reception the night before. Looking at him, I was glad that I'd taken extra care with my hair and makeup, that I'd put on a wrap dress and heeled boots, dressing like I would for a regular work day rather than the jeans and sweater I'd worn earlier as I ran errands closer to home.

"Belinda," he said. "So glad you could make it out here. Come on in."

He stepped out of the way so I could enter the house. Directly ahead was a short hallway with a set of stairs to my right, but beyond that was a large open space with a wall of glass that looked out onto an expansive yard, one that had a large covered patio and a pool. Beyond the yard, though, was exactly what I'd hoped for—a breathtaking view of Los Angeles in all its gleaming nighttime glory. Just the faintest red glow rested on the horizon where the sun had set beyond the Pacific Ocean.

"It's spectacular," I said honestly, and he smiled, looking pleased.

"Well, let me show you around a bit. Then you can give me your thoughts."

I nodded, and he gave me a brief tour of the ground floor, showing me the kitchen—plenty of space there for catering staff to do any on-site prep that might be required, thanks to the expanse of pale quartz counters and the equally oversized island—the large dining room, the den and the living room. Somewhat to my surprise, a white baby grand piano had a place of honor there.

"Do you play?" I asked. For all I knew, the piano was merely a prop and nothing more. It certainly fit the pale, neutral palette used in the rooms I'd seen so far.

"A little," Allan replied without pausing. "Not as much as I should, though. Let's go outside."

He opened the huge sliding glass door and ushered me onto the patio. It was built on a scale to match the rest of the house, with a long dining table on one side and an outdoor living room with couches and chairs and a slate-topped table. Around the corner, off the dining room, was a sectional arranged around a fire table, and beyond that was the pool, glowing like a brilliant aquamarine in the darkness. And of course, shimmering in the distance was the skyline of Los Angeles, looking about as magical as I'd ever seen it, with the lights of its skyscrapers creating bright patterns against the deep cobalt blue of the night-time sky.

"This is a perfect setting," I said. "Honestly, you'd never be able to do as well as this in a rented venue—at least, not one that would still be available at this late date."

The compliment to his house made him smile again. "I'm glad we're in agreement on that."

I glanced around the yard and patio again, this time looking at them with a professional's eye. "About how many guests are you anticipating? The number doesn't have to be exact, since I assume you're not expecting to serve a sit-down meal, but—"

"Around a hundred, maybe a hundred and fifty, but no more than that."

That sounded reasonable. Enough to make the event lively, but not so many that people would start to feel squeezed. My peculiar gifts would ensure that the weather was fine, and so we'd also be able to utilize all this lovely outdoor space without having to worry about contingencies in case a sudden downpour decided to visit L.A. on New Year's Eve.

"Do you want me to take care of the invitations as well?" I asked.

For a moment, he seemed to consider, and then he shook his head. "No, I'll manage that part of things. I want you to focus on the catering, the floral arrangements, the entertainment."

All the things I was best at. Obviously, I could have assisted with the invitations as well, but all I would have done was pass on Allan's specifications to a graphic designer and a printing company. "What would you like for entertainment?"

"Live music. I was thinking a jazz trio, something that wouldn't be too overpowering."

"I can arrange that," I told him, already flipping through the files in my head to see who might be suitable…and available. At the same time, the breeze picked up, almost cold on this exposed hilltop, and I shivered.

The lighting wasn't all that bright out there on the patio, and yet Allan still seemed to pick up on my discomfort. "It's getting chilly. Let's go inside."

No arguments from me. I followed him back into the living room, then waited as he closed the sliding glass doors behind us. After going over to the coffee table, he bent and picked up a small remote, and pointed it at the narrow, horizontal fireplace built into the travertine on the far wall. At once, a gas fire came to life, sending flickering orange light over the bed of black glass in the hearth.

"Better?" he asked.

"Yes, thank you," I replied, my tone carefully

neutral. Maybe he'd turned on the fireplace to warm up the room a little…or maybe he simply thought having the fire going would make the space a little more romantic.

Don't be silly, I told myself. *He's been all business tonight. It's pretty obvious that he's not going to try anything. For all you know, the only reason he asked you out for coffee last night was so he could talk to you about his party. But you immediately assumed he was making a move on you and shut him down. Typical.*

Apparently not noticing my mental turmoil, Allan headed over to the kitchen and opened the enormous stainless steel refrigerator, then produced a bottle of white wine. "How about a glass of wine to seal the deal?"

On second thought….

"Oh, I don't drink on duty," I said, and his blue eyes lit up with a sort of inner laughter.

"I wouldn't call this 'on duty,'" he responded. "It's not like you're herding wedding guests or something. Just one glass."

My instincts told me that arguing with him would only showcase my reluctance. One glass was definitely not a make-or-break amount of alcohol. And if it made my client happy, then that's what I would do.

"Sure."

He flashed me a grin. "Perfect. Go ahead and sit down—I'll be over in a moment."

I took a seat on one of the long white sofas in the living room, then busied myself with opening up the satchel I'd had slung over one shoulder so I could extract the contract inside. At least by doing that, it looked as though I was focused on business…and I hoped when I handed the contract over to Allan, he'd understand that business was the only reason why I was in his house that evening.

A glass in each hand, he came over to the living room and sat down on the couch next to me. Not too close; he'd definitely made sure to maintain a respectful distance. However, even that modest eighteen inches or so was still close quarters for me, since I could see all too easily the slight wave in his thick, dark blond hair, the fascinating diagonal creases over his deep-set eyes. And he smelled really good, too, something crisp and faintly green, so subtle that I only caught a faint hint of a scent when he moved.

"Um, here's the contract," I said, laying it out on the travertine coffee table, along with a pen.

"A drink first," he countered, then handed me one of the glasses he held.

Since arguing would also attract attention, I accepted the glass and managed to smile. "Here's to a successful venture," I told him.

"And a very happy new year," he added.

Well, I supposed it was a proper toast for a party that would take place on New Year's Eve. We clinked glasses, and I took a sip of the wine. Clean and bright, a faint mineral aftertaste that told me it was pinot grigio, most likely Italian and not domestic. While I didn't pretend to have a sommelier-level knowledge of wines, it was important for me to know something about them so I could help to make educated pairing choices for the events I organized. Of course, some of my clients preferred to ignore my advice, which was their prerogative...even if the results on a few notable occasions had been close to disastrous.

But if the pinot grigio we were currently drinking was any indication, then it didn't seem as if I would have to worry too much about any wine choices Allan D'Alessandro might make.

After he took a second sip, he set down his glass. "Where do you need me to sign?"

I blinked at him. "Don't you want to read it over first?"

The corners of his eyes crinkled in amusement. "I don't think that's necessary. You have a very good reputation, Belinda. I know my friend Luke wouldn't have hired you to manage his wedding if you weren't a consummate professional."

A warm flush touched my cheeks at the praise.

Of course, I did my very best to provide all of my clients with an experience that was as smooth and trouble-free as possible, but I wouldn't deny that I enjoyed hearing Allan say such a thing.

Or maybe there was an entirely different reason why I'd blushed right then.

I took another sip of pinot grigio and said, "Still, I'd feel better if you'd at least glance at it."

Expression still amused, he responded, "All right. Just to make you feel better."

He picked up the contract and glanced over it, blue eyes flickering as he scanned the contents of the document. It wasn't very long, just one sheet of paper printed front and back, with a place for both of us to sign and date it at the bottom. At one point, he paused, took the pen I'd set out for him, and then scratched something out on the contract and wrote something else in its place.

"Is there a problem?" I asked, internal alarm bells going off.

"Not at all," he said. His mouth quirked. "I was just crossing off the part about you getting a fifteen-percent commission so I could change it to thirty percent."

"Oh, right. Thank you."

"I wouldn't want to cheat you, not after you agreed to take on such a last-minute project."

Normally, if a client wanted any changes to my standard boilerplate, I would have entered the updates before I ever left the house and brought an updated contract with me to a meeting. But since Allan had sprung this all on me last-minute, of course I hadn't had a chance to make the necessary alterations.

Even so, I should have thought of that before we sat down to go over the document. That I'd forgotten was a pretty good indication he had me a lot more rattled than I wanted to admit.

Since I'd already thanked him, I managed a smile and swallowed some more of my pinot grigio. Probably not the wisest thing I could have done, since I hadn't eaten anything since noon, and I could feel that gulp of white wine hitting my system almost immediately.

Keep it together, I told myself. *Once the contract is signed, you can get out of here…and then find someplace to grab a bite to eat so you're not driving all the way back to Santa Monica on an empty stomach with all this wine sloshing around in there.*

Allan continued to study the contract, although he'd already moved on to the reverse side of the paperwork. A moment later, he set the paper down on the coffee table so he could sign and date the document. His signature was bold and black, and pretty much exactly what I would have expected it to look like.

When he was done, he handed the pen to me.

For less than a second, his fingertips brushed against mine, and an odd little thrill moved down my spine. Then I pulled in a breath and scolded myself for the second time.

Don't be an idiot. Sign the damn contract.

Which I did, although not with quite as much as flair as Allan had. Still, that signature signaled we had moved past the courtship phase and were now committed to this thing.

Okay, probably not the best way to think of our party-planning partnership.

"Great," I said, in the crispest, most professional voice I could summon. "I already looked over my calendar this week, and I have an opening on Wednesday late morning to go over the menu and floral arrangements. I was thinking of a great caterer in West Hollywood I've worked with many times before—if that works for you."

"It works just fine," Allan replied, again with amusement glinting in his blue eyes. Had he noticed my reaction to him, and was he entertained by the effect he seemed to have on me?

God, I hoped not.

He went on, "I'm actually taking the entire month of December off to get my agency up and running, so my schedule is very flexible. I am at your beck and call."

Was he hinting at something more than

merely being available for appointments with caterers and florists and musicians?

I had to pretend that he wasn't, or I knew I'd never get through this meeting with my dignity intact. "Great," I said. "I'll get in contact with the caterer and the florist tomorrow and let them know our timeframe, and then I'll be in touch with you to confirm."

"That sounds like a plan."

I was pretty sure I smiled. Mostly, I was concentrating on picking up the contract and sliding it back into my satchel, because that way I wouldn't have to maintain eye contact. "Then I think we're all set," I told him. "I'll scan the contract in when I get home and send you a .pdf. Should I text it to you, or would you rather I email it?"

"Text is fine," Allan replied. "My laptop is in for repairs right now."

"Oh, I'm sorry."

"It's nothing. My own clumsiness."

"Then I'll text it to you." I got up from the sofa, satchel slung over my left arm. "You have a good evening, Allan."

He rose as well, gaze intent on my face. "I was hoping I could take you to dinner—my way of saying thanks to you for coming all the way over here on a Sunday night."

There it was. So much for thinking his offer of

coffee the evening before had only been because he wanted to discuss his party with me.

Or maybe I was reading too much into his invitation. He did look almost apologetic, as if he knew that asking me out to dinner wasn't supposed to be part of the program but had wanted to make the gesture anyway.

"Oh, no, that's fine," I said hastily. "Travel is part of my job, after all. And I have a long day tomorrow—lots of meetings—so I think it's better if I get home and make it an early night. But thank you for the offer."

To my relief, he didn't appear too disappointed. "No worries. I'll look for your text with the contract—and I'll wait to hear about our meetings on Wednesday."

His words gave me an opening for a graceful exit. "I'll be in touch as soon as I have everything firmed up," I told him. "Good night, Allan."

"Good night, Belinda."

He walked me to the door but didn't say anything else, only offered a wave as I headed down the front walk to where I'd left my car in the driveway. And he remained standing in the entry while I got in the vehicle, as if to make sure I wouldn't be attacked by any muggers who might be hiding in the shrubbery that separated his lot from the equally imposing property next door.

It was only as I began to back out onto the

street that he closed the door, eclipsing the rectangle of yellow light that had silhouetted his tall frame…and it was only then that I let out a breath I hadn't even realized I was holding.

The next two weeks were going to be…interesting.

CHAPTER FOUR

THE NEXT MORNING AT WORK, DEE WASN'T quite as contrite as I'd expected her to be.

"Well, you got a gig paying double your rate, didn't you?" she asked as she stirred milk into her coffee. I took it black, but she always doctored hers to the point where it must have tasted more like coffee ice cream than the real thing.

"That's not the point," I said. "You know you're not supposed to give my private number to clients."

She blew on her coffee, probably using the action as cover to decide how best to respond. There was no way in the world I would ever fire her over this sort of thing—I valued her help way too much for that—but she also needed to know not to do it again.

"Sorry," she said at last. "I guess I felt sorry for

him. I mean, it can't be easy to get dumped as horribly as he was."

I couldn't argue with that observation. Probably Allan had given Dee a sad puppy-dog look, and that was all it took. I had a feeling he probably also mentioned Luke Nicolini, which would have provided another point of connection to my company.

"He seems to have recovered," I said, then sipped from my own mug of coffee. We were sitting in the little conversation area at the front of the office; Dee and I both had desks toward the back of the space, but we often met with clients on the love seats in this more casual setting, just because it generally helped to relax people and made them think they were sitting down with friends to talk over their weddings and parties, rather than being confronted by someone using a formal desk to maintain space between them.

"Well, good," Dee said. "He seems like a nice guy. Cute," she added, although with the slightest upward inflection at the end of the word, as if she wanted to know what my reaction to him had been.

However, I'd had a feeling my assistant might undertake that particular line of questioning, so I was ready for her. "I suppose so," I replied, my tone careless. "I wasn't paying much attention."

But of course, being Dee, she wasn't about to

let it go that easily. "You *never* pay attention. When was the last time you went out on a date?"

"It's hard to date when you work almost every Friday and Saturday night," I pointed out.

"*I* date."

Which was only the truth, so I couldn't exactly tell her she was wrong. How she managed it, I wasn't sure, but Dee somehow managed to have a fairly active social life. Either she was extraordinarily good at finding men whose schedules were as weird as hers was, or they were willing to be accommodating because they just liked her that much. Whatever the case, she was able to make things work, whereas I…wasn't.

Then again, I didn't want things to work. My whole romantic existence basically revolved around making sure things wouldn't work, no matter how hard a guy might try. Problem was, I couldn't tell Dee that. I had to pretend that I really was trying, and I was simply the victim of bad timing or bad luck, or maybe a combination of the two.

"And I'm glad for you," I said. "Really. But it shouldn't matter how good-looking Allan D'Alessandro is or isn't. He's our client. End of story."

Her mouth compressed, but I could tell from the way she gave a fatalistic lift of her shoulders that she wasn't going to argue the point any further. She knew as well as I did that dating clients was unprofessional. I wouldn't say it never happened in our line of work, but it definitely wasn't going to happen with me. I'd make sure Allan had a great party and would wish him luck with his new agency, and that was all.

And maybe if I was really, really lucky, about five or ten years down the line, Dee would realize that I had no interest in being with anyone. Marriage was a great institution—or so I'd heard —but it simply wasn't anything I was destined to have in my life.

Not for the first time, I reflected on the irony of being in this line of work when the fabled "happily ever after" just wasn't in the cards for me, but, to be fair, I really hadn't set out to be a wedding planner. I'd always had a knack for arranging flowers, and at first I'd thought I might want to be a florist, but then I started doing the window displays at my grandmother's bakery back before she'd sold the business and retired, and those displays caught the eye of a local event planner. Margie had taken me under her wing and began showing me the ropes the summer after I graduated from high school, and then offered me a job as her full-time assistant. I'd been at sort of loose ends—I was signed up to start getting my associate of arts degree from Santa Monica Community College, where my mother had taught ceramics for more than twenty-five years—but deep down, I'd known college wasn't for me. My grades and scores were good, and yet I didn't have a burning desire to spend more time in school. I'd wanted to get out there and do something.

Working for Margie had given me that chance, even though neither Faye nor my mother were very happy with my decision. I understood why; both of my moms worked in education—Faye was a special ed. teacher—and they didn't like the idea of me setting out with only a high school diploma to shelter me from the cruel realities of the world.

But then Margie passed away very suddenly—a massive stroke no one could have predicted—and it turned out she'd left her entire business to me, since she had no children of her own. The five years I'd spent as her assistant had given me connections I could never have managed otherwise, and I was able to build on them and expand the business in the years that followed. Once I started earning more than what my mother and Faye made combined, the complaints about my not having a college degree faded away. I was good at what I did, and it kept me busy enough that most of the time, I simply didn't have the leisure to bemoan the fate that being a Carson witch had bestowed on me.

Except on the very rare occasions when someone like Allan D'Alessandro crossed my path.

Luckily, Dee didn't have the chance to argue the point about the supposed unprofessionalism of dating clients, because nine-thirty had rolled around, and so had Melissa Blankenship and Jack Holloway, stepping through the door right on time.

"Melissa!" I said brightly as I rose from the love seat where I'd been sitting. "How are you?"

She flashed me a smile, showing newly bleached teeth. "I'd like to say great, but my father just texted me this morning saying he wants to bring a date to the wedding, and I told him he couldn't, and then he said he wasn't going to come if he couldn't bring Bimbette—"

"Barbara," Melissa's fiancé Jack put in. He was lean and lanky, with mid-brown hair and friendly hazel eyes. Not the sort of guy I'd probably crane my head to look at if I passed him on the street, but I had a feeling Melissa was more in love with his bank account than anything else.

"Whatever," Melissa snapped. She flipped a lock of bright blonde hair over one shoulder and pouted. "She's still a bimbo. And I don't want her horning in on my wedding."

"Coffee?" Dee asked, probably thinking it was a good idea to distract our client with a beverage.

At once, Melissa shook her head. "Can't. It'll stain my teeth."

"Mineral water, then."

She let out a sigh, as if she'd been hoping we'd offer her champagne or something more interesting than water. However, while I liked to provide some refreshments for my clients, I drew the line at supplying alcohol. "Sure," she said, adding almost as an afterthought, "Some for you, too, Jack?"

He paused for a few seconds, then said, "Actually, I'd like some coffee."

"Jack, your *teeth*."

"My teeth will be fine, Melissa."

Dee shot me a sideways glance, and I allowed myself the barest of shrugs. "It's a chilly day," I said. "Coffee for Jack, please."

My assistant hurried off to get him the promised cup of coffee, while Melissa rolled her eyes but didn't quite dare to intercede. She definitely ranked in my upper tier of Bridezillas, but even she could tell when her fiancé had had enough.

Being Melissa, however, she had to find something to complain about. She sidled over to the window and peered out onto Montana Avenue, the corners of her glossy pink lips turning down somewhat. "It looks like it's going to rain," she complained. "I thought you said it wouldn't."

"I said the weather on the day of your wedding would be clear," I reminded her gently. And that wasn't me working weather magic, but only the long-range forecast supplied by the National Weather Service. However, as the day itself approached, I'd do what was required in order to make sure Mother Nature cooperated. "I didn't say anything about the days leading up to your wedding. Wouldn't you rather the weather got any rain out of its system now?"

She heaved a sigh, one that made her oversized chest strain against the thin sweater she wore. "I suppose. But I'd rather not have to go tromping around Greystone Mansion in the rain."

"Well, let's hope for the best," I said lightly as Dee came over and handed Jack a mug of coffee. He shot her a grateful smile and took a sip. "Besides, we'll probably be spending more time indoors there than out, so even if it does rain a little, we should be fine." I paused there, wondering if I should pick up the thread she'd started about her father's new girlfriend. For the moment, though, Melissa seemed distracted, and I figured it was better to let the topic go for now. If she brought it up again, well, I'd figure out something. The seating charts had already been set, but it wouldn't be too difficult to slide someone else in if necessary.

My cell phone, which I'd left sitting on the

coffee table in the conversation area, began to ring. I shot Melissa and Jack an apologetic smile.

"I need to take this," I said, guessing it was probably the caterer I'd reached out to earlier that morning, right after I got in. "But then we can head out afterward."

I scooped up the phone. Sure enough, the call was from Aux Delices, the company I wanted to use for Allan's party. I hadn't been sure about their availability, but it turned out that the New Year's gig they'd previously booked had been canceled unexpectedly, and they were only too happy to pick up a replacement job to fill in the sudden hole in their schedule.

"Perfect," I told Marcelle, the owner of Aux Delices. "Allan and I will be in Wednesday morning at eleven to go over the menu."

"See you then," she replied, sounding relieved. "I'll put together some samples that I'm sure will impress your client."

I said that sounded great, and ended the call. As I slipped the phone into the pocket of my jacket, figuring I'd transfer it to my purse as we headed out the door, Melissa sent me a disapproving glance.

"Who's Allan?"

From her tone, you'd think I'd been caught cheating on her or something. And while I could partially understand her wanting to make sure I didn't have any other big clients that would distract me from making sure every single detail of her wedding was perfect, I still experienced a flicker of annoyance. I'd been juggling multiple projects for years and knew how to manage my time.

"A client who's having a New Year's party," I said calmly. "You'll be happily off to the Seychelles long before that."

Dee put in, "He's the guy Nina Nomura dumped."

Melissa's brown eyes widened, and an expression of practiced sympathy spread over her features. "Oh, wow. No wonder he wants a party. That girl kicked him to the curb like whoah."

Which she had, but I had a feeling Allan wouldn't really appreciate me sitting around and gossiping about his personal life with my clients. I made a show of glancing at my watch—it always felt more effective to do that than look at the time on my phone, which was the main reason why I wore a watch in the first place—and said, "Well, we need to head out if we're going to make it to Greystone by ten. You'll be following me, right?"

"Yes," Jack replied. He looked relieved that we were about to get the show on the road and not waste any more time talking about Allan D'Alessandro's woes. "Melissa and I are going to leave from there. She has one more final fitting we have to get to."

I nodded, murmuring an inner prayer of relief that I hadn't been invited along on that particular expedition. While I'd been at the boutique for the initial gown selection—a four-hour ordeal that consumed an entire afternoon when I had other matters I needed to handle—once the all-important dress had been chosen, I was no longer required to attend any subsequent fittings. That honor went to Melissa's mother, who appeared as though she'd spent a good chunk of her divorce settlement on plastic surgery to keep herself looking like her daughter's older sister, rather than someone at least a quarter-century older.

Luckily, though, Loretta Blankenship had declined to go on the final walk-through at Greystone Mansion, so I wouldn't have to deal with her during this particular outing. A good thing, because although I'd gotten home early enough the night before, I hadn't slept as well as I would have liked, thanks to my thoughts continually straying to Allan D'Alessandro.

What would have happened if I'd accepted his dinner invitation?

Absolutely nothing, I told myself. *And nothing is going to happen. Period.*

"Shall we?" I said, and ushered Jack and

Melissa out of the office, then waited as Dee followed and locked the door behind us.

Greystone Mansion was located in Beverly Hills, about fifteen minutes away from the Carson Creations office on Montana Avenue. The historic site, originally built by the Doheny family, was operated by the city as a public park, with the mansion itself only open for special events, but on a threatening day like the one we were currently enjoying, there weren't many people out and about on the grounds.

From the dubious glance Melissa sent upward as she climbed out of Jack's Range Rover, I could tell she was rethinking her decision to have an outdoor wedding in December, although I knew she had nothing to worry about. The day of the ceremony would be mild and clear, with temperatures hovering right around seventy degrees. Yes, it would be cooler once the sun began to go down, but I'd already arranged to have outdoor heaters set up for the reception, which would be held in the mansion's courtyard.

The site's event coordinator, Lorraine Chao, met us as we approached the formal garden where the ceremony itself would take place. I'd worked with her several times before, and so I knew we wouldn't have to worry about any surprises on the day of the event. And she was so calm and yet enthusiastic as we walked from location to location, making the final determinations as to where the tables would be placed and the dance floor set up, that even Melissa began to relax, and seemed almost cheerful by the time we were done.

Not a moment too soon, because rain began to fall as we were saying our goodbyes. The bride let out a little screech and put up a hand to cover her artfully curled hair, and Jack guided her back over to his SUV as Dee and I made a break for my little Mercedes.

"That went well," Dee said.

I sent her a sideways glance, just to make sure she was being serious. Actually, I knew things had gone just about as well as they possibly could, but that last-minute rain had most likely gotten Melissa all worked up again. I had a feeling I'd probably get a panicked call from her sometime that afternoon once she was done at the bridal boutique and needed me to hold her hand and assure her for thousandth time that her wedding day would be absolutely perfect in every way.

"About as well as it could, yes," I agreed, maneuvering the car onto Loma Vista Drive so I could guide us down to Sunset and then westward to Santa Monica. The rain had picked up, and I switched on the windshield wipers.

Dee looked at the moisture sluicing down the windshield with narrowed eyes but knew better than to comment on the weather. She'd worked with me long enough to know that there would be miraculously clear skies on the actual day of the event, even if it rained continuously between now and then.

We drove for a few miles in silence, and then she said, "Are you going to need me to work on New Year's, now that you've got Allan D'Alessandro's party to manage? Because I made plans, since I thought we'd be off until after the first of the year once we were done with the Blankenship wedding, but—"

I'd already been anticipating her question, so I shook my head immediately. "No, I won't need you there. He's only planning on a hundred guests or so, and it's not going to be a sit-down meal or anything. I can handle it."

The expression of relief on her face was obvious, but then she frowned. "It doesn't seem right to have you working New Year's by yourself."

"It's fine," I said. "It wouldn't be the first time. And this should be a pretty mellow event. Allan doesn't strike me as the high-strung client type."

"No, he seemed pretty cool." Dee shifted in her seat and gave me a very direct look. "Maybe it's good that you'll be alone with him on New Year's."

Oh, boy. I could feel my fingers clench on the steering wheel and deliberately relaxed them. If I snapped at Dee over her remark, then she'd know that maybe I was just a little more interested in Allan than I wanted to let on. Better to play it cool; she was going to think what she wanted, but there was no need for me to give her any additional ammunition. "Yes, alone with a hundred other people."

A wry grin pulled at her mouth, and she gave a slight hitch of her shoulders, as if to show that she knew I'd scored a point. "Okay. But still."

"But nothing," I said smoothly. I had to return my attention to the road because the rain had begun to come down harder, and, as usual, people were driving as though the streets were dry as a bone. The sooner we got back to Santa Monica and off the road, the better. "I took the gig because I knew I could handle it on my own and wouldn't need to make you change your plans to help me out. Otherwise, I would have told him no."

"Even at double your usual fee?"

"Even with that," I replied, my voice firm. "It's not like we're starving for clients and need the work. Your mental health is more important."

Dee smiled a little, but then she sent me another of her patented laser-focused glances. "And what about yours?"

What about mine, indeed.

But I only shrugged and said, "After the Blankenship wedding, managing Allan D'Alessandro's little soirée is going to be a walk in the park. Honestly, it's probably a good thing it came along, because otherwise, I probably would have been climbing the walls from boredom by the time the first of the year rolled around."

Since Dee had been working for me for the greater part of four years, she knew that remark was nothing more than the simple truth. I hated the phrases "workaholic" and "Type A," but I was sure I'd been labeled with them on more than one occasion. Working hard was just part of the job if you were an event planner, and yet I knew that I put in longer hours than most simply because keeping busy was a good way to distract myself from the wasteland of my private life. Although I'd never confess it to anyone else, I secretly hoped that if I stayed busy enough, focused enough, then one day I'd look up and be my mother's age and well past the point when anyone would bother me about why I wasn't dating anyone or ask why I wasn't married.

My assistant grinned. "I was actually kind of surprised that you hadn't booked anything over the holidays this year. I have to admit, I was having kind of a hard time imagining you having a quiet Christmas."

Most likely because we'd had Christmas weddings the past two years in a row. The brides in question had wanted to combine the magic of the holiday with the enchantment of their wedding day, and I had to admit, it generally wasn't too difficult to get family members to visit California in December, when the weather would be mild and pleasant. Snow was beautiful to look at, but—at least from what I'd been able to tell, having never lived in a cold climate—it could turn into a mess real fast.

"Oh, Christmas will be quiet," I said. "Just Mom and Faye and Grandma and me, as usual. But we like it that way."

Rather, having small, intimate holidays was the only thing I really knew—same for my mother, who, as a Carson witch, had been the only daughter of an only daughter. Faye came from a big family, but they were apparently super-conservative and religious, and they'd basically disowned her after she came out and moved in with my mother. I got the feeling that her parents were still around, but she never talked about them, nor about her brother and sister and various nieces and nephews. More than once, I'd wondered what it must be like to have family out there in the world somewhere and not have any contact with them. However, I'd known better than to ask Faye about the situation, because even after so many years, the topic was still a touchy one for her. No, we made our own small but close family, and my grandmother had always treated

Faye like a second daughter, so she knew we Carsons accepted her even if her own relations didn't.

Dee fingered the shoulder strap of her seatbelt and nodded. "I have to admit, sometimes I'm jealous. A quiet little holiday would be a nice change of pace for me."

That was for sure. Dee came from a big Mexican-American family who'd lived in Highland Park for several generations, and so when they got together for Thanksgiving or Christmas or what-have-you, her parents' big Craftsman-style house was always packed to the gills. I knew this for a fact, since I'd gone there with her several times and always came home afterward feeling a little shell-shocked from all the hubbub.

"You know you can come to my mom's any time," I told her.

"Yeah, but my mother would never let me hear the end of it if I bailed on the Rodriguez Christmas." She shrugged. "It's okay. Besides, I know you'd be disappointed if I didn't come back with a big pan of my mom's tamales."

Oh, yes, those tamales. Dee's mother Isabel made them from scratch every year, pans and pans of them that went home with the various relatives as part of their presents, along with homemade cookies and sweet bread. Dee always brought some of her loot to the office after the holiday, and it had become sort of a Boxing Day tradition for us to sit on the love seats and eat tamales and pore over the January issues of the various bridal magazines.

"True. It's not Christmas without your mom's tamales."

"I'll tell her you said that. It'll make her day."

I grinned. By that point, we were back on Montana Avenue and headed toward the block where Carson Creations' office was located, and so I had to focus on making a left turn at the uncontrolled intersection that would lead us to the parking area behind the building. We were allotted two spaces, thank God, or otherwise we would have had to fight for street parking—never an easy task in Santa Monica, even on a rainy day like this one.

However, I was able to pull into the lot without incident, and Dee and I hurried inside, laughing about the rain, glad that we had our one outdoor task for the day handled. Right then, I figured I could handle just about anything Melissa Blankenship—or the world—might throw at me.

Even my conflicted feelings about Allan D'Alessandro.

UNTITLED

Interlude

Rain beat down against the sliding glass doors in the living room and made a pattern of expanding circles on the surface of his swimming pool, but Asmodeus found he actually enjoyed the view. There was something rather magical about the foggy gray skies, the way the low cloud bank obscured parts of L.A.'s downtown skyline, making it look like a city on a floating island.

And besides, if it poured today, then there was a good chance the weather would be clear on Wednesday for his meeting with Belinda at the caterer in West Hollywood.

In his opinion, things were going quite well. She'd agreed to plan his party, which meant he'd already gotten past the first hurdle. True, she hadn't accepted his dinner invitation, but in all fairness, he really hadn't expected her to. He'd made the offer mostly to see how she would react. As he'd guessed, she'd offered a plausible if not completely bulletproof excuse for why she needed to head home after they'd shared that one glass of wine, and then had gotten away as quickly as possible.

Funny how she could seem so poised and self-assured, making her seem older than the middle or late twenties he guessed she must be, and yet at the same time skittish as a wild horse. He had the impression that Belinda didn't have a lot of experience with men, which he found strange in someone as attractive as she was. Maybe it was only that she was so busy planning other people's weddings, she didn't have any time left over for her own personal life, and yet Asmodeus couldn't shake the feeling that some other factor was at play here.

If he could claim all of his master Lucifer's powers—or at least, the powers Lucifer had once possessed before he became the mortal Luke Nicolini—then Asmodeus would have been able to peer into Belinda's life, to see her thoughts and those of everyone around her. However, while he commanded an array of otherworldly talents that made his existence here on Earth far easier than it ever would be for a mere human, he couldn't read

Belinda's mind, nor the minds of her close family and friends. True, he did have the ability to possess people, and therefore could gather much the same intel that reading minds might have provided.

The problem was, he didn't feel comfortable doing such a thing in this particular situation. He couldn't ignore his attraction to Belinda Carson, nor his hope that the attraction he already felt might turn into something greater, might become affection, followed soon after by love. If he succeeded in this venture and they truly ended up loving one another, he would have to tell her the truth of who he'd once been…and such a revelation would most likely also have to include confessing that he might have possessed her mother or grandmother or assistant, just so he could take a peek into their minds.

While Asmodeus didn't pretend to know everything about human women, he had a feeling that such a revelation probably wouldn't go over very well.

As he frowned, considering how he might go about gathering more information about the lovely but far too cautious Belinda Carson, his former compatriot Beelzebub materialized a few feet away, staring at the white baby grand directly in front of him with his usual expression of jaundiced disapproval.

"Rainy days and Mondays, eh, Asmodeus?"

Asmodeus couldn't quite keep himself from frowning. The whole time he'd been with Nina, he hadn't seen hide nor hair of the other demon. At the time, he hadn't questioned Beelzebub's conspicuous absence, except possibly to be glad that he didn't have to deal with his former partner-in-crime's cutting remarks about his current love interest. Why he should turn up now, Asmodeus had no idea.

He doubted the reason was anything good, though.

For a moment, he was silent, eyeing Lucifer's right-hand demon, now the *de facto* lord of Hell. Despite his scorn for earthly diversions, including fashion, Beelzebub was wearing a downright natty blue plaid suit, complete with bow tie and expertly polished lace-up brown wingtips. His head was cocked to one side as he appeared to wait for his former partner to make some sort of reply.

Asmodeus had often wondered about the variations in their appearance, why they all had a particular look they wore when they mingled with mortals. While they could change certain elements about their looks, they all had a particular default—Lucifer tall and black-haired and blue-eyed, with the sort of presence that people naturally deferred to even if they didn't quite know why. Asmodeus himself was perfectly content with his own dark blond hair and gray-blue eyes, although he didn't know whether he would have chosen that coloring on his own if given the option.

Beelzebub, on the other hand....

Possibly it had been a small joke on the part of their Creator to make the other demon so smoothly handsome, so innocent in appearance, that more than once Asmodeus had mentally referred to him as "baby-face Beelzebub." Nothing he would ever say aloud, because even though the two of them were evenly matched when it came to physical confrontations, he knew that Beelzebub was far more devious and would eventually concoct the kind of revenge that might leave a lasting mark. Still, it was a phrase he repeated to himself now, just to give himself a bit of an edge in whatever stratagem his former friend might be about to launch.

"Hello, Beelzebub," he said smoothly. "Love the suit."

"You would."

The demon came around the side of the piano and let his fingers drift in a dissonant *glissando* down the keys. Asmodeus tried not to wince. He hadn't been lying to Belinda when he'd said he liked to play. The skill came to him easily enough, and he'd found himself sitting here on a surprising number of occasions, songs moving through his head and gliding down to his fingertips, all with unhurried ease.

He hoped he would be able to retain that talent when he became mortal.

If he became mortal. Then again, Lucifer didn't seem to have suffered too much in the transition. True, he couldn't transport himself instantaneously from place to place any longer, and he had to suffer in traffic like every other mere mortal, but it was much easier to contend with that particular hardship when doing so from behind the wheel of a Bentley.

"To what do I owe the honor of this visit?" he asked, then waved his hand. At once, a tray with a couple of glasses of wine appeared on the low table in the conversation group placed a few feet past the spot where the piano stood.

Beelzebub glanced at the wine and smirked. "I'm not interested in such mortal foolishness."

"Pity," Asmodeus said. He left the place where he'd been standing by the window and went to pick up one of the glasses, and took a sip. The wine he'd conjured was a soft, fruity pinot noir from Washington State, something that seemed to go well with the misty gray day outside. "You have no idea what you're missing."

"I'm not missing anything at all," Beelzebub returned. A frown creasing his smooth brow, he went on, "As to your question…well, I just thought I'd drop in to see how you were doing after your little play relationship dissolved."

Play? Asmodeus set his jaw, but he didn't bother to argue, since he knew that was what the other demon wanted. Things with Nina hadn't ended well, true, and yet he knew he hadn't been playing at that relationship. He had wanted it to work—would have wanted such a thing even if his continuing existence in this world wasn't at stake.

No point in telling Beelzebub any of that, though. For one thing, he would never believe that his former friend was capable of genuine affection or concern, mostly because those emotions had certainly never darkened that particular demon's black heart. Also, if he guessed that Asmodeus was being sincere, he would only have mocked him for allowing a mortal to have such power over his feelings.

"I am very well," he said politely. "In fact, I'm planning a New Year's Eve party—you should come, if you're free."

A very slight barb, that one. Because of course Beelzebub was free to come and go from Hell as he liked, as long as he didn't stay on this plane for too long…and also because the current master of Hell had nothing remotely resembling a social life, and certainly didn't have any plans for New Year's.

"What a foolish custom," Beelzebub sneered.

"As if there is any particular line of demarcation from one year to the next."

"I suppose not," Asmodeus said, in his most off-hand tone. "Still, I'm fine with any excuse for a party."

"You would be." The other demon paused for a second or two, then smiled. It wasn't a pleasant smile, though. Probably the expression would have been even more off-putting if worn by someone whose features hadn't bordered on cherubic, but it was still effective enough. "Or are you allowing yourself one last bash before you return to Hell where you belong?"

Irritation flared, but Asmodeus made himself have another swallow or two of wine before he would allow a reply. After all, Beelzebub had said much the same about Lucifer, believing until the end that their master would fail in his attempt to make a mortal fall in love with him and would be forced to return to Hell. It was probably a good thing that Asmodeus had already made his bargain with God and therefore was safely topside when word came down that Lucifer had found his redemption after all. He doubted he would have wanted to be anywhere near his fellow demon after he got that particular piece of news.

With any luck, he'd be able to prove Beelzebub wrong in this particular instance as well.

"I still have some time," he said.

Beelzebub made a derisive noise. Eyes narrowed, he replied, "You had months and months, and what did it get you? A public flogging. You should have returned to Hell last month after Nina dropped you like a hot coal. What makes you think you can succeed now, with so little time left to you?"

Another swallow of wine, and Asmodeus said, "I've already met someone. She is very…promising."

"Who?"

As if he would make the mistake of telling Beelzebub anything about Belinda Carson. Part of the reason she made such a good prospect was that Asmodeus knew he had a perfectly legitimate reason for being in contact with her, one that had nothing to do with pursuing her romantically. Yes, his fellow demon wouldn't have too difficult a time divining that the lovely young event planner might be the object of his intentions, and yet there was no reason to make things easier for him.

"Someone I already knew," he said, still in that mild tone. The statement wasn't too much of a stretch, since he'd first seen her at Luke and Christa's wedding, even if he hadn't actually spoken to her that night. But her path had crossed his, albeit tangentially. Besides, he felt no compulsion to tell Beelzebub the truth. They weren't angels, after all.

That comment made his fellow demon frown, expression distracted, as if he was mentally paging through all the people Asmodeus might have encountered during his time here on Earth and doing his best to see which, if any of them, could possibly be a likely romantic prospect. This was probably a waste of Beelzebub's time, simply because Asmodeus had been quite active socially all these months, meeting literally thousands of people at all the parties, movie premieres, gallery openings, and other outings he and Nina had attended during their months together.

Not that he minded throwing Beelzebub off the scent for a bit. That would give him a little more breathing room to zero in on Belinda Carson and do his best to figure out why she was working so hard to keep him at arm's length. Almost any other time he'd approached a mortal woman, she'd been all too receptive to his advances. The thing was, he got the impression that Belinda was receptive, although on a level she didn't want to acknowledge. He'd noted the way her gaze would suddenly shift away from his, as if she'd realized that their eye contact was a little too intense…and he'd seen the way her mouth parted slightly and her pupils dilated when they were in close proximity. Those were subtle signs of human attraction, ones she probably didn't even know were betraying her, even as she did her best to seem calm and cool and professional.

Because of those small signs, Asmodeus guessed that Beelzebub's vision of him failing miserably and having to return to Hell with his figurative tail between his legs just might be a bit premature.

Still scowling, the other demon said, "Well, I suppose you'll just have to hope that she doesn't mind being your second choice."

"What a peculiar way to look at the situation," Asmodeus returned. "It is a natural human reaction to look for another relationship after one has ended, for whatever reason. They don't think of themselves as being a second choice, but rather a more promising prospect."

"Or a rebound," Beelzebub shot back, surprising Asmodeus. He wouldn't have thought his fellow demon knew such a term.

He shrugged, and drank some more wine. While he couldn't actually get drunk, even while wearing this human form, alcohol still relaxed him —and he needed all the help he could get while dealing with the other demon.

"I suppose that's between the two of us," he said. "But if there wasn't anything else you wanted—"

Annoying as he could be, Beelzebub at least

knew how to take a hint. "Just you back in Hell, Asmodeus. See you soon."

And he disappeared, blue plaid suit and all. Looking at the spot where his former friend had been standing a few seconds earlier, Asmodeus drained the rest of the wine in his glass. Then, with a philosophical shrug, he went over to the table and picked up the glass Beelzebub had ignored, then took a sip from it as well.

No point in wasting good wine, after all.

CHAPTER FIVE

I'D JUST PAUSED AT THE FRONT DOOR OF AUX Delices, the catering company in West Hollywood where I was meeting Allan, when he pulled into the recently vacated spot right in front.

Money and parking karma, I thought. *Must be nice.*

He opened the door of his sleek white Tesla roadster and got out, the bright morning sunlight picking out gleams of dark gold in his hair. Looking at him, I couldn't quite stop myself from thinking how handsome he was in his pale gray dress shirt and charcoal slacks, casual and ultra-stylish at the same time, like James Bond on his day off.

Almost as soon as that thought popped into my head, though, I pushed it aside, and made myself put on a bright, professional smile as I went over to him. "Hi, Allan. I hope you didn't have any trouble finding the place."

"None at all," he replied. "The nav brought me right in."

My gaze slid past him to the car, which sat at the curb looking like a shiny white Star Wars stormtrooper helmet on wheels. "I thought the new Tesla roadster wasn't on the market yet."

Now it was his turn to smile. "Let's just say I pulled in a few favors."

Apparently. What, was he buddies with Elon Musk or something? Thinking of that glossy, ultra-expensive house in the Hollywood Hills, I guessed I wouldn't put it past him. "Well, Marcelle is waiting for us. Let's go see what she was thinking of for your party."

"Of course."

He opened the door for me and I went inside, my high heels clacking a little on the pale drift-wood-hued wood floor. I didn't want to reflect on how gentlemanly he was, how he hadn't even paused to see if I would let myself in. Not that I minded one way or another, but I supposed I wasn't used to that kind of consideration.

Marcelle Chalumet, the owner of the catering company, stepped forward, hands outstretched. She was a cheerful ball of energy in her late forties, with a dark brown pixie cut and bright red lipstick on her wide, friendly mouth.

"So good to meet you, Mr. D'Alessandro," she said, her French accent still pronounced, even though I knew she'd been living and working in the L.A. food scene for more than two decades.

"Allan, please," he responded, and her smile broadened a little.

"Of course, Allan. This way."

She spread a hand to indicate that we should follow her out of the main room, which contained several tables adorned with framed photos of some of their more luscious creations but not much else. Down a short hallway was another, more private room, where she had a variety of small plates set out, each one showcasing a different hors d'oeuvres.

"Belinda didn't mention any particular dietary restrictions," Marcelle said, "and so I thought it best to provide a variety, enough that you should have something for everyone. And also small bites with protein, since it will be New Year's and people will be drinking. You will want us to provide the bartender and full bar service as well, yes?"

That was something Allan and I hadn't discussed in any detail, but I'd assumed he'd want the full Monty, if only because probably not everyone would want to drink champagne all night. To my relief, he nodded.

"Yes, all that. And plenty of champagne as well."

"Of course," Marcelle said. "Do you have a preference?"

"Perrier Jouët," Allan replied.

The caterer looked pleased that he'd requested French champagne. Mentally, I added a few more thousand dollars to the overall budget…not that I guessed it would be a problem.

"Very good," Marcelle said, making notes on the clipboard she held. "And now…the tasting."

Allan looked at the dizzying array of hors d'oeuvres displayed on the table in front of him and appeared vaguely dismayed. "I have to taste all of that?"

"Just a bite each," I said, trying not to smile. "But you need to make sure it all works for you."

"Okay," he said. "Just let me roll up my sleeves."

Which he did, revealing nicely tanned forearms and a slim Patek Philippe watch. I probably didn't want to think about how much that little bauble had set him back…which made me wonder exactly how much a Hollywood agent actually earned. Enough to own a house that was probably worth at least five or six million, and to drive a quarter-million-dollar car that wasn't even available to the general public yet?

I told myself it didn't matter, but I knew that

wasn't exactly the truth. Not that I suspected Allan of laundering money or selling stolen art on the black market or something, and yet, I couldn't quite figure it out. I didn't run in A-list Hollywood circles, but I'd rubbed elbows with enough people in the business that I had a decent idea of who earned how much...and what they spent it on. Something in his portfolio didn't quite match up.

However, I knew nothing about his past, about what he'd done before he came here to Los Angeles. I supposed it was possible that his family back in New York had money, and he was just playing at being an agent because it gave him something to do.

And unless his checks bounce, it's no concern of yours where it all comes from, I told myself as I watched him take a bite of an herb-crusted lamb lollipop.

Or at least, it shouldn't have been my concern. I'd always been one of those people who wanted all the "i"s dotted and the "t"s crossed, and whenever something didn't add up for me, then my brain started poking at the problem, trying to figure out where the short-circuit had originated.

Any questions I might have been entertaining needed to remain unanswered for the time being, though. Like Marcelle, I took notes as Allan tasted filet mignon with shallot marmalade, prosciutto-wrapped cantaloupe, chardonnay goat cheese tartlets, and more. Everything he tried got his seal of approval, and eventually we had the menu worked out, as well as the number of servers— seven—and bartenders—two. That seemed like heavy staffing to me, but I could tell he wanted to make sure his guests didn't have to wait too long for another appetizer tray to be passed, or to have another martini mixed up.

"And you are working with Secret Garden Flowers?" Marcelle asked me. A logical question, since Secret Garden was my go-to florist, although of course I always encouraged my clients to suggest their own if they had someone else in mind. But since Allan seemed content to let me go with my usual vendors, that was the plan. In fact, we'd be heading over to their shop after we were done at Marcelle's, since they were located just a block away.

"That's right," I said. "After Allan and I have made our choices there, then you and Tori can coordinate."

Tori was the owner of Secret Garden, and also someone who was very easy to work with. I often felt blessed in my vendors, because they really helped to smooth the way even if I might be dealing with that month's special flavor of Bridezilla. Not that I had to worry about diva behavior with Allan.

Marcelle said that would be perfect, and not too long afterward, my client and I emerged into the bright sunlight on Pico Boulevard.

"I thought we could walk," I told Allan. "The florist is only a block or so away."

"Good idea," he said with a grin. "I need to walk off some of that filet mignon."

His smile was so dazzling, I was glad I'd put on my sunglasses as we left Aux Delices. And it was probably just the sun blazing down from the clear blue sky that sent a wave of warmth over me.

Or at least, that was what I tried to tell myself.

We headed off toward Secret Garden Flowers. Since I thought silence would be even more awkward than some form of stilted conversation, I made myself say, "I was thinking of muted tones for the flowers…shades of white and cream and pale green. The palette in your house is already neutral, and I thought having anything bright would be a bit too jarring. Does that sound all right?"

"It sounds fine," he replied. "I trust your judgment—you're the expert, not me."

Quite a change of pace from someone like Melissa Blankenship, who'd fought me on pretty much everything from the exact shade of pink roses used in the reception centerpieces to the earrings her bridesmaids—all ten of them—would wear. While I was gratified by Allan's trust, in a way, it put even more pressure on me. I had to make sure everything was perfect.

No worries, I reassured myself. *You've got this.*

The meeting with Tori went as smoothly as the tasting with Marcelle had gone. We agreed on pale hydrangeas in heavy, low blown-glass vases for the tables where the stationary hors d'oeuvres would be served, and tall cylinders of the same bubbly blown glass with submerged lights at the bottom and green amaranthus trailing down the sides as accents in the corners and other places where a festive touch was required. Allan listened to us and nodded at the appropriate intervals, looked over the photo albums of samples Tori provided, and in general echoed all my suggestions.

Less than twenty minutes later, we were back outside and walking toward the block where we'd left our cars. By then, it was a little past twelve-thirty and I was feeling hungry, although I told myself that once I got back to the office, I'd just have one of the Chobani yogurts Dee and I left in our work fridge for occasions such as this when we were going from meeting to meeting and didn't have a lot of spare time.

However, Allan apparently had other ideas.

"How about some lunch?" he asked, just as we were passing a restaurant with a crowded patio full of lunchtime diners. We Angelenos would eat *al fresco* at the drop of a hat, although I had to admit that it was an exceedingly nice day for December. It wasn't as though anyone was shivering under an outdoor heater and pretending they were having a good time.

Despite my current famished state, I made myself say, "I thought you just ate your weight in hors d'oeuvres."

He laughed. "I think I left some room. Besides, you didn't eat anything. You must be hungry."

Of course, I was, although I didn't want to admit it to Allan. While going out to lunch seemed considerably less fraught than the dinner he'd offered me on Sunday night, I still didn't know whether sharing a meal was a very good idea. I didn't want to give him the wrong impression.

At that moment, my stomach gave a very unladylike growl, and he chuckled again.

"I'd say that sounds like a yes. After you."

I murmured a silent curse at my traitorous tummy and then headed into the restaurant, Allan holding the door open for me once again. Although I had to admit I'd been neatly trapped into this lunch, I told myself that if the wait was too long, I'd beg off anyway and use the excuse that I needed to get back to the office for another meeting. It wasn't a complete lie—I did have a client consultation later that afternoon, but it wasn't until three. I had plenty of time to have lunch here in West Hollywood and still make it back to my office in Santa Monica without breaking a sweat.

As luck would have it, though, several groups of people were leaving as we came in, and so we only had to wait a minute or two while a table was bussed for us. Then the hostess seated us and let us know that our waiter would be over shortly.

A fresh breeze played with the edges of the patio umbrella that shielded us from the sun, but it was still comfortable enough, although I was glad that I wore a lightweight sweater over my camisole and skirt. Allan took off his sunglasses so he could get a better look at the menu; out in the daylight like this, I could better see the shifting blues and grays of his eyes, the way the lashes that shaded them were several tones darker than his hair, making the color of those eyes stand out even more.

And then I realized I was staring, and I quickly picked up my menu and pretended to be absorbed in its contents.

The waiter came by, a guy around my own age, slick and perfect, most likely an aspiring actor. Sometimes, I wondered if there was any other kind of waiter in this town.

Before I could ask for an iced tea, Allan

ordered a bottle of chardonnay. I opened my mouth to protest but realized doing so would only highlight my reluctance to drink at lunch, and so I pushed my misgivings aside. One glass wouldn't kill me. If we didn't finish the bottle, the waiter could cork it up and Allan could take it home with him in the trunk of his car.

"I hope you didn't mind," he said, after we'd placed our orders—lemon piccata chicken for him and pasta primavera for me. "It just seemed like such a nice day, we should have some wine to celebrate."

"We're celebrating the nice day?"

His gaze lingered on my face for a second or two, and I had to fight to look back at him without blinking, to pray that the heat in my face wasn't a flush of embarrassment but only a reaction to being outside on a sunny day. "That, and getting everything squared away with the caterer and the florist. I had no idea the process could be so easy."

"You've never thrown a catered party before?" I asked, somewhat surprised. It seemed to me that he must have done this on a regular basis—if not here in Los Angeles, then back in New York before he relocated to the West Coast.

He shook his head and reached for the glass of water that had been waiting at his place setting. "No. I tend to go to other people's parties. I suppose I figured it was time I returned the favor."

I allowed myself a small smile. "Oh, so your motivations for hosting this New Year's bash are purely altruistic, then."

"Well, not purely," he returned, his gaze never wavering. "I'll admit that I do have the ulterior motive of showing my former partners at Hart Hathaway that I'm doing just fine on my own."

Hart Hathaway was one of L.A.'s largest agencies. They repped a bunch of A-list celebs—including Nina Nomura, which I assumed was how Allan had met her in the first place. From what I'd been able to piece together from reading the gossip sites, Allan had been the representative who signed her to the agency, but then at some point, Brian Hart, the company's founder, decided he wanted to take a more "personal" interest in her career. I wasn't sure exactly how it worked to have two members of the same agency fighting over one of their clients, but I assumed that Brian wanted a bigger slice of Nina Nomura's pie.

Well, at least a bigger cut of the substantial earnings she was now generating. Ahem.

Anyway, I could see why Allan wasn't thrilled with Hart Hathaway in general and Brian Hart in particular. Throwing a splashy party to launch his new company would be a good way to show that his former boss's betrayal hadn't hurt him in the slightest.

Figuring that asking a few questions about his new venture should be a neutral enough topic, I said, "And how are things going with your new agency?"

"Great," he replied. "I just signed a lease on an office in Century City, and I'm bringing several agents from Hart Hathaway with me. They're eager for a chance to prove themselves in an environment that isn't as top heavy as their former employer."

Meaning, I supposed, that Brian Hart and his partner, Trace Hathaway, tended to skim the choicest clients off the top, leaving everyone else to fight for the leftovers. If that really was what had been happening, then I could see why some of the more junior members of the firm were looking forward to starting over in an environment that wasn't stacked so heavily against them.

"And you'll be starting up after the first of the year?"

"More like the end of January," Allan responded, then paused as the waiter returned with the bottle of wine. He poured chardonnay for both of us and departed, and Allan lifted his glass. "A toast to A.D. Enterprises."

I raised my glass as well and clinked it against his. "That's what you're calling your new agency?"

"Yes. I want it to be the first thing people think of when they're considering representation."

"It works," I said. "Short, easy to remember."

"That's what I was hoping."

We both drank some more wine, and then he set down his glass and sent me a considering glance, one that was very different from the admiring gaze he'd worn a few minutes earlier.

"What about you?" he asked.

"What about me?" I said, then raised an eyebrow at him. "I'm not interested in getting representation, if that's what you're asking. I'm probably one of the few people living in L.A. who never had any interest in show business."

My frank reply made him chuckle, and he shook his head. "No, what I meant was, how did you end up in the event planning business? How long have you been doing this sort of thing?"

"Nine years," I said, an answer that seemed to surprise him.

"What, did you start when you were in high school?"

"No," I replied, "but close. I was eighteen."

I wondered if he was going to ask whether I'd gone to college, since it seemed to be the standard question that came up whenever I went into any detail about my career path, but he seemed satisfied by my reply and instead asked about how I'd even gotten started doing this kind of work. Since

I'd told the story plenty of times, it was easy enough for me to explain how I'd gone to work for Margie Fitzgerald in her event-planning business, and how she'd left the company to me in her will, since she didn't have any heirs.

"And so, here I am," I finished, then reached for my glass of wine to take a much-needed swallow of chardonnay. "I'm sure if someone had asked me ten years ago what I planned to do with my life, I wouldn't have said I'd be an event organizer, but I really enjoy it."

"You don't get tired of working weekends all the time?"

Was that his subtle way of trying to find out exactly how I managed my personal life with a job as demanding as mine? Maybe, but I wasn't going to tell him that I hadn't had an actual date in more than a year, and that the only social life I currently had consisted of going to the movies with my mother and her wife. All right, Dee and I went out shopping together sometimes, and even had gone to a concert or two, but a social whirl, my life was definitely not. Getting close to someone was too risky. I certainly couldn't talk about my family and its curse, and I was sure if I told anyone I was a witch—albeit a very low-level one—they'd think I was even more woo-woo than most native Californians. Maybe there were still some witches back in Massachusetts, a place the

Carsons had fled centuries ago, but I'd never met a single one here in our adopted state.

"I love my work," I told Allan, which was only the truth. Yes, I had some clients who drove me right up a wall, but I'd still rather deal with temperamental brides than some middle-management jackass who needed to make himself feel bigger by dumping on his subordinates. Most likely, I would have lasted about a day in a corporate job...if even that long. "I guess I don't mind working weekends because it's sort of like people are paying me to go to their parties, you know?"

That answer made him smile, laugh lines crinkling at the corners of his eyes. "I suppose I never thought about it that way. But then, it's not exactly like going to a party during your free time, though. After all, you're still on the clock if there are any fires that need to be put out."

"True," I admitted. "Although I'd rather have to put out fires than make small talk with people I don't know."

"Isn't that what we're doing now? Small talk?"

I supposed maybe it was. Then again, he was my client; it wasn't as though I intended to tell him any of my secrets. Taking care to keep my tone light, I said, "Well, but we know each other, right? It's not as though we've never met before now."

"You have a point." He shifted in his chair,

leaning forward slightly. "And actually, I can't think of anything I'd rather be doing than sitting here and talking to you."

Once again, his gaze caught mine, only this time I found myself looking down at the napkin in my lap, fussing with it rather than continue staring back at him. That seemed more awkward than meeting his eyes, though, and so I glanced up again and said, "All part of the service, Mr. D'Alessandro."

A glint entered his cool blue eyes, and, rather than tell me to call him "Allan," he only said, "Good to know, Ms. Carson."

The waiter came over with our food then, and so for the next minute or so, we busied ourselves with focusing on our meals. Or rather, that was what I did; Allan continued to watch me for a moment before he finally began to eat, although I didn't know what he expected to see in my face. Over the years, I'd gotten very good at being neutral with men who showed the slightest interest in me, so I knew he wasn't going to find any encouragement in my expression.

I wished there could have been. No, I wouldn't have engaged in outright flirtation with him, not when he was my client. However, he'd only be my client until the end of the year. After his party was over and done with, I would have been free to let Allan know I was interested in pursuing a romantic relationship. That is, if circumstances had been normal, then there wouldn't have been anything preventing me from seeing whether the chemistry I'd noticed between the two of us might work out in the end.

Problem was, circumstances weren't normal, and I knew that better than anyone else. Luckily —or unluckily, depending on how you wanted to look at it—this wasn't the first time I'd experienced a physical attraction to someone. I knew that if I ignored the way my body responded to him, eventually, the feeling would go away. And if I kept suppressing those reactions, then they'd die a natural death, like a fire smothered by damp earth.

No, it wasn't fun, but I couldn't encourage him. I didn't want to be responsible for what might happen if he actually began to develop feelings for me. It had been a long time since a man had perished thanks to loving a Carson witch, and I sure as hell wasn't going to break that streak.

After I'd taken a few more bites of my pasta primavera, I managed to say in a normal enough voice, "I think I have the entertainment narrowed down to three candidates. I'll text you some .mp3s of their work after I get back to the office."

"Good," he said. "And after that, we're mostly done?"

His tone was also neutral, and I wasn't going

to try to figure out what might have been going through his head. Had he acknowledged to himself that he'd been shot down, if in the subtlest way possible? I couldn't know for sure, but at least it seemed as if he was willing to focus on the problem at hand, namely, his party.

"Mostly," I said. "Tori will want to do a walk-through with me at your house closer to the date of the party. I was hoping maybe the twenty-sixth or the twenty-seventh?"

If he was disappointed that I was willing to skip right past Christmas, he didn't show it. "That should work. I'll be in town for the holidays."

"So, you won't be going back to New York?"

He blinked at me for a second, as if he didn't quite know where that question had come from. Then he smiled and said, "No. There are some who might say Christmas in New York is magical, but what's magical to me is not having to worry about snow and black ice."

No threat of those kinds of hazards in L.A., that was for sure. "Then why don't we pencil it in for the twenty-sixth, and I'll let you know more about the timing as we get closer to the date?"

"Sounds good."

From there, I went off into brisk logistics, asking if he wanted any kind of pavilion for the backyard, or whether he planned to keep most of the "action," so to speak, inside the house. As before, he seemed agreeable to all my suggestions, and by the time our lunch had concluded, I'd thought we'd done a pretty good job of hammering out the basic framework for the party. I knew Marcelle and Tori would manage their particular details, and therefore I probably wouldn't have a lot to do until after I was safely past the Blankenship wedding and Christmas as well.

And although I didn't want to admit such a thing to myself, I was inwardly relieved that there shouldn't be any need for me to see Allan in person until we met at his house on the twenty-sixth. Even then, I should be safe enough, since Tori would be there and Allan wouldn't have the opportunity to try to get cozy the way he had during our first meeting.

After that...well, I'd only have the party to manage, and then we could be safely out of each other's lives. While I didn't like the idea of never seeing him again, better that than the alternative.

I liked him too much to wish him any harm.

CHAPTER SIX

To my relief, the rest of the work week that followed my meeting with Allan was so full of managing all the last-minute details of the Blankenship wedding, I really didn't have much time to worry about the odd ways I missed him, even though we'd only been in each other's company on two different occasions. Oh, I didn't ignore him completely—I sent him the promised .mp3s from the three different bands I'd selected, and I also forwarded him some sketches Tori had put together for the proposed floral arrangements. However, all that contact was via text and email, and I didn't have to deal with the extremely distracting reality of his physical presence.

In the midst of final bridesmaid gown fittings and a frantic call to an expert colorist in Brentwood to fix the maid-of-honor's hair—she'd tried to go auburn and had somehow managed to turn her long locks a bright orange—I still found myself pausing from time to time, though, thinking of the flash of Allan's smile, or the warm, friendly tones of his voice…such a nice voice, really, smooth enough for a radio announcer but without any of the phoniness.

So much for hoping that his absence would allow him to slip quietly from my mind, that I'd realize I'd only manufactured an attraction to him because the holidays were coming up way too fast and I didn't like the idea of being alone any more than anyone else did. Except…I knew that excuse was utter b.s. I'd survived plenty of Christmases—and New Years' and Fourth of Julys and frigging Arbor Days—without having anyone at my side. This Christmas shouldn't have been any different.

But it was, because I'd met Allan D'Alessandro. And honestly, I tried to be objective about him. The afternoon of the bridesmaids' dress fittings, I'd sat in the boutique and done my best to find every single fault about Allan that I could possibly think of—his eyes were too deep-set, or his lips a little fuller than I liked, his hair a little too perfect—but I had to admit that those small imperfections actually made me like him that much more, since I'd never been one for pretty boys anyway. And by the time I was done, I realized that I hadn't accomplished much except to convince myself that he was probably the ideal man for me.

Which I knew was stupid. There wasn't any such thing as an ideal man, especially not for me. No, I couldn't even have the world's least perfect man, since I wasn't allowed to have a man at all. Not in the way it counted, at any rate.

At that point in my musings, I was compelled to stop torturing myself and step in to prevent Melissa from haranguing one of her bridesmaids —Ashley—over gaining a couple of pounds. Now her gown would have to be let out a bit, which wasn't the federal case Melissa was trying to make it out to be. Once I'd gotten all the ruffled feathers smoothed and had talked Melissa down from going completely nuclear, Allan D'Alessandro had been pushed to the back of my mind.

Mostly.

Saturday, December twenty-second rolled around. As I'd assured Melissa, the day dawned bright and clear, without a cloud to be seen in the entire Los Angeles basin. I was up at six, did my usual stair-step routine while watching YouTube videos in the living room, ate breakfast, and was out the door by seven-thirty. While Dee had gone on to Greystone Mansion to oversee the placement of the reception tables and the deliveries of the linens, flowers, and other odds and ends— including two dozen pure white doves, which would be released as the couple was making their triumphant recessional amongst their hundreds of well-wishers—it was my job to meet Melissa and her wedding party where they were staying at the Viceroy L'Hermitage in Beverly Hills. In the back of my little Mercedes SUV, I had my emergency stash, which included a first aid kit, a sewing kit, duct tape, extra florist's tape, rechargeable batteries, disposable cameras, eye makeup remover, thumb tacks, and just about anything else that might possibly come in handy. I also had my own little bag of makeup, heels, jewelry, and a dress; I dressed casually in the morning because I knew I'd be on my feet all day, and no one except the wedding party was going to see me before I got to the site anyway.

The Royal Suite at L'Hermitage was utter chaos when I arrived. Or rather, it looked and sounded that way, with ten bridesmaids, plus the bride, her mother, three makeup artists and three hairdressers crammed into a space that on paper should have easily accommodated all of them. After all, that particular suite's square footage was roughly double that of my modest home in Santa Monica. However, once you included all those women and their gowns, shoes, makeup bags, hair styling appliances, makeup kits, and various other accoutrements, it was easy to imagine that a bomb had hit the upscale $10k-per night suite.

As soon as I entered the room—Ashley, the bridesmaid who'd earned Melissa's ire by gaining a few pounds, let me in—Loretta Blankenship descended. "You're late," she said in accusing tones.

I actually wasn't, since it was 7:59 a.m. and I had told everyone that I would be there at eight o'clock. However, I'd learned years earlier that arguing with the mother of the bride was never a good idea. "Sorry," I said, hoping I looked at least halfway contrite as I manufactured a plausible lie. Luckily, traffic problems were the one excuse that pretty much always worked in Los Angeles. "There was a nasty wreck on Sunset, and I had to detour. Everything looks like it's under control, though."

Another lie, but Loretta appeared at least partly mollified. "Well, I've done what I could. I'm not sure there are enough plugs for all the curling irons, though."

"Not a problem," I said, then reached into the top plastic box on the rolling cart I'd trundled up to the suite and pulled out a multi-prong power strip. "This should help."

She actually smiled, and in that moment, I could see a hint of the weariness she'd been doing her best to hide behind her brassy bravado. Probably, she was ready for this whole thing to be over with as well.

I went and plugged in the power strip, and got a chorus of "thank-you"s from the hairdressers in attendance. And actually, they did look as though they were managing pretty well, with the hairstylists on one side of the long table in the dining area, working on the bridesmaids two at a time, while the makeup artists had set up on the opposite side of the table, doing their work in tandem so no one would have to wait too long to get buffed and polished to perfection.

As befitted the bride, Melissa sat alone in the dressing area off the bedroom while Yvonne, a stylist at a top Beverly Hills salon, smoothed her long blonde hair into a perfect waterfall of curls designed to look artless and natural but only achievable by someone earning two hundred dollars an hour for her expertise. When I peeked in to see how she was doing, Melissa frowned.

"I'm just sure I'm getting a zit right in the middle of my forehead," she complained, then pointed a French-manicured finger at her brow.

Casey, her makeup artist, was standing off to one side and shook her head. "You really aren't, Melissa. Your skin is perfect."

"But I can *feel* it," Melissa complained, and I stepped forward, knowing that I would have to be the tie-breaker here.

I leaned down toward her where she sat in her chair and frowned as I scrutinized the skin on her forehead. As Casey had said, Melissa's skin was perfect, smooth and tanned a very light golden brown, enough to give her a healthy glow but nothing that would seem too over the top for a Southern California winter wedding. "You look fine," I said in soothing tones. "There isn't a zit. There isn't even a little spot that looks like it's *trying* to be a zit. Take a breath."

Melissa inhaled, but then her mouth turned down again. "I need a drink."

Don't we all, I thought, but I only sent her an encouraging smile. "Now, we talked about that, Melissa. I can go get you a glass of champagne if you really want one, but it could make you puffy. You don't want to be puffy for your wedding pictures, do you?"

As I'd hoped, the mere threat of looking anything less than model-perfect in her wedding photos was enough to make her shake her head. "No, I don't. Can you get me some mineral water, though? Evian, though…not Perrier. The bubbles make me gassy."

"Right away," I promised, and left so I could pick up the phone in the main room and call room service to have a flat of Evian water delivered. I could have bought some from the grocery store and schlepped it over here for about a quarter the cost, but I had to draw the line somewhere, and that was where I'd drawn it. Besides, I doubted Jack Holloway would even notice that teeny line item when he finally got around to looking at the bill for this suite.

Getting eleven women fully styled, made up, and dressed took time, even when you had makeup artists and hairstylists working in concert. It wasn't until noon that everyone was ready to head downstairs and get into the line of limousines that were waiting at the front entrance. During the morning, I'd ducked out several times to check on the groom and his attendants, but they were all doing fine—there was generally a lot less drama on the guys' side of things, mostly because their hair didn't require a lot of work and they didn't have to worry about makeup or squeezing into strapless bras and heels. Or at least, I didn't think they did…I wasn't about to check what was going on under their tuxes.

Because Melissa wanted to make sure she was absolutely perfect in her wedding photos, she'd decided on a "first look," meaning the bulk of the pictures would be taken before the ceremony actually took place. This ignored the tradition of the bride and groom not seeing each other before the wedding itself, but really, with a couple who were already living together, that tradition seemed a little silly anyway. The limos whisked the wedding party off to Greystone Mansion, with me following in my own car once I'd made sure all the stylists were out of the suite and that the house-keeping staff knew to come back in and tidy everything up, set out the flowers I'd ordered, and have the dessert basket waiting on the table in front of the fireplace and a bottle of Cristal chilling in the fridge.

I'd ducked into a bathroom to change and apply my own makeup before I left the suite—I'd styled my hair at the house earlier that morning—and so I was about as presentable as I was going to be. As usual, I wore a simple knee-length dress in a neutral shade just this side of pale rose, with pearls at my throat and ears, but bare fingers and only my watch strapped on my left wrist, just because rings and bracelets could get in the way if I was required to do anything physical during the day. As I drove, I directed my car to call Dee. I'd checked in earlier, but now that D-day was approaching, I had to make sure there hadn't been any last-minute hiccups.

"Hey, Dee, the bird is in flight." That was our code for saying the bride and her party were on their way. Silly, maybe, but wedding days could be long and tiring, and these little games were our way of getting through them with—we hoped—smiles on our faces.

"Copy that, chief," Dee responded. "Base camp is a go."

Which meant that the flowers had been delivered, the tables set up, and everything else at the site was as ready as it could be. I let out a little sigh of relief. Although I'd had no reason to believe everything wouldn't go smoothly, sometimes little glitches popped up at the worst time. At least Mercury wasn't retrograde. I generally preferred to avoid ceremonies during those problematic periods, but doing so wasn't always an option.

"Great," I said. "Arrival in T minus five. See you then."

"Got it. Over and out."

I pushed the button on my steering wheel to disconnect the call and guided the car the rest of the way to the mansion. Because I was working the wedding, I didn't have to use the public lot, but was able to go around back and park next to the caterer's van. I got my little rolling cart of emergency supplies out of the cargo area in my SUV and trundled it through the service entrance, waving a hello at Max, the weekend site manager. He sent me a smile and a quick thumbs-up, meaning there hadn't been any snafus so far.

Dee met me as I was putting my cart in a safe alcove off the kitchen. As usual, her hair and makeup were on point, and I had to wonder how much time she spent getting herself ready in the morning before she left for an event. Still, she'd never been late yet, so I supposed it didn't matter how much time her preparations took.

"Loretta was poking around the courtyard," Dee told me as I headed out toward the formal garden to make sure all the flowers had been placed correctly. Yes, she'd already let me know that "base camp" was ready to go, but I'd be neglecting my duties if I didn't check for myself. Besides, Troy, the photographer, would be waiting for the limos and would handle herding the wedding party for the all-important pictures, so I had time to do a visual inspection of everything. "But she couldn't find anything to complain about, so she headed out front to wait with Troy."

Well, thank God for that. There really shouldn't have been anything for the mother of the bride to find fault with, but that had never stopped anyone before. "And the father of the bride?"

Dee grinned, red lipstick blazing in the clear early afternoon light. "Oh, he showed up about ten minutes ago with his new girlfriend in tow. No wonder Loretta was breathing fire about that."

Lovely. I'd put Barbara—the girlfriend—at a table with a group of the groom's cousins, figuring it was close enough to the head table that she wouldn't feel completely left out, but also not someplace where she would be in Loretta's line of sight. Although more and more couples were opting for "sweetheart tables" these days, where the newly married couple would sit alone apart from the wedding party, Melissa had wanted the traditional setup with a head table, probably so she could sit on a dais and be on display like the royalty she obviously thought she was.

"How bad is it?" I asked, pausing to make a minute adjustment to one of the sprays of white orchids and pale pink roses that adorned the entrance to the aisle on the formal garden's green lawn.

Dee's mouth twitched. "Let's just say that if they'd made her implants any bigger, she probably would have tipped over."

Just about what I'd feared, but there wasn't anything I could do about the situation except hope that Barbara knew enough to stay out of Loretta's orbit. While I might fume inwardly about Joel bringing his new girlfriend to his daughter's wedding, it wasn't the first time I'd encountered this kind of sticky situation, and I knew it wouldn't be the last.

"I guess we'll have to hope for the best," I said. "Everything looks in order here. Let's take a quick trip through the courtyard and along the terrace, and then we'll head over to be with the bridal party. I don't want Melissa to think I'm shirking my duties or something, even though there really isn't much for us to do while the photographer is working."

Dee nodded, and we progressed to the court-yard, which, as she'd already told me, looked picture perfect, with multiple round tables spaced evenly around the flagstone-paved area. At the center of the space was a small walled pond, and arrangements of woven twigs and roses floated there already, the glass candleholders they contained each set with a votive just waiting for the appropriate time to be lit. All of the center-pieces were in place, and tall urns filled with roses and orchids guarded the entrance to the mansion proper.

"Okay," I said. "Looks good."

"Like you were expecting anything else?" Dee inquired, her tone arch.

Of course, I hadn't been; Dee was a profes-sional. I lifted an eyebrow at her, and we headed over to the terrace, where bar-height tables and chairs had been set up, and a fully stocked bar stood to one side. In fact, the bartender was already present, polishing glasses. He flashed Dee a smile and she grinned back at him.

"Hi, Marco," she said.

"Hi, Dee," he returned. "Just getting every-thing ready."

He offered me a smile as well, and I nodded at him. Technically speaking, he really didn't have to be on duty until five, since that was when the ceremony would be concluded and people would head out in search of drinks while the remainder of the wedding photos were taken, but I'd taken the precaution of having Marco manning the bar as early as possible, simply because experience had taught me that members of the bridal party tended to go in search of fortifying drinks while they were waiting for the happy couple to finish having their own portraits done.

Thus satisfied that everything was managed, we went inside the mansion, where Melissa and Jack were in the process of having some photos taken on the gorgeous black marble staircase in the foyer. Standing off to one side and looking at her, I had to admit that she did look very beautiful in her form-fitting shantung gown with her bright gold hair flowing over her shoulders. And Jack was handsome and obviously very proud to be standing next to her.

In moments like those, I could forget all the petty annoyances and early morning phone calls and manufactured crises. The two of them were happy and practically shining from within, and that made it all worth it, right?

Of course, I was probably being a little premature. These were just the wedding photos, not the ceremony itself. Until that was over with, I couldn't quite let myself breathe easy.

But the photo session went beautifully, and I wasn't called to do much more than wait off to the side, my emergency packet of sewing supplies stashed in my pocket while I watched Troy arrange the various groupings of attendants. Then it was time to get everyone in place for the ceremony, and Dee ushered the groom off to the formal garden, while I waited in the house with Melissa and her bridesmaids, getting them water, helping to touch up lipstick that might have faded a bit during the preceding hour.

At last, though, the strains of Pachelbel's *Canon* began to drift into where we waited at the side entrance of the mansion, and it was time to send the bridesmaids and their groomsmen off one by one, until at last Melissa and her father were the only two left.

"You're perfect," I told her in a gentle whisper. "This is your time. Go on."

She smiled at me and blinked—I could see tears shining in her eyes, although I knew she was too much of a professional to let them slide down her cheeks and ruin her makeup—and then she looped her arm through her father's. As they made their way down the steps, I bent and made a quick adjustment to her train, then stepped back out of the way.

Once they were in the garden and had begun to slowly walk down the aisle, I allowed myself to leave the mansion as well, positioning myself behind the back row of chairs so I could see everything clearly. The timing couldn't have been more perfect—a warm glow from the setting sun illuminated the hedges of white roses to either side, and caught in the fountain that would serve as the backdrop for the ceremony itself, the splashing water glittering in fiery jewel tones of citrine and amber and topaz.

I didn't need to listen to the words the minister spoke; I'd heard them many times before. No, I only wanted to stand there and look at how beautiful the scene before me was, how all those hours and weeks of work had boiled down to this one perfect moment. Some people might have thought I was torturing myself by watching a scene play out that I would never be able to experience for myself, but I thought it was exactly the opposite. Maybe I couldn't have a happily ever after, but by watching these couples get married, I could reassure myself that mine was a special case, and definitely not the norm. And as long as I could have that reassurance, I knew everything would be all right.

Then it was done, and Melissa Blankenship was now Melissa Holloway—she'd been adamant about not wanting to keep her maiden name. Part of the job done, but another starting, as Dee herded various family members off to one side for their portion of the wedding photos and I guided the remainder of the guests toward the terrace for the cocktail reception.

It really wasn't too much work, since most people were in the mood for a drink. I brought up the rear, making sure there weren't too many stragglers. As they headed toward the bar, where Marco had been joined by a second bartender, I paused to look back over my shoulder. However, I wasn't able to see very far, because someone was blocking my view. Recognition flared, even as a pair of blue eyes laughed down into mine.

"Hello, Belinda," Allan said.

CHAPTER SEVEN

I GAPED AT HIM FOR A SECOND OR TWO, THEN demanded, "What in the world are you doing here?"...right before I realized that using such an accusatory tone on a client probably wasn't the smartest move in the world.

However, he didn't look offended. Eyes crinkling with amusement, he said, "Last-minute addition. I've been in talks with Jack about representing him for certain TV and print advertising he's considering. He told me about the wedding and asked me to come."

"You weren't on the list," I said flatly.

"Like I said, last-minute addition. I think Jack talked to your assistant this morning, since he knew you were busy 'herding bridesmaids,' as he put it."

That sounded like something Jack would have

said, so I didn't much see the point in arguing. Caterers always padded the number of portions anyway, just in case of little last-minute emergencies or additions to the guest list. No, feeding Allan wasn't the problem…having him here at all was my real concern.

I told myself not to be dramatic. After all, I was working. If he'd thought he could drop in and indulge in a little casual flirtation, he was due for disappointment.

"I see," I said. "Well, I have several things I need to check on, so enjoy yourself."

He still wore that amused look. I noticed that he had on an expertly cut charcoal gray suit with a subtle pinstripe, meaning it was a different one from the suit he'd been wearing at the Lowell wedding the weekend before. Did I want to know how many five-thousand-dollar suits he owned?

Probably not.

And I didn't want to stand there and look at him, because then I'd be forced to notice once again how well he wore a suit, how it showed off his broad shoulders and slim hips and long legs. Luckily, I could make my escape without seeming too obvious about it.

"I'll catch you later, then," he said, and sauntered off toward the bar. Even though people were mobbing Marco and his assistant, they miraculously got out of the way as Allan approached, allowing him to go up directly and ask for a drink.

Magic?

I doubted it, although I was the last person who would ever deny the presence of some very strange supernatural forces in this world. Whatever the reason for the easy way he slipped in and got his martini, I wasn't going to be able to figure it out then. I had far more important matters to attend to.

Shaking my head a little, I left the terrace and went in search of the caterer.

Several hours later, dinner had been served, and everyone was relaxing into drinks and dancing. So far, the only mishap had been a guest tripping and splashing some red wine on the hem of Melissa's gown. Luckily, the accident occurred well after all the wedding photos had been taken. Even so, I got out my emergency kit and took care of the stains. That is to say, I pretended to use baking soda and some white chalk to hide the stains, when in actuality all I did was rub a forefinger over the dress's hem while the red wine magically disappeared.

The air had cooled as the sun set, but the heaters set out on the courtyard were doing their job to keep things comfortable. Overhead, stars glittered in a midnight-blue sky, and a thin finger-nail of a moon hung off to the west. All in all, the wedding was another in a long line of successes I had under my belt, and I had to hope that working on one this high-profile might net me some celebrity clients. That was where you could earn the really big money, although I had to admit that Dee and I had done very well on this partic-ular go-'round.

I hadn't seen much of Allan, except to note that he'd been placed at a table with several of Jack's teammates and their wives. He'd been talking animatedly, hands gesturing, and I wondered if he was trying to talk contracts with any of them, although I never got close enough to actually hear what he was saying.

As I stood to one side, watching as people slow-danced to "Moon River," his voice came at my ear.

"We should dance."

I turned to look at him, glad I hadn't jumped. He did seem to be very good at sneaking up on me…or maybe it was simply that I tended to get lost in the clouds at the worst possible times.

"That again?" I asked, making sure I sounded amused and not irritated. "I'm working, Allan. The Blankenships aren't paying me to dance."

For a moment, he didn't reply, only stood

there as he appeared to survey the crowd before us, from those actually out on the dance floor to the people who seemed content to remain in their seats and nibble on the remnants of their wedding cake as they sipped champagne.

Then he said, "As far as I can tell, your work here is done. The ceremony is over, the food and the cake have been served, and it seems as if this group is better-behaved than the one at the Lowell wedding, so I doubt you'll have to arm-wrestle any drunks. Why not have a dance?"

Since everything he'd said was only the truth, I didn't have many arguments I could offer. However, I did have one very good objection. "That may well be," I admitted, "but you're still my client, Allan. It's just not…proper."

"'Proper'?" he repeated, that amused glint back in his eyes. "What is this, the Victorian age? Anyway, it's not like you're my attorney or my doctor or something. You're planning a party for me. That's all."

Was he belittling my work? I stared up at him for a second, trying to decide whether I should be offended. He was right, though. While I thought I provided an important service for people, it wasn't quite the same thing as performing open-heart surgery or representing someone in a divorce case.

"Still," I said, drawing out the word to show my reluctance.

"'Still,' nothing."

I retreated to the only protest I had left. "I don't know how to dance."

One dark brown eyebrow lifted. "Belinda, they're slow dancing, not doing the tango."

"I—"

He took my hand, his fingers warm and strong against mine. "Just one dance. If the Blankenships have a problem with it, they can talk to me."

Probably if I'd dug my heels in, he would have let go. I didn't know him well, but I could already tell he wasn't the sort of man to ever force the issue. No, it was more that he could tell my reluctance was feigned, wasn't something I actually felt. Even the touch of his fingers against my skin was enough to make my heartbeat speed up and my cheeks feel flushed. I reacted to him way too easily…and that was the whole problem.

It's the last wedding of the year, I told myself. *What's the harm?*

Only, I knew what the harm could be. It could be me allowing him into my life in small, incremental ways, opening myself up for the inevitable disappointment that had to follow. And yet….

And yet, I wanted to know what it felt like to have his arms around me. Just one dance, in a very public place. It should be safe enough.

I hoped.

"All right," I said.

He smiled, his fingers tightening on mine for a second or two. Then he led me out to the dance floor, put his other hand on my shoulder. I was surprised by the weight of it, although maybe that was only because I felt hyper-sensitive to everything about him, the faint scent of his cologne, the difference in our heights, even though I wore three-inch heels that boosted my modest five foot five to a more imposing five foot eight.

My heart pounded, and I prayed that he wouldn't be able to sense the way it was racing, nor the way my breaths seemed labored, even though we weren't moving very fast and this wasn't the sort of exertion that would have normally increased my heartbeat the tiniest bit. No, this was all his proximity, the warmth of his body as he held me and I did an awkward little box step in time to the music.

It was glorious and awful at the same time, mostly because I couldn't stop wondering whether everyone was staring at us, couldn't prevent myself from thinking how good it felt to be in his arms, even for something as innocuous as a slow dance at a wedding with hundreds of people watching. This was probably a huge mistake, and yet…I was very glad I'd agreed to dance with him.

He didn't try to speak, only moved softly with

me in time to the music. I was relieved by that, mostly because I feared I would have sounded far too breathless if I'd talked to him right then. Instead, I wanted to focus on the soft, sweet sounds from the band, the twinkling of the stars overhead, the wonderful sensation of being in a man's arms.

Not just any man's arms, though…Allan D'Alessandro's arms. And that made all the difference in the world.

Eventually, the song was over, and I pulled away from him at once, pretending to fuss with smoothing the skirt of the fit-and-flare dress I wore. "Well, you've had your dance. Now I really need to check on—"

He still held on to me by one hand, though, and twined his fingers with mine so I'd have a difficult time disentangling myself without making it very obvious. "Belinda, you don't really have something to check on, do you?"

I could have lied, of course—how could he have known what claims I had on my time? I didn't want to, though. Bad enough that I'd already tried to say I had something to do when I really didn't. "No," I said, after a pause that seemed hideously long to me.

However, he didn't appear angry, or even annoyed. Instead, he asked, "Can we go for a walk?"

That sounded dangerous, even though the entire grounds of the mansion were lit up for the event, since the Blankenships had rented the whole place. Still, enough people came and went from the courtyard to the terrace to the garden that I guessed Allan and I wouldn't be completely alone.

"Just for a few minutes," I told him. "I don't want to leave Dee hanging in case something comes up."

"I understand."

Still with his fingers wrapped around mine, he led me away from the courtyard and over to the terrace. People lingered there as well, talking and drinking, but most of them were clustered around the bar, while he led me to the edge of the outdoor space, away from the tables and the wedding guests. Off in the distance, the lights of Los Angeles gleamed in the darkness—a different view from the one I'd seen out Allan's living room window, but no less spectacular for the altered perspective.

For a moment, we stood there in the semi-darkness. A cool breeze blew in from the ocean, pushing past the outdoor heaters that clustered on the flagstones, and yet, I still didn't feel chilled. Maybe it was only the sensation of his fingers against mine, some kind of odd afterglow from the dance we'd just shared.

Then he said, "It seems you're surprised that I'm interested in you."

Warmth touched my cheeks again, and I was glad that the lighting wasn't bright enough to reveal my flush. "Allan, we hardly know each other."

"True. But I'd like to get to know you better." He paused for a second or two, then added, "If I'm completely off base here, tell me now. It's just that I can feel some kind of connection between us. I know that sounds like a line. I don't mean it to be, though."

His voice was calm, almost gentle, with maybe the slightest undercurrent of amusement, as if he was surprised at himself for speaking to me so honestly. I was a little surprised, too; I wasn't sure what I'd expected him to say, but it hadn't been something like that.

He wasn't handing me a line. I'd felt the connection…attraction…whatever it was…just as he had. The problem was, I knew I couldn't do anything about it. Not really.

"I like you, Allan," I said. Even confessing that much felt as if I'd just crossed a line, but I knew I had to keep going. "But I just don't have time for relationships or a personal life."

Maybe I'd jumped the gun by mentioning relationships this early in the game. However, I knew I had to head him off at the pass before this…whatever it was…between us went any further.

"I can tell you're very busy," he replied. "I understand that. But maybe we don't need to be so formal about things."

I raised an eyebrow, not sure what he was trying to say. "What do you mean?"

He released my fingers so he could rest his hands on the stone balustrade before us. Staring out at the lights of the city rather than looking at me, he said, "Come January, I'm going to be really busy with getting the agency up and running. So, maybe…maybe we should allow ourselves to have a little fun between now and then. No strings. Just a couple of people enjoying the holidays together."

That suggestion sounded almost too good to be true. "You want us to see each other until the end of the year, and then go our separate ways?"

"Exactly." Allan turned back toward me. He wore a slight smile, but I wondered if he was using that expression more to conceal what he was really feeling than to let me know what was going on inside his head. "This was your last event of the year except for my party, right?"

"Yes," I replied.

"Then why not relax and let yourself have a little fun?" His smile stretched into a grin. "I've been told that I know how to have a good time."

Oh, I had no doubt of that. I'd been able to read between the lines of the gossip sites and could tell that there didn't seem to have been many parties, openings, or premieres he and Nina had missed. If I let him, he could probably run me ragged between now and New Year's without even breaking a sweat.

And if he did…where was the harm in that? Nine days wasn't enough time for him to fall in love with me. We could be together, play at being in a relationship, and then go on with our separate lives when we were done. It might be the only chance I ever had of being in a couple, of learning what it felt like to know someone would be at my side when I went out to dinner or to a party. By that point in my life, I was used to being alone… but I was also heartily sick of it.

"Just until the end of the year," I told him, and he nodded.

"When the clock strikes midnight on December thirty-first, we can both turn back into pumpkins and go our own way and be good productive citizens when the first of the year rolls around."

Well, when he put it that way….

"All right," I said, and he smiled at me.

"Get ready to have your best Christmas ever."

"You and Allan D'Alessandro?" Dee asked me, her eyes wide. "Since when were you a thing?"

"We're not a 'thing,'" I replied. We stood in the little cubbyhole off the kitchen where I'd stashed my rolling cart of emergency supplies; the wedding guests had left, and Jack and Melissa had been whisked away to their opulent suite. I was about to do my final walk-through of the party site but needed to change into the flats I'd stored with the rest of the emergency stuff. "We just shared a dance. That's all."

She put a hand on her hip and tilted her head to one side, surveying me for a moment. "I have never once seen you dance with anyone at one of your events. Not once."

"Maybe no one asked me before tonight."

"Wrong. I've seen you give a bunch of guys the brush-off."

Since that happened to be the truth, I didn't bother to deny it. "Well, maybe they didn't ask as nicely."

She chuckled. "Oh, he's charming. I'll give you that. And don't take me wrong—I'm glad you danced with him. I hope it was the first of many more dances. I'm just...surprised."

Well, that made two of us. I still couldn't quite believe that I'd agreed to Allan's little arrangement. Possibly it had been the admittedly romantic atmosphere of the evening, or maybe I'd been a little off balance from his proximity. Whatever the reason, it seemed I was committed to this course, and I'd just have to see what happened.

The first sign of him having any true feelings for me...of it turning into anything more than a brief diversion for the two of us...and I was pulling the plug, though. I couldn't take the risk of anything bad happening to him.

"Guess he just swept me off my feet," I said lightly, and Dee shook her head.

"I don't think you're really the type that gets 'swept,' Belinda," she replied. "Obviously, there's something at work here that I can't quite understand. But it's cool. Right now, I just want to walk the grounds and get out of here."

"Amen to that," I told her, and it seemed my words put an end to her speculations about Allan, since she and I headed out to walk the grounds after that, collecting any abandoned personal items we found. Once we were done, we handed everything over to Max, thanked him for staying so late, and then got out of there. I headed for Santa Monica, while Dee drove eastward to her apartment in Hollywood.

Of course, thinking about Hollywood made my thoughts drift to Allan and his house in the Hills. Was he still awake, or had he gone to bed already, sleeping the sleep of the just now that he knew he had me fairly caught?

Thinking about him in bed probably wasn't the smartest idea, though. I hadn't seen the upstairs at his house and therefore had no idea what his bedroom looked like, but I still imagined him lying on a king-size bed, bare chest just visible above the sheets, with the lights of the city twinkling through the windows.

If this little arrangement of ours went the way I thought it would, then there was a pretty good chance I'd get to see those city lights...and that bare chest...in the not-too-distant future.

And that was okay. It was all right to be with him and sleep with him and have a good time together. None of that would trigger the curse. I could even let myself care for him, because the curse didn't care about my heart. In fact, it *wanted* me to hurt.

I wouldn't let the situation go that far, though. Just keep it easy and light, keep things bobbing along on the surface. Fun, and laughs, and hopefully some good sex. It had been a long time for me, mostly because it was more work than people probably thought to find a guy decent enough to hook up with but not so wonderful that you wanted to spend any more time with him than you already had in the sack.

Well, Allan was definitely decent. And since we'd be saying goodbye after our nine days were up, I didn't have to worry about him getting clingy. I hoped we could stay friends afterward, if for no other reason than he would be a valuable contact to have.

Then I wanted to laugh at myself. "Valuable contact"…sure. I could try to fool myself, but I knew better. I couldn't allow him to care for me…

…but I knew I already cared for him, far more than I should.

"It's all right," I whispered to myself as I turned off Wilshire Boulevard and down 22nd Street, heading for my house. "He'll never know.

"I won't let him."

Asmodeus whistled to himself as he drove home from the Blankenship wedding, ignoring the Tesla's state-of-the-art sound system. He thought he could be forgiven for feeling pleased with himself—he'd come up with the idea of wooing Belinda with a no-strings, limited-time relationship the day before, had figured it was probably the best strategy to get her to agree to spend some time with him that had nothing to do with planning his party. Because he knew she was already attracted to him, he figured she would agree to the plan, even as she told herself that this was probably the safest way to get a little closer without worrying about a long-term connection.

Of course, everything rode on the contingency that she wouldn't want to leave once their nine days together were up, would realize she'd fallen in love with him and wanted to share his life. However, he didn't think achieving that end would be too difficult. He would treat her like a queen, prove how thoughtful and devoted he was, and then she would understand that it would be foolish to do anything except promise to share her days with him. She would come to live with him in his house in the Hollywood Hills, and they would settle down to a cozy earthly existence together, just as Lucifer and his own mortal bride had done not so long ago.

None of these calculations were made with a cold heart, however. While Asmodeus wanted to be free of Hell forever, he'd known that the object of his affection would have to be someone worthy, someone he could easily imagine spending the rest of his life with. In Belinda Carson, he had found a woman he ached to be with—pretending to be cool and casual the past few days had been more difficult than he'd imagined. Seeing the sun bring out glimmers of copper and bronze in her lustrous hair…seeing her full mouth lift in a smile…gazing at the smooth, creamy skin at the base of her throat…all of those delicious attributes had made him want to take her in his arms and kiss her, even as he'd known it wasn't yet time for those kinds of intimacies.

But he'd gotten to dance with her earlier that evening, had been able to feel her slender form pressed up against his body. She'd seemed very different from Nina, smaller, far more delicate, and yet he sensed a strength in her that told him she would only allow herself to be pushed so far.

Not that he planned to push her at all. He wanted her to come willingly to him—and, if the way she'd reacted to that one precious dance was any indication at all, she was definitely more than willing.

He wanted to send her flowers, but he'd have to wait until Monday and have them delivered to her office, since of course, she didn't have any idea that he knew where she lived. Asmodeus guessed she would be unnerved by such a revelation and would probably think he was stalking her, and that was the last thing he wanted her to believe about him.

A phone call, though. If he made the first move, then she'd know he was serious. He didn't want to wait on her, partly because he feared she might rethink her impulsive decision of the night before, and therefore pull back and not contact him at all. That just wouldn't do. They had such a short amount of time to make this work.

And it *had* to work. Otherwise…well, otherwise, he'd be back in Hell, stuck listening to Beelzebub complain about the prisoners and whatever else was plucking his last nerve that day.

Asmodeus couldn't bear to contemplate such a fate.

It was all right, though. He knew that Belinda was already half in love with him. All he had to do was make her fall the rest of the way, and this would be a done deal.

Easy.

Beelzebub strode to the top of the north tower and cast a baleful gaze across the dark, dull plain that stretched far below him. Once upon a time, this spot had been the favorite place *he*— Beelzebub still thought of his former master in italics, refusing to allow Lucifer's name to take up space in his mind—would come whenever *he* wanted to brood over something, but *he* had been absent from the underworld for more than six human months and wasn't coming back. This tower was now Beelzebub's, along with everything else in the palace…everything else in Hell, really.

It wasn't supposed to be this way, though. He was supposed to be running Hell with Asmodeus as his second-in-command. But no, his former comrade had decided he wanted the same sweetheart deal *he* had gotten, wanted to stay topside so he could play footsie with some insipid mortal woman and pretend that he'd never been a

demon, had never been one of Hell's top lieu-
tenants.

He had to be stopped.

But how? Beelzebub couldn't indulge in any of
the more obvious forms of spying on his fellow
demon, because Asmodeus would sense his presence immediately. What exactly he might do to
stop him, Beelzebub didn't know, but he couldn't
preclude the possibility of divine intervention.
That would be disastrous. It was already obvious
that the Man Upstairs had extended some obvious
favors to Beelzebub's erstwhile friend, and drawing
down His wrath was something to be avoided at
all costs.

All right, then. He couldn't openly spy on
Asmodeus, and he knew better than to go
anywhere near his former boss and *his* new bride,
the only other people in L.A. who might know
something of Asmodeus's current activities.

Well, except one. Asmodeus had spent six
months with the woman and she'd dropped him
like the proverbial hot potato, but that didn't
mean she might not know something of what he
was up to these days, or who he was seeing. In
fact, Beelzebub thought that she might very well
be a little put out to learn that Asmodeus was
pursuing a new love barely more than a month
after he'd been kicked to the curb, as the mortals
so quaintly put it.

That seemed to settle things. It had been quiet enough in Hell lately, and so he thought a quick jaunt topside shouldn't be too much trouble. While he supposed that he was pushing things just a little by visiting a friend of Christa Simms, *his* new bride, Beelzebub had gotten the impression that the two women didn't talk as much as they used to, thanks to Nina Nomura's now-frenetic schedule. In fact, approaching the newly famous young woman posed its own set of problems, although he thought he should be able to get around any possible restrictions without too much trouble.

After all, being a demon did have its perks.

A blink of his eyes, and then he was topside, in an exclusive enclave in Malibu where each home laid claim to its own private little stretch of beachfront property. Not in his own body, of course; Beelzebub was very good at possessing people, and had decided his best course of action was to take up residence in the person Nina was currently living with, a man named Brian Hart, her lover...and her new agent.

Beelzebub wondered what had rankled Asmodeus more, that Brian had replaced him as Nina's agent, or as her lover. Not that it mattered much. What mattered was that Nina wouldn't see any reason why she shouldn't confide in Brian.

After all, he'd helped to engineer some of her current success.

The day was cool and windy, but the couple still sat on their deck overlooking the Pacific Ocean, both of them bundled in bulky sweatshirts and jeans. Nina's heavy dark curls were pulled back in some kind of fabric-covered elastic band, but the wind kept whipping Brian's overlong forelock into his eyes, making Beelzebub frown in annoyance.

Nina was scowling as well, although not because of her hair. No, she had a laptop open on the table in front of her as they drank their morning coffee, and appeared to be scrolling through images from what looked like some kind of overblown, extravagant wedding.

"Do *you* know what he was doing there, Brian?" Nina asked, the set of her full mouth almost petulant.

Although Beelzebub generally had no use for human women, even he could see why Asmodeus might have fallen under her spell. There was something very lush about her appearance, a sensual quality that seemed calculated to draw every male eye in the vicinity.

However, he didn't have time to contemplate Nina Nomura's physical charms. Instead, he had to stop and take a quick peek into Brian Hart's consciousness—still there, if submerged beneath that of the invading demon—and get up to speed on what they were talking about.

Ah, there it was. Nina had been scrolling through some sort of gossip website, and had come across photos from an expensive wedding that had taken place the evening before. Apparently, the groom was a member of a local sports team. Which one didn't really matter. What apparently mattered was that Nina had spied Asmodeus—in his guise as Allan D'Alessandro— in one of the pictures. Worse, he had been dancing with someone.

"Can I see that again?" Beelzebub asked.

Nina looked puzzled that he'd want to look at something he'd viewed just seconds earlier, but then she lifted her shoulders and pushed the laptop across the table toward her companion. Beelzebub took it and angled the screen so it wouldn't get hit with quite so much glare from the sun, and peered at the photo in question.

Yes, that was definitely Asmodeus, even though his face was partially turned away and the picture was a little blurry. In his arms was a slender woman, probably in her late twenties, although Beelzebub couldn't tell for sure, since she also was looking away from the camera. She had long red hair that cascaded over her shoulders in loose curls, and appeared to be smiling up at her partner, although the angle made it hard to see her expression. Really, her hair was the most striking thing about her; despite the angle, he thought he could see enough to tell him she wasn't much more than passable, certainly no one nearly as eye-catching as Nina.

However, beggars couldn't be choosers, he supposed.

"Who is she?" Nina demanded.

"How would I know?" Beelzebub returned, figuring that was a safe enough reply. After all, Brian might have been an agent, but that didn't mean he had the face of every woman in L.A. under thirty memorized. A quick scan of the man's memories proved that Brian didn't know who the unknown woman was any more than Beelzebub did. "A wedding guest, I suppose. The bride isn't anyone famous or even in show business, so I would assume her friends aren't famous, either."

Nina's luminous green eyes narrowed, and then she picked up her cup of coffee and took a sip. "So, why would he be dancing with her?"

About all Beelzebub could do was shrug, even as he experienced an inner stab of disappointment. The photo wasn't captioned, and since obviously neither Nina nor Brian recognized the woman, he didn't seem to be any closer to his goal than he had been before he slipped into Brian's brain. However, he could feel the human's consciousness squirming around underneath his, and realized that Brian probably wouldn't be too thrilled with his current love interest asking questions about her ex-boyfriend. "How the hell should I know?" he responded, hoping he'd injected the correct amount of irritation into his tone. "I suppose he wanted to enjoy himself. And why should you care, anyway?"

"I don't care," Nina said immediately, then swallowed some more coffee.

Beelzebub wasn't so sure about that. Was it possible that she still harbored some sort of feelings for her former lover? No, he doubted she was pining away over him. More likely, she just didn't want to see him moving on so quickly. "As for your other question," he said, once again picking at Brian's thoughts to get the information he needed, "I heard a rumor that Allan was going after Jack Holloway for representation, so I suppose that's probably why he was at the wedding. Kind of scraping the bottom of the barrel, if you ask me, but I guess he has to start somewhere since he's not with Hart Hathaway anymore."

A snide remark, but again, one Beelzebub knew was completely in character for Brian Hart. Nina seemed to accept it at face value, giving the barest of nods as she picked up her coffee and drank again. Her gaze was fixed on the ocean, almost contemplative, and he could tell she'd already begun to lose interest in the topic.

"So, a work thing," she said. "No biggie."

"No biggie," Beelzebub agreed, and pushed the laptop back over toward her. She shrugged and closed it, then asked about the dinner they had planned for that evening with a couple of producers and their wives.

Her comment seemed to be the signal for Beelzebub to leave. He vacated Brian Hart's body with a sigh of relief, although he didn't go straight back to Hell. No, obviously he would have to stay here and do a little research. The underworld had its attractions, but free wi-fi wasn't one of them.

He'd seen the photo, and the bright red hair of the woman in Asmodeus' arms. That was all he needed. Someone had to know who she was…

…and, sooner or later, he would track her down.

CHAPTER EIGHT

I ROLLED OVER IN BED AND STARED UP AT THE ceiling, feeling strangely blissful. Yes, I'd slept well, but I didn't think that was the real reason for my current relaxed state. Usually, as soon as I opened my eyes, my brain started racing a mile a minute, thinking of all the tasks I had to get done that day, making detailed mental lists for the upcoming week and everything that needed to be handled. In that particular moment, however, I found myself smiling. I felt like a kid waking up on the first day of summer vacation…and it wasn't simply because I didn't have any more weddings scheduled until mid-January.

No, I was happy because I'd danced with Allan D'Alessandro the night before, and I'd agreed to spend the next nine days with him. What exactly we'd be doing during that particular stretch of time, I didn't know for sure, but I had a feeling he would make it memorable no matter what we did to fill our days together.

I sat up and reached for my phone to check the time. Almost nine, which was rare for me. As if to draw attention to my sloth, Mr. Mittens stood in the doorway to the bedroom and gave a loud meow.

"Working on it, cat," I said affectionately, pushing myself out of bed. I left my cell phone lying on top of the quilt while I went to fetch my robe, then retrieved the phone and headed down the hallway to the kitchen. Mr. Mittens had one of those water fountain setups and a bowl with a dry food dispenser attached, since I often had days where I was gone for twelve hours or more and couldn't be home to take care of the cat, but when I was there, he wanted wet food, damn it.

After putting the phone down on the counter, I fetched him a can of food, opened it, and dumped it into his bowl. His water situation looked okay for the moment, so I got some coffee started. Once the Keurig was working away, I allowed myself a big stretch, arms wide as if to embrace the morning.

Maybe it was crazy, but I couldn't remember the last time I'd so looked forward to a day. Yes, I would get excited at dress fittings or when I went with a client to choose flowers, but that was different. This wasn't about a client. This was about me…and Allan.

Almost as if his name in my thoughts was a trigger, my cell phone chimed, indicating that I had a text message. I picked up the phone and looked at the home screen.

Hope I didn't wake you. Call me when you're ready to get your day started.—A

I noticed the text had come in at precisely nine o'clock. It looked like he hadn't wanted to wait any longer than that, which had to be a good sign he was just as excited about our upcoming shared week as I was.

No, I'm up, I texted back. *I could probably be out the door by 10:30. What did you have in mind?*

That's my little surprise. Can I pick you up at 10:30? I'll need your address.

For just a second, I hesitated. Was I ready for him to know where I lived? But then I realized I was being silly. What, I was okay with dating the guy and possibly even going to bed with him, but I didn't want him to come over to my house?

I took a breath and typed, *2215 22nd St.*

Thanks, he replied. *See you in a bit.*

And that was the end of that.

Since I had a definite time when he'd be arriving, I knew I couldn't allow myself a slow, leisurely morning. He hadn't said anything about break-fast…or brunch. Should I eat something?

Ten-thirty sounded like it possibly could be a brunch date. I decided to have some yogurt with my coffee but leave it at that. Once I was done with my abbreviated breakfast, I hurried into the shower. Luckily, I'd washed and curled my hair the day before and it still looked presentable, so I didn't have to waste time on anything beyond making sure it was brushed and more or less held in place by setting spray. No, instead I could hem and haw over what to wear. A skirt or a dress seemed way too much. Jeans could be a problem if he ended up taking me someplace fancy.

In the end, I decided on my new dark gray skinny jeans, boots, and a muted sage green jacket over a tank top. Put together, but not trying too hard. At least, I hoped that was the impression the ensemble gave. I had to admit that I wasn't very good at the whole "casual going out" thing, mostly because I spent most of my time in work clothes, and during my off hours, I schlepped around in jeans and sweatshirts in the winter, or jeans and tank tops in the summer.

Promptly at ten-thirty, the doorbell rang. I took one last look in the mirror to make sure my eye liner hadn't decided to smudge itself or my lip gloss hadn't taken the opportunity to smear all over my teeth, ascertained that everything still looked pretty much intact, and headed over to open the door, all the while praying that I'd gotten things right, that I didn't look as though I'd tried too hard…or not hard enough.

And okay, Allan looked great in a suit…but he also looked pretty damn good in faded jeans, a dark T-shirt, and a leather jacket.

"Um…hi," I said, knowing I sounded like some inexperienced high school kid about to go out on her first date. "Come on in."

I stepped out of the way, and he entered the living room and glanced around. Good thing I'd tidied up on Friday and hadn't been home enough on Saturday to make any kind of a mess. My place wasn't as fancy as his, but I liked the casual, beachy vibe of the off-white linen sofa, the flat-weave rug on the floor in shades of soft blue and cocoa, the oceanscapes on the walls.

"Do you want some coffee?" I asked, not sure what else to say.

He smiled, as if noting my awkwardness. "No, I wanted to take you to brunch. If that's okay."

"Brunch sounds great," I said. "Let me get my purse."

I hurried off to the bedroom to collect the item in question, and then returned to the living room to see Mr. Mittens winding his way around Allan's calves and purring loudly. The cat's open friendliness startled me, since he really didn't like strangers and generally took a long time to warm up to anyone. Even when I'd brought him home from the shelter, he hadn't really showed any open signs of affection until he'd been living with me for more than a week.

"I guess he likes me," Allan remarked, bending down to scratch Mr. Mittens behind the ears.

"I guess so," I said, even more startled. It was one thing for my cat to decide to be friendly toward someone, but he never let anyone except me touch him.

That had to be a good omen, right? After all, if the cat liked Allan, then that must mean we were supposed to be together.

Well, except for the tiny problem of me not being allowed to be with him on anything resembling a permanent basis. Mr. Mittens had better not get too attached, because this relationship wasn't going to last very long.

And since that was definitely not the sort of thing I should be thinking at the start of our time together—even if it might have been nothing more than the truth—I pushed the thought right out of my head and smiled at Allan.

"Well, I'm ready. Try to extricate yourself if you can."

He shook his head, then bent down to pet Mr. Mittens one last time before he stepped away. The cat looked wounded at this defection, but then gave the feline equivalent of a shrug and stalked off toward the kitchen, tail in the air. Good thing my cat was a short-hair, or the lower section of Allan's pants probably would have been covered in fur.

"I think I offended him," he remarked.

"Probably," I said. "He's a cat. But he'll get over it."

We went out, and after I'd locked the front door, we headed down the front steps and over to where the Tesla was parked at the curb. Allan had the expansive sunroof panel removed, basically turning the car into a convertible, and I sent him a sideways glance.

"Do you think it's warm enough for that?"

"Probably not," he said cheerfully. "But the sun's out, and I'll turn on the heater."

Thankful that I always kept a scrunchie in my purse in case of any emergencies where I might need to get my hair out of the way, I climbed into the car and let Allan shut the door behind me. The vehicle was quite low-slung, and he had to perform a serious bend to slide in on the driver's side, but I supposed he thought the contortions were a small price to pay to get behind the wheel of such a slick piece of automotive perfection.

He started it up, and I was surprised at how quiet the car was. But then, of course it was silly to have been expecting the growl of a typical sports car in an all-electric vehicle. Despite the silence, I could still sense how powerful the motor was, how much the roadster wanted to leap forward when Allan put his foot on the accelerator. However, he kept it at a sedate speed as we headed west on Wilshire and then turned right to go north on Pacific Coast Highway. Despite his cautious driving—or maybe because of it—I was acutely aware of heads turning as we glided past. This part of the world definitely saw its share of exotic automobiles, but I doubted many of the people who stopped to stare had ever seen this particular model Tesla roadster in person before.

The breeze whistling overhead was cool, and yet I was comfortable enough, thanks to the warm air drifting out from the climate-control system's vents. It felt good to relax against the luxurious leather seat and let Allan pilot the car. Honestly, I couldn't even remember the last time I'd had someone drive me someplace. When Dee and I shared rides, I was always the one driving, and when I met my mom and Faye to go to the movies or out to lunch or something, we rarely drove together, since I often had to dash off to another appointment once I was done seeing them.

This felt good…probably too good.

"Did everything work out okay at the reception?" he asked as we passed Temescal Canyon

Road and the outskirts of Pacific Palisades. "I left a little after ten, so I don't know if there was any last-minute drama."

"None, thank God," I replied. All right, the mother and father of the bride had shared a fierce *sotto voce* exchange at one edge of the terrace, a convo probably fueled by Loretta's fifth glass of champagne and an all-too-clear look at her ex-husband dancing with his new girlfriend, but at least they'd had the consideration to argue off in a corner where not too many other people were around. I didn't think Melissa or Jack had heard any of their heated conversation. "No after-midnight panicked messages, nothing from the venue this morning. I wasn't really expecting there to be, but you never know."

"And now you're free," he said, a certain warmth entering his voice.

"Well, except for your party," I reminded him. "Speaking of which, I'm expecting Marcelle and Tori to send me their final estimates tomorrow, so I'll get those over to you as soon as I have them."

"And then I can cut you a check."

It seemed odd to be thinking about him paying me when I'd basically told him we could date for the next week and a half, but I knew I had to attend to business no matter what happened. My standard practice was to ask for fifty percent up front once I had the finalized estimates from the vendors, with the balance due seven days after the event in question.

"Right," I said, hoping I didn't sound too awkward.

"Well," he went on, "that works out perfectly, actually. You can bring the estimates over tomorrow night—Christmas Eve, in case you forgot. Does that work?"

It did, mostly because my family tradition had always been to get together on Christmas Day. Over the years, I'd had just enough Christmas Eve parties or receptions to manage that it seemed foolish to try going to Faye and my mom's place when I never knew whether I'd be booked or not. This year, of course, my Christmas Eve was free, and so it was perfectly fine for me to go over to Allan's.

"Sure," I replied. "Just let me know what time."

He smiled then, a small, somewhat secretive smile. "I'll let you know."

We drove in silence for some time, while I looked out the window at the steep hillside to my right and the enormous expanse of the Pacific Ocean to my left. Since it was fairly windy that day, the dark blue waters were choppy and topped with whitecaps, but beautiful nonetheless. Actually, I reflected that it was sort of sad how seldom I even went to the beach, considering how close I lived to the ocean. Maybe sometime during this little winter break I'd given myself, I could head over to the shore and take a walk, although December probably wasn't the best time of year for that sort of outing.

I could see we were approaching the Malibu pier, and in fact, Allan turned into the long, narrow parking lot on the south side, managing to snag a prime spot near the restaurant at the pier's entrance. This show of luck might have surprised me, except that I'd seen him do almost the same thing in front of Aux Delices just a few days earlier.

Malibu Farm Restaurant, the sign outside read, and I gave a nod of comprehension. "Oh, I've heard of this place," I told Allan as he turned off the motor. "I've always meant to come out here, but I somehow never got around to it."

"Then I'm glad I decided to bring you here," he said. "I'd heard it was good, too, but I haven't had much reason to hang out in Malibu. Give me a sec, and I'll come around and get your door."

He let himself out and I waited in the passenger seat, reflecting that I also wasn't used to men opening car doors for me. It really wasn't necessary, but if he wanted to act the gentleman, then I wasn't about to stop him.

I took his hand as he helped me from my seat, while with my free hand, I reached up to remove the scrunchie from my hair so I could slip it back into my purse. The scrunchie had served its purpose, but I didn't want to walk into the restaurant wearing the damn thing.

The place was open and airy, and a little more casual than I'd expected. Still, that was good, since I didn't have to worry about being underdressed. The restaurant also offered a breathtaking view of the ocean and the pier, since the entire west wall was made of glass.

The hostess led Allan and me to a table for two up against that wall, and I sat down, wondering how we'd managed to get a seat, since the place was obviously packed. Maybe he'd had a reservation, but he hadn't said anything about one to the girl, who looked like she was probably a college student, maybe at Pepperdine, since the campus was just up the road.

Well, however he'd gotten us these seats, we were sitting in them now, and at one of the best tables in the restaurant.

"This is great," I told him as I picked up my menu. "It really feels like I've gotten far away, even though we only drove about ten miles up the coast from Santa Monica."

"Good," he said. "I wanted to give you a little bit of an escape. You work very hard."

I supposed I did, although sometimes what I did really didn't feel like work at all. However, I'd be the first to admit that the hours could be brutal, although the rewards were equally as great. After all, I got to help my clients make memories that would last a lifetime. How many people could truly say that about their jobs?

"It just looks hard," I said with a smile, and although my reply made him raise one eyebrow ever so slightly, he didn't bother to contradict me.

The waitress came over then, and Allan ordered a bottle of Schramsberg champagne. Now it was my turn to raise an eyebrow, but he looked singularly unconcerned. He waited until the waitress had departed to get the champagne before he said, "I thought you deserved a celebration after surviving the Blankenship wedding. Besides, is it really brunch if you don't have champagne?"

"Truly an existential question for our times," I responded, and he grinned, that dancing light I liked so much returning to his blue-gray eyes, almost the same color as the water that lapped against the pier outside the window. "I don't think I'll try to figure that one out...but I'll also admit that I was sort of hoping there would be champagne."

"Well, then." Allan picked up his menu and glanced through it, although I got the impression he wasn't all that interested in its contents, was more focused on my expression, my reactions.

"The last thing I'd ever want to do is disappoint you."

A little shiver went through me. So far, he'd been anything but disappointing. In fact, despite his obvious pursuit of me, I honestly couldn't think of another man I'd felt as relaxed around. True, I tended to be on guard whenever I was with a member of the male half of the species—a natural enough reaction, considering what the Carson curse had done to my love life—but even though I knew my relationship with Allan couldn't really go anywhere, I didn't feel any of that same tension. I liked talking to him, being around him. And actually, I didn't mind being quiet when I was with him, either, as if I could somehow detect that he was simply happy to be in my company and didn't feel the need to try to force anything.

Which meant he was looking more and more perfect…and therefore more and more off-limits. And it just wasn't fair. Why should I be held responsible for something my great-great-to-the-umpteenth-power grandmother did three hundred years before I was even born?

Unfortunately, I'd had this mental conversation many times before, and it always ended up in the same place. It didn't matter how much I railed against my current circumstances—I couldn't change them. About all I could do was try to bend the rules just the teeniest bit, not so much that anyone would get hurt, but only enough that I could enjoy myself for a little while and pretend there wasn't anything terribly strange about my life or the men I allowed in it.

I smiled at him but didn't have to reply, since the waitress returned with the champagne, expertly uncorked it, and poured us both a glass. Of course, I hadn't even bothered to look at the menu yet, so I picked it up and glanced hastily through the offerings while Allan ordered a Greek omelette. I'd actually eaten a good bit at the Blankenship reception—the food had been excellent—and so I asked for a kale/ricotta scramble, feeling slightly virtuous.

Once the waitress had left to put in our order, Allan lifted his glass. "To the next nine days."

"To the next nine days," I echoed, and we clinked our glasses together. I sipped some of my champagne—all right, *méthode champagnoise* wine, since Schramsberg came from California— and enjoyed the fizz of it going down. We'd already agreed to spend the next week together, but somehow, making that little toast and drinking together made it feel as if Allan and I had actually sealed the deal.

He sipped again, then settled against the back of his seat. "So, tell me all about yourself."

I laughed. "That's kind of a tall order for

breakfast. Besides, there really isn't all that much to tell."

Well, not much that I could actually share with him. I couldn't tell him about the curse, and I thought it better to leave out the part about being a witch, especially since my talents were so modest. It wasn't as though I could snap my fingers and make a unicorn appear in the middle of the restaurant. Honestly, none of the little magics I was able to command were the sort of thing that were even really visible to the naked eye. Small household magics, really, stuff that came in handy if you were a wedding planner, but nothing that would change the world.

But since he kept watching me expectantly, champagne glass held in his elegant fingers, I knew I had to say something. "You already know about how I got into the wedding planning business," I said, then sipped at my champagne. "What else did you need to know?"

"What about your family?" he asked. "Have you always lived in Santa Monica?"

My family was always a dicey subject. True, the world had changed a lot in the past five years or so, but sometimes it was really hard to tell how accepting someone would be about openly gay parents. However, nothing Allan had said or done so far seemed to indicate he was anything but open-minded. Besides, better to get it out there and see how he dealt with my not-so-standard family life.

"My mom's a lesbian," I said bluntly. "She's been with Faye since before I was born."

Obviously, he hadn't been expecting that particular backstory, because his eyes widened for just a split-second before he gave a very small nod, as if accepting that piece of information and then moving on. "And your father…?" he ventured, letting the question trail off delicately.

I shrugged and drank some more champagne. At the rate I was going, I was going to need another refill in the near future. "I have no idea who he was. Is. I mean, assume he's probably still alive, but you don't get much information about sperm donors except the basic biological facts."

"Ah." Allan set down his champagne glass and leaned forward, gaze intent on my face. "Do you ever wonder about him?"

"Of course, I do," I said. "But I know that subject is a dead end. Those donors are anonymous for a reason—they don't want the offspring they might have possibly fathered showing up on their doorsteps, after all."

At least, that was always what I'd told myself. I'd be lying if I said I hadn't hoped in my inner heart of hearts that maybe the anonymous man who'd donated his genetic material all those years ago had regretted his choice to keep his identity a secret, that maybe he wanted to know if he had a son or daughter out there somewhere, but I knew that hidden hope was a very long shot. And honestly, except for those few times when I didn't have a "real" dad to accompany me on a school's father-daughter outing or something, I really didn't miss having a father. My mother and Faye took such good care of me, were always so present as parents, that I never thought I lacked for anything.

"I suppose you have a point." Allan picked up his champagne again and sipped from the glass while I did my best not to stare at his mouth. He hadn't made a move yet, but I still couldn't help wondering what it would be like when he finally did kiss me.

I had a feeling it would be pretty spectacular.

"So, that's all you needed to know about me," I said. "No big family or anything—it's just my mom and Faye and my grandmother and me. And Mr. Mittens, of course."

"The cat, I presume."

"Yes. You're lucky he likes you. He's a very good judge of character."

The corner of Allan's mouth lifted ever so slightly. "I suppose I should be flattered."

I was about to reply with an off-hand comment about Sadie, Faye and my mother's hyperactive little Chi/Jack Russell mix, but I didn't get the opportunity. An odd little murmur swept through the restaurant, and the next moment, a shadow fell over our table. Standing there was probably one of the most spectacular-looking women I'd ever seen, with brilliant green eyes and a fall of perfect spiral chocolate-brown curls down her back. Immediately behind her was a dark-haired man probably only an inch or so taller than her statuesque five foot ten, but I barely noticed him as my brain registered who this apparition must be.

None other than Nina Nomura.

CHAPTER NINE

"Hi, Allan," she said, barely even looking over at me. "What are you doing in Malibu?"

"Having brunch," he replied imperturbably. I was glad he appeared so unaffected, because I knew I hadn't quite recovered from my shock. Yes, I supposed there was always a remote chance that Allan might run into his ex at some point, but L.A. was a pretty big place; I would have said the odds were stacked against such a thing actually happening.

Yet here we were.

He went on, still in that casual tone, "Nina, this is Belinda Carson. Belinda, this is Nina Nomura."

Her gaze slid over toward me, and I was surprised to see the flare of recognition in her striking green eyes. Honestly, I hadn't expected her to remember a mere mortal like me, but obviously, I was wrong.

"Oh, we've met," she said. "Christa's wedding planner, right?"

I nodded and managed to find my voice. "That's right. How have you been, Nina?"

"Just fine," Nina replied. She looked over at Allan again, her expression now almost amused. "Planning a wedding, Allan?"

"Hardly," he said. He still appeared as unflappable as ever, but I thought I detected just the slightest tightening of the muscles of his throat. "As it happens, Belinda is helping me plan my New Year's party. You and Brian are welcome to come, of course."

Nina's companion, who must have been Brian, shot Allan such a condescending smile that I wished I actually was a real witch who could cast hexes or something. That guy definitely needed to be turned into a toad.

"Sounds awesome," he drawled, "but we're already going to Roland's party that night. You understand."

"Of course," Allan said. If he was disappointed by their refusal—or by Brian's dismissive tone—he didn't show any sign of it.

"Excuse me," the waitress said. She'd just appeared behind Brian's elbow, looking slightly irritated by the way our table was being blocked. However, her annoyed expression shifted to one of surprise—with a mixture of awe—when she realized exactly who was standing in her way. "I mean, I'm sorry, Ms. Nomura, but—"

"It's all right," Nina said. She stepped to the side, unblocking the table. "We were just saying a quick hello." Her gaze moved back to Allan. "Enjoy your brunch."

She looped her arm through Brian's, and together they headed toward the restaurant's front door. Most likely, they'd come in for breakfast earlier and by pure bad luck had passed by our table on the way to the exit.

The waitress eyed both Allan and me with newfound respect as she set our plates down in front of us. "Was there anything else you needed?"

"I'm good," I said hastily, and Allan echoed that sentiment. She headed off toward the kitchen, and I picked up my fork, not sure what to say. At last, I blurted, "Sorry about that."

His lips twitched. "Why are you sorry? You had nothing to do with them being here."

True, but I did feel sorry that he'd had to run into his ex-girlfriend on what was supposed to be the first day of our little holiday fling. I told him as much, and he gave an eloquent lift of his shoulders.

"Actually, I'm glad I ran into her."

I stared at him in surprise. "You are?"

"Yes." Ignoring the food in front of him, he reached for his glass of champagne instead. "Because I saw her again and didn't feel anything at all. It appears I've moved on." He lifted his glass, tilting it toward me in a sort of salute. "And I have you to thank for that."

How was I supposed to respond to that particular remark? If the circumstances had been different, I might have been gratified to learn I'd had such an effect on him, but in that moment, I couldn't help but feel a wash of guilt. I didn't want him to care for me...or at least, not to the extent where that caring might put him in danger.

Somehow, I managed to smile and say, "I'm glad. It's always good when we find someone no longer has the power to hurt us."

And then I dug into my food, not waiting for his reply. Our whole conversation was starting to get a little too close to the bone for me. Also, although I would never have admitted such a thing to Allan and really didn't want to admit it to myself, I knew I was feeling a little shaken by that encounter with Nina Nomura. Yes, I'd met her before, but back then, she was only Christa Simms' maid-of-honor, not someone who happened to be the ex-girlfriend of the man I was dating. Now I couldn't help comparing myself to her...and knowing there was no real comparison. Under normal circumstances, I would have said I was an attractive enough person. But my level of prettiness could in no way survive a comparison to Nina's almost insane gorgeousness.

As I was taking a bite of my ricotta/kale scramble, Allan said, "Are you comparing yourself to her?"

"No," I mumbled around a mouthful of eggs.

He set down his champagne and reached for his fork. "You shouldn't. There's no need to do that. She's in my past. And honestly, I find you much more fascinating."

Somehow, I managed to swallow my food. "I find that hard to believe."

"It's the truth. Nina is a lot of fun, and she's beautiful and lively and smart…but she also hasn't had to work for very much in her life. Her family is very wealthy, you know."

I supposed I knew that sort of peripherally, since I thought I recalled reading somewhere that her father was a plastic surgeon and she'd grown up in Pacific Palisades or some other similarly upscale area. About all I could do was manage a small shrug.

"But you," Allan went on, "you're not even thirty years old, and you're running a successful business all by yourself. I do find that much more interesting."

"I inherited the business." I felt compelled to point out that particular not-so-insignificant fact.

He didn't seem too concerned by the reminder. After finally taking a bite of his Greek omelette, he said, "Lots of people inherit businesses. Not all of them manage to hang on to those businesses, let alone expand them and make them even more successful."

I wasn't sure where he'd dug up that little detail. Quite possibly, he'd been doing some research on me. At any rate, it was true—Margie had given me her business, but I'd taken it and run with it, expanding my repertoire beyond simply weddings, gradually getting a clientele that was more and more upscale. The previous year, Carson Creations had grossed just a little more than three quarters of a million dollars, and I knew I would surpass that number this year, even though I wouldn't close the books until December thirty-first rolled around.

"All right, maybe," I conceded, then reached for my drink. The glass was nearly empty by that point, so Allan tipped some more bubbly into the champagne flute and waited for me to go on. "Still, she's so...so...."

"She's someone who was destined to be a star," he said. "I'll grant you that. But stars can get tiring after a while. When you're around them, you end up squinting all the time from the glare."

I tilted my head at Allan and sent him a side-ways look. "Now you're teasing me."

"Maybe just a little." He picked up his fork and returned to his food. "I just don't want you to think that I still have a thing for Nina, because I really don't. And no, I didn't bring you here thinking that maybe our paths would cross. Honestly, I didn't even know she was staying at Brian's place—he's the one who has a house in Malibu. I know Nina rented a house in Beverly Hills after she moved out of my place."

Actually, the traitorous thought had crossed my mind that maybe Allan had suggested Malibu because he thought he might "accidentally" bump into Nina, even though such a ploy really didn't seem like him, or at least what I thought I knew about him. However, I brushed that niggling concern aside as his words seemed to finally sink in. So, he and Nina had shared that gorgeous house in the Hollywood Hills? I really didn't like to think about how she must have spent months and months there, thereby imprinting the place with her presence.

All right, I had to admit that there was defi-nitely no sign of her there now—not a photo, nothing to show she'd been Allan's companion in the place. Then again, I hadn't seen the upstairs. For all I knew, he had a wall-size Warhol-esque portrait of her hanging in the master bedroom. Somehow, I doubted it, though.

"It's fine," I said. Was it fine? I couldn't say for sure. What I knew for certain was that I needed to get past this silly spurt of jealousy. Nina was obviously in Allan's past, and besides…

…besides, I wasn't his future. The best I could hope for was this present…and I needed to make sure I didn't screw it up.

Brunch was a little subdued after that, but we moved on to less fractious topics and did our best to pretend the interruption had never occurred. Afterward, Allan suggested we go up to the Getty Museum—the old one, the villa-style place perched on a Malibu hillside less than a mile from the restaurant.

I would have said this was a spur-of-the-moment decision, except that I knew you had to have a reservation to go to the museum. Well, I wouldn't hold his forethought against him; I guessed that he'd wanted to come up with something fun to do during our time together, and I hadn't been to the villa for years and years, not since my mom and Faye took me there when I was thirteen. Admission was free, so if we'd ended up doing something else, it wasn't as though Allan would have wasted any money…not that he probably had even taken such a thing into consideration.

Because it was the weekend before a holiday, the place was full almost to capacity. Even so, Allan exhibited his usual parking karma by getting a space very close to the path that led up to the villa. We got out, and he asked, "Have you been here before?

"Not since I was in junior high," I replied. "What about you?"

He shook his head. "I'm new enough here that I haven't gotten to see all the sights yet. The County Museum of Art, and the big Getty Museum off the 405, but not much more than that."

"When did you come here from New York?"

By that point, we'd reached the entry pavilion, where we waited for the elevator that would take us up to the main level where the museum itself— a replica of an ancient Pompeian villa—was situated. Allan hesitated for a moment, then said, "Not quite a year ago. I relocated in February."

I grinned. "Probably a good time to get out of New York."

"The weather here was definitely better, although still rainier than I was expecting."

True enough—we'd had a wetter-than-normal winter, although I'd managed to keep the rain away from any weddings I was planning. Still, it hadn't been easy.

"Do you miss it?" I asked, once we'd stepped inside the elevator and were headed upward. Despite the packed parking lot, we were the only ones riding up to the museum right then. Probably, a lot of people had gotten there earlier in the day; we hadn't left the restaurant until a little past one o'clock.

"New York?"

I nodded.

His expression went a little vague, as if he was focusing on something very far away from our current location. I guessed he was remembering the East Coast and all the reasons why he'd left it. "Not really. Los Angeles suits me much better."

That was understandable. Even though L.A. real estate was absolutely insane, it sounded like it was even worse in New York. His house in the Hollywood Hills had to be worth millions, but it was a three-thousand-square-foot, two-story home on a decent plot of land with a swimming pool and views for days. That same amount of money in New York would probably get you a large condo in a nice neighborhood, but I'd rather have the house and the pool, thank you very much.

"I'm glad it suits you better," I said, feeling bold.

His eyes met mine, and another of those

strange but welcome thrills ran down my back. "Me, too."

The moment had to end there, because the elevator doors opened and we were confronted by a group of tourists who looked annoyed that someone was already inside and they had to wait for the two of us to exit. After that, we pushed our way to the entrance, where Allan checked in with the attendant on duty and we were allowed to roam free in the villa.

It was really a beautiful place, despite the crowds. We went from room to room, looking at the statues and the paintings in the various galleries, stopping to read the little plaques next to each piece. And if we wanted to go outside and breathe in the fresh ocean air, well, all we had to do was step out of a gallery and walk around the peristyle, a formal garden with a long, narrow reflecting pool in the center.

We talked about the differences between Los Angeles and New York—well, Allan did most of the talking, since I'd never been to the East Coast and had no basis of comparison—and wandered from garden to garden, getting our fill of the beautiful scenery and the serene nature of the museum and its accompanying gardens. Eventually, though, we'd seen all there was to see, and made our way back down to the car.

By that time, it was nearly five o'clock, and

the sun had already almost disappeared, was now a fiery half-disk setting beyond the deep blue of the ocean. We got in Allan's car, and he headed south on Pacific Coast Highway. However, as we were approaching Wilshire, where I expected him to turn left so he could take me home, he stayed to the right instead.

"Um…are we going somewhere?" I asked. Not that I minded spending more time with him—in fact, I'd sort of been dreading having to say goodbye—but I generally wasn't the kind of person who liked to have surprises sprung on her.

"It's such a lovely evening," he replied, apparently apropos of nothing. "I thought we could stay out a little while longer."

"Sure," I said, knowing I sounded less than enthusiastic. "Where?"

"The pier, of course."

Well, just earlier that day I'd been thinking that I needed to spend some time at the beach. Either Allan was a mind reader, or he'd also thought that a trip to Santa Monica merited a visit to the pier.

I didn't bother to protest that we'd have a hard time finding someplace to park on an early Sunday evening—especially one that wasn't a school night, since of course all the schools were out for the long Christmas holiday. Allan had already shown that he had a knack for parking that beat anything I'd seen in all my time in L.A., so I'd just roll with it.

"Sounds fun," I said, and left it at that.

As I'd expected, he got a primo spot in the north parking lot, and we made our way across the boardwalk and then up the stairs to the pier itself. With the sun nearly gone, the wind was a lot colder, and I hoped my thick twill jacket would be enough to ward off the chill. Allan would probably fare better, since he had on a leather jacket, but I hadn't thought about dressing to stay warm, since I'd figured this would be a daytime outing and nothing more.

Once we reached the Pacific Park fun zone, though, it felt a little warmer, probably because we were surrounded by people on all sides, and there were also buildings that housed food stands and souvenir shops and carnival-style games, and they helped to block the brisk ocean breeze. Towering over everything was the enormous Ferris wheel, brightly lit against the gathering dusk.

Allan gazed up at it for a moment, then asked, "Have you ever been on that?"

"Sure, when I was a kid." I sent him a dubious look. "What, did you want to ride on it?"

"I'd like to," he said. "I've never been on a Ferris wheel."

"You haven't?" I said, surprised. "You never

went to Coney Island when you lived in New York?"

For a second, he stared at me blankly, as if he wasn't quite sure what I was asking. Then he shook his head. "No, I never made it out there." A pause, and he added, "It's not quite as close to Manhattan as you might think."

I'd have to take his word for it, since my knowledge of the five boroughs was more than a little hazy. "Well, then we definitely need to go for a ride on the Ferris wheel. I hope you're not afraid of heights."

"If I were, I wouldn't have a house on the side of a hill."

I couldn't argue with that remark, so I nodded and said, "It looks like we can buy tickets over there. Let's take a look."

The two of us headed over to the kiosk I'd just spied, and a minute later, we were proud owners of a pack of tickets that would get us not just on the Ferris wheel, but all the other rides in Pacific Park. I really wasn't sure I wanted to go on some of them—anything that spun around too fast tended to get my stomach churning—but I decided to go with the flow and see what happened.

We handed the attendant our tickets and climbed into one of the cars, and he shut the door behind us and latched it. A moment later, we were moving—but just enough so another car could get in position and its passengers could climb aboard. A few more delays, and then at last we began to move, the huge wheel slowly rotating so that the fun zone shrank below us and the glittering lights of Los Angeles seemed to shimmer all around.

Unlike traditional Ferris wheels, the Pacific Wheel had round cars, so we could choose which direction we wanted to look. To the east was all of the glittering L.A. basin, while to the west was the vast darkness of the Pacific Ocean, broken up here and there by blinking lights that I guessed belonged to oil platforms.

"It's beautiful," Allan said, and I nodded.

"I've never been on this at night. It's really gorgeous."

Actually, that last word came out more as "g-gorgeous," because up there, the wind was much stronger and colder, and I could feel my teeth begin to chatter. At once, Allan moved closer to me. "Cold?"

"A little."

He slid over a bit more on the fiberglass seat, and the next thing I knew, he'd dropped his arm around me and pulled me close. It felt good to be snuggled up against him, and not just because of the welcome warmth his body provided. No, it was also that he felt strong and reassuringly solid, and he just smelled so damn good.

"Better?" he asked.

"Much," I said, letting myself relax into the somehow simultaneously thrilling and comforting sensation of his arm around me and my head on his shoulder. The big wheel spun around, dropping us down almost to the wooden platform where we'd first boarded, then moving back up into the dark sky, the noise from the pier and the blended scents of ocean salt and hot grease fading the higher we went.

And then the wheel stopped, and we hung there in the cool air, the car swaying ever so faintly.

"Is it supposed to do this?" Allan said, although he didn't sound too concerned.

"They pause it sometimes, I think...I can't remember for sure." I had a hazy recollection of the Ferris wheel stopping when I'd ridden it years and years ago, except I hadn't been lucky enough to get stuck in the prime position at the apex of the wheel's revolution.

He was silent for a moment, chin lifted as he stared out into the darkness of the ocean. What he was trying to see, I had no idea, since there really wasn't much out there. A few seconds later, though, he murmured, "Well, I'd say it was fortuitous timing."

A shift in position, and then his hands cupped my face, fingers warm against my wind-chilled cheeks. For one endless moment, our eyes met, his now almost the same night-dark blue as the sky above our heads. Then he bent and touched his lips to mine.

I'd been kissed before then, of course. Not as often as I would have liked, but enough that I knew what it was supposed to feel like. That kiss, though…my body seemed to flare to sudden life, flushing with heat as our mouths opened and we tasted one another, pressed closer as his hands moved from my face so he could pull me against him. We were both fully clothed, and yet I didn't think I'd ever felt that naked before, so utterly exposed, as if by kissing me, he was somehow able to reach down into the depths of my soul, to see who I was, to want me because of it, to recognize me in a way no one else ever had.

It was too much. I couldn't allow this to happen. I knew that, and yet I also somehow knew I wouldn't stop this, wouldn't stop what was happening between us. My soul craved this closeness, needed to feel cherished, even if I knew that feeling wouldn't last…*couldn't* last.

But I would let myself be happy for these few short days.

The Ferris wheel gave a sudden jerk, and we started moving again. Allan lifted his lips from mine, but he kept his gaze fixed on my face. I thought I could see surprise in his expression, as if he, too, had felt an echo of the shock that had shuddered through my body.

For his sake, though, I hoped it wasn't quite the same. I couldn't let him fall in love with me. In lust, sure. Anything else, though….

"Wow," I said, knowing I had to shatter the moment somehow, needed to bring us back to the here and now with the kind of remark that would break the spell we'd begun to weave between the two of us. "I wasn't expecting that."

At once, he smiled, although at the same time, I thought I glimpsed a brief hint of something else in his expression—disappointment? hurt?—before the familiar pleasant mask slipped into place. "I hope you didn't mind."

"No," I replied at once. "I was kind of hoping you would do that."

His hand reached over to clasp mine. I wrapped my fingers around his and gave them a gentle squeeze, signaling that I welcomed his touch. "I'm glad."

We were both silent then, holding hands until the ride was over and we were able to climb out of the little fiberglass car. The sounds and smells of the fun zone surrounded us again, but I was still acutely aware of the pressure of his hand on mine, the way he walked a little closer to me than he had previously.

Which was good. I wanted to relish his closeness as long as I could.

"Hungry?" he asked as we headed out to the
main section of the pier.

It actually had been quite a while since
brunch, since my watch told me we were coming
up on seven o'clock. "Yes," I said. "There's a
Bubba Gump's here on the pier, but I'm not much
into chain restaurants."

"Neither am I," Allan said. "What else is good
around here?"

"Depends on what you're in the mood for."

Maybe it was just the dancing lights from all
the midway games, but I thought I saw a twinkle
in his eyes. "Surprise me."

That comment sounded like a challenge.
There actually were quite a few good restaurants
within walking distance, but I thought we should
go to one of my old favorites, a place that was a
Santa Monica institution.

"Get ready to be surprised," I told him, and
began to walk toward Ocean Avenue.

Allan stayed by my side, although his
eyebrows lifted slightly. "Don't we need to move
the car?"

"No. It's only a few blocks away."

He shrugged and followed me as I crossed
Ocean, then turned to our right so we could go

down Santa Monica Boulevard. Another block up, and we'd reached our destination.

"A pub?" he asked, looking up at the old-fashioned sign that hung above the King's Head's front door.

I put a hand on my hip. "What, are you too fancy for some fish and chips?"

"I like fish and chips very much," he said. "Lead on."

Well, at least it appeared he was ready to roll with the punches. Also, my casual tone seemed to have told him that I wasn't quite ready for it to all be moonlight and roses, and he seemed fine with that, too.

A man after my own heart. Too bad my heart really wasn't mine to give.

We went inside. The pub was crowded on that Sunday night, feeling even more cramped than usual because of the holiday decorations that had been crammed into every possible spare inch of the interior, but it felt good to me—cozy, and a welcome respite from the damp night air. A group had just gotten up from one of the tables at the window, and the hostess promised us that one—"just as soon as it's had a wipe," she told us in an accent that seemed to indicate she was a recent transplant from the U.K.

The delay was only for a minute or so, and soon enough we were ensconced in the vinyl-upholstered booth, where we could watch the crowds pass by on Santa Monica Boulevard outside. Allan picked up his menu and studied it for a moment, then set it back down and shook his head.

"This really isn't the sort of place I expected you to hang out," he remarked.

"Just because I organize high-end events doesn't mean I want to live like that every day. Sometimes I want to put on a pair of jeans and get comfy."

"Which I find admirable."

Our waiter came by and took our drink orders —Allan rose to the occasion and requested a Guinness, while I got my favorite pub drink, a "snake bite," which was a mixture of hard cider and Harp lager. Once again, my companion looked a little startled, but he didn't comment on my order, only leaned against the back of the booth and smiled at me.

"So, how long have you been coming here?"

"Since I was a kid," I replied. "Faye and my mom started bringing me here when I was probably around seven or eight. And after that, it was just one of the restaurants in our regular rotation. I like eating here when I can because there isn't much chance of me running into any of my clients in a pub."

He chuckled. "No, probably not. Their loss, I suppose."

I agreed. The place was very low-key, but I knew plenty of British celebs stopped in when they were visiting L.A.—in fact, my family had had a David Beckham sighting in the King's Head when I was in high school. And yes, he was that gorgeous in person—I had to tease my mom and Faye about the way they'd gotten all googly over him, since they didn't have a hetero bone in their bodies, but even they had to acknowledge he was a pretty fine specimen of a man.

Our drinks arrived, and Allan and I clinked glasses, although we weren't really toasting anything except maybe simply being together. Which, I thought, was a good enough reason to celebrate.

After we'd both had several swallows of beer, he said, "Are you all right with coming over to my place in the late afternoon tomorrow, maybe around four-thirty or five?"

"Sure," I replied, although I wondered why so late. Then again, it was Christmas Eve. I never thought of it as the sort of holiday where a lot of daytime activities were involved. "That'll give me a chance to run some errands before everything closes down for the holidays."

His eyes laughed at me over the rim of his pint glass, which he'd just lifted to his mouth to take another drink. "Does anything really close in Los Angeles?"

"Some things," I replied, "but you're right—probably not that many. Do you need me to bring anything?"

"Just yourself. Well, and the finalized budgets, assuming your vendors get you the information you were waiting on."

Funny how he could be all business now, when less than fifteen minutes earlier, we'd been sharing the most breathtaking kiss I'd ever experienced. However, the human mind could be a strange thing—the human heart even more so—and so I didn't feel too thrown off by his comment.

"They will," I said. "They wouldn't leave me hanging like that over the holiday."

"I'm glad to hear it."

Then we went on to talk about the museum and what we'd seen that afternoon, and I told him a little more about growing up in Santa Monica and how I used to spend what felt like my entire summer at the beach—carefully slathered in sunscreen, since I had the fair skin to go with my red hair. Because both Faye and my mother worked in education, we were all off for summer at basically the same time, which made childcare a lot easier.

Just light small talk, carefully avoiding the

subject of our kiss at the top of the Pacific Park Ferris wheel. We ate, and laughed, and eventually the meal was over, and it was time to retrieve Allan's car so he could take me home.

As he drove, I wondered how best to handle our farewells. Yes, we'd kissed, but I wasn't quite ready to invite him in and ask him to stay over. Or rather, although my body was probably ready enough, I didn't want to let him think that one kiss was quite enough to get me into bed…even though in this case, it probably was.

We got out of the car, and he walked me up to the front door. I dug my keys out of my purse, then paused, trying to think of something to say that didn't sound too dismissive.

"It was a wonderful day," I said simply, and his expression warmed as he gazed down at me.

"It was," he echoed. He bent and kissed me, but it was a gentle kiss, not much more than a press of his lips against mine. For just a second, he glanced toward the door, and a corner of his mouth lifted. "And it was all I needed. Good night, Belinda…I'll see you tomorrow."

Having delivered his goodbye, he turned and headed down the porch steps. I stood there for a moment, watching him go. Part of me was relieved, while the other part wondered if I should have invited him in, should have thrown my scruples aside.

There's always tomorrow, I reminded myself as I unlocked the door and went in. Mr. Mittens was lying on the living room sofa, and he cracked one eyelid and sent me a very bored stare before he closed his eye again. Well, he was used to me coming and going at odd hours.

And as for the next day…I had a feeling it was going to end very differently.

CHAPTER TEN

As expected, the estimates from both Marcelle for the catering and Tori for the flowers and other decor were in my inbox by ten o'clock the next morning. They both wished me a happy holiday, and said they'd be in touch later if I had any questions. Tori also said that she didn't think she needed to come over to Allan's for a walk-through as long as I sent her enough photos, and I replied that I'd take care of getting her images of the property and send them to her after Christmas.

All that handled, I made copies of the estimates for Allan and slipped them into a manila folder, which I placed in my tote bag. Also in that tote bag was what I liked to think of as my "emergency kit"—a personal one this time, not something intended for my brides. That kit contained a travel toothbrush and toothpaste, face wipes, travel-size deodorant, and a spare pair of underwear. No, I didn't know for sure that I would be staying the night at Allan's house...but I also didn't know that I wouldn't, either.

My mother called and asked if I wanted to come over that evening, even though the main festivities would be taking place on Christmas Day itself.

"I can't," I told her, cell phone held up to my ear with one hand while I had a small plastic watering can in the other. I made sure to only have very low-maintenance houseplants, but eventually even they needed some TLC. "I have a date."

"'A date'?" she repeated, sounding surprised. "On Christmas Eve? Who is it?"

"Um, a guy I met at the Lowell wedding," I replied. "No one you would know."

"Ah," she said, which could have meant anything. I knew she did her best not to interfere in my love life—not that it was exactly a love life, but I didn't know how else to think of it— but she'd expressed concern from time to time that I was skating a little too close to the edge with some of the men I'd dated. And maybe I had, but I was careful to keep things casual, always broke off a relationship if it looked like things were getting too serious. Of course, lately

I'd skirted around the problem by not seeing anyone at all, and yet even that forced celibacy seemed to bother her on some level, as if she kept hoping I'd secretly discover I'd been gay the whole time.

That would have made my life a lot easier, but I knew it was never going to happen.

"He's an agent," I went on, taking care not to mention Allan by name. No, my mother didn't haunt the celebrity gossip sites the way I did, but I figured it was better to be safe, just in case. "He's launching his own agency in January and so will be super-busy. It's perfect, really, because we can see each other over the holidays and then go our separate ways."

A long pause, and then she said, "Belinda, do you honestly think it's going to be that easy?"

"Sure," I lied, even as I recalled the touch of his fingers brushing against my skin, the way my entire body had come alive at his kiss. "This is just a…fling. A way to spend time together at a fun time of the year. He doesn't have time for a relationship, and neither do I."

That was a nice way of sugarcoating the situation. However, my mother didn't call me on it, because she knew I needed to have my coping mechanisms so I wouldn't drive myself crazy.

"So, you're seeing him tonight?" she asked, sounding resigned.

"Yes. But don't worry—I'll be at your place right on time tomorrow afternoon."

We always gathered around two o'clock on Christmas Day to open presents and have a nosh of some sort, usually gourmet cheese and crackers and wine. After that, we sat down to a real holiday dinner of free-range turkey and all the trimmings —Faye was a wonderful cook, so the real challenge of the day was to avoid eating so much that they'd have to roll me out the door at the end of the feast.

"Great," my mother said, now with a forced cheeriness that didn't fool me one bit. But at least she hadn't tried to convince me that going over to Allan's that night was a bad idea. "You have a lovely Christmas Eve, darling, and we'll see you tomorrow afternoon."

"Merry Christmas, Mom," I replied.

"Merry Christmas, sweetie."

I ended the call, telling myself that I should be relieved she hadn't asked me to give her more information about Allan. But then, there was no real reason for her to do so. She knew as well as I did that there was no way he'd be around after the holidays, and so there wasn't any point in learning more about him.

Well, that was a depressing thought. I put down the phone and finished watering the plants, then made sure everything was as tidied up as possible. Since I spent so much time away, I never did much decorating for Christmas, although I had a fresh pine swag on the mantel, and a pair of cheerful poinsettias sat on the two side tables in the living room. I eyed them for a second, then sighed and took them into the bedroom and shut the door. While Mr. Mittens was in general a well-behaved cat, I couldn't be sure he wouldn't get so irritated with me about being gone overnight that he might not knock them over or worse, try to take a nibble. Better to be safe than sorry.

Of course, that assumed I actually would be staying at Allan's, which was far from a given. But I didn't want to take the chance.

I allowed myself one last peek in the bathroom mirror, just to make sure my makeup looked fine and the curls I'd set in my hair earlier that day hadn't decided to go all limp. Red wasn't a good color for me, so I didn't have anything really festive and holiday-appropriate, but I hoped the close-fitting dark teal sweater, gray wool skirt, and high-heeled black boots I wore looked dressy enough for Christmas Eve at Allan's house. Underneath, I wore my favorite green satin bra and panties.

Would he get to see them?

I supposed I'd just have to wait and see what happened.

A double-check of Mr. Mittens' food and

water supply, and then it was time to sling my purse over one shoulder and gather up the tote bag with the budget paperwork and my little emergency kit. I went out to the garage—my house was originally built in the late 1940s, and the garage was detached—and sent a wary glance up toward the sky. Unlike the night before, which had been clear and starry bright, this afternoon was cloudy and gray, almost threatening. There hadn't been any rain in the forecast, but....

Holding back a sigh, I stowed the tote bag in the cargo compartment of my little Mercedes SUV, then hurried back to the house, let myself in, and grabbed my black leather coat and a small folding umbrella from the closet just inside the front door. While I could meddle with the weather if necessary, I really tried to do so only for my clients, since California needed whatever rain it could get, even if it did come on Christmas Eve.

Back on the sofa, Mr. Mittens sent me a jaundiced look, as if annoyed with me for disturbing his nap.

"Sorry, kitty," I said. "See you soon."

Then I shut the door and locked it again. The lights in the living room were on timers, so I didn't have to worry about leaving my cat home alone in the dark—or letting anyone casing the neighborhood know that no one was home on this particular Christmas Eve. Not that I had much to steal, except my big, newish iMac in the home office. My laptop was in the tote bag, and I'd never been the kind of person to collect expensive jewelry. There were probably much better prospects on my block when it came to that sort of thing.

Having reassured myself that a Christmas Eve burglary was probably not anything I needed to worry about, I got in the car and backed out of the garage, then cut over to Sunset Boulevard so I could head east. It might have been the lead-up to a holiday, but it was also a Monday, meaning there was still plenty of traffic on the roads, possibly more than usual, thanks to people trying to get out of town a few hours earlier than they normally would.

I watched the brake lights of the car ahead of me and tried not to curse. After all, Allan had said "sometime between four-thirty and five," so it wasn't as if I had a hard deadline I needed to hit. Still, my work had turned me into a very punctual person, and I disliked running late.

Eventually, though, I was able to turn left on La Brea and then head up toward the streets that would lead me toward Allan's hillside home. Here, the roads were a lot less crowded, and I was able to pull into his driveway at almost exactly four forty-five.

As I put the car in park, a few drops of rain hit

the windshield. Good thing I'd gone back to get my coat, although I hoped it wouldn't start raining hard enough that I'd have to deploy the umbrella. Hurriedly, I grabbed my purse and got out, then went back to fetch the tote bag from the cargo area. A few drops of rain hit my hands, but I thought my hair should be able to survive intact unless a downpour started in the next couple of seconds.

Luckily, though, I was able to make it to the front door and the safety of its overhang without getting anything more than a few droplets on me. I rang the doorbell, noticing that a pair of large cream-and-red poinsettia plants in elegant urns now adorned the entry. They hadn't been there during my last visit, so apparently Allan had gone out and gotten them to make the house look a little more festive for the holiday.

He opened the door, looking very elegant in a dark blue dress shirt and gray slacks. At once, he stepped aside, saying, "Come on in. Is it raining?"

"It's trying to," I replied as I entered the foyer. Allan took my tote bag and purse from me, allowing me to shrug out of my coat.

"Let's trade," he said, and reached for the coat so he could hang it in the closet behind him.

I gave it to him, accepting in return the tote and my purse. "I like the poinsettias."

That comment earned me a smile, although he

said, "Oh, that's nothing. Come in—let me get you a drink."

I followed him into the living room and saw that he'd only been telling the truth. Fir boughs decorated with pale gold ribbon and glittering glass ornaments lay on the low ledge that hugged the stacked-stone fireplace, and a tall, slender tree adorned with white lights and ornaments in the same soft gold palette stood against the window. Over in the dining room, the table was covered in a white cloth with a gold beaded runner in the center, and more greens decorated with gold ribbons had been artfully wrapped around a long bronze candleholder that flickered with a dozen votives.

"Wow," I said. "You've been busy. No wonder you wanted me to come over later in the afternoon."

He looked almost absurdly pleased, like a kid whose finger painting just got the coveted place of honor on his mother's refrigerator. "Well, I didn't do any of this, except make a few calls. Tory was busy, but she gave me the names of a few people who could take care of some last-minute decorating for me." A pause, and he went on, "I wanted it to feel like the holidays for you."

"Well, it does," I told him, knowing I'd flushed a little at the thought that he'd done all this just for me. "It's beautiful."

"I'm glad you like it. I told Leslie what I was thinking of, and she just sort of ran with it." As he was speaking, Allan went into the kitchen and got a bottle of white wine out of the fridge. "Some chardonnay?"

"Sounds great," I said. After the drive over there from Santa Monica, I definitely needed a drink.

He poured wine for both of us and then came over and gave me a glass, which I took with the hand that wasn't holding the tote bag. "Why don't we sit in the living room?"

That sounded like a great idea, since he had a fire going in the hearth, and everything was about as cozy as a cool-toned modern house like this would ever be. I followed him over to the couch and sat down next to him. The last time we were in this room together, I'd maintained a much greater space between us, but there was no need for those constraints now that so much had changed between us.

"Merry Christmas," he said.

I echoed the words as we touched glasses, then added, "I have the estimates from Marcelle and Tori. I figured you'd probably want to get that over with first so we can relax."

"Definitely," Allan replied. He allowed himself another swallow of chardonnay, then set down his glass. I did the same, freeing up my hands so I could reach in the tote and pull out the manila envelope and hand it over to him. He removed the paperwork in question and began to scan its contents.

Since he didn't speak right away, I wondered if he was taken aback by the amounts in question. He'd acted as if money was no object, but maybe I'd misread him. "If it's coming in a little high, there are probably a few places where we can trim things," I suggested, and he immediately shook his head and sent me an amused sideways glance.

"No, this is all fine," he said. "I don't want to change a thing. Let me go write you a check."

It felt strange to sit there on the couch as he got up and went around the corner to a room I hadn't seen yet, presumably the office. However, I sipped my wine and gazed out the window—well, the part of it that wasn't obscured by the Christmas tree—and saw how the rain had begun to pick up in earnest, dimpling the surface of the swimming pool. The fire was warm, though, and the house smelled good, of some kind of potpourri or candle or something scented with orange and clove, festive without being cloying.

Allan returned and handed a check over to me. I glanced down at it, then frowned.

"This is for the whole amount."

"Yes, it is," he said, his tone casual. "But I don't see the point in fussing around with deposits when I know everything is going to go perfectly. Isn't that your stock in trade…organizing events that are worry-free?"

Well, it was, although I thought it would be tempting fate to acknowledge the fact quite so baldly. "I do what I can," I replied lightly. "But I'll hold the check until the party's over, just in case."

"You really don't need to do that."

"I know," I said, then tucked the check into the binder in my tote bag. "But I'll feel better if I do."

For a moment, he was quiet, watching me carefully. I tried not to flush under that steady gaze, but it was hard, especially since I was acutely aware of how close we sat, of the lightly tanned skin at his throat where his shirt collar was open, the strength of the hands that lay on top of the expensive wool trousers. When he spoke, though, it was with a faint chuckle in his voice.

"I think I may have found the one honest woman in L.A."

All I could do was shake my head. "I think that's an overstatement," I protested. "There are lots of good people here. But if all you do is hang out with entertainment industry types, I can see why your point of view might be a bit…jaded."

That remark made him laugh out loud. "You're probably right. Still, I have to say, it's refreshing. Here's to being honest."

We clinked glasses again and drank, the chardonnay slipping happily down my throat. It was very good, not oaky at all. Since I hadn't gotten a look at the label, I didn't know what it was, although I supposed I should have known to trust Allan when it came to choosing wines.

A bit of silence as we sipped our wine, and then he said, "And it's really all right that you're not with your family tonight?"

"Yes," I replied. "We're all set for tomorrow, so you don't have to worry about me abandoning my mom and Faye and my grandmother on Christmas Eve. Honestly, we would have just sat around and watched *A Christmas Story* or *Scrooged* or something anyway." I paused, scanning his face for a moment. There wasn't much to read in his expression, except possibly a bit of amusement at my family's choice of entertainment. Still, he knew quite a lot about me, while he'd told me very little about himself. "And your own family?" I asked. "It must be hard, if this is your first holiday away from the East Coast."

At once, something in his face went closed and quiet. "I'm afraid I don't have much of a family anymore," he said. "Just a…brother…and we're rather estranged, I'm afraid. You know how it is."

Actually, I didn't, because even though my family wasn't large, just the four of us, what we lacked in size we more than made up for in togetherness. However, planning weddings had introduced me to a wide range of family dysfunctions, so I had some exposure to the ways people managed to screw each other up, even if I hadn't been forced to deal with any of those neuroses on a personal basis.

I made a noncommittal sound. "I'm sorry."

"Don't be," Allan responded at once. "I came to L.A. to make a fresh start, and I've been having a wonderful time. I don't miss New York, or…him."

Whoever this brother was, he must have been a piece of work. I couldn't think why else Allan would get that expression on his face when talking about him, since in general, he seemed remarkably sunny and equable, even when confronted by his famous ex-girlfriend in probably one of the last places he'd expected to see her.

Well, I wouldn't pry. If he wanted to tell me more, I'd listen, but it was probably better to leave it alone, especially since we were supposed to be having a cozy Christmas Eve together.

"Fair enough," I said. "So, tell me about your plans for your agency."

His eyes crinkled at the corners, as if he'd seen right away what I was doing with that particular change of subject, but he didn't call me on it, only went on to talk about how he'd lured away a couple of the junior agents from Hart Hathaway, and how the finishing touches were being put on the new office and they'd be able to move in the week after the new year. Jack Holloway had already signed with them, and the new forward for the Lakers, along with several TV personalities who were less than enchanted with their current representation. I didn't pretend to know all that much about the ins and outs of Hollywood management, but it sounded to me as if Allan's agency was going to hit the ground running. He definitely was taking it seriously, which seemed to disprove my private theory that he was merely a rich East Coast dilettante looking for something to amuse himself while he was out here in L.A.

"And what about you?" he asked. "You said you were going to be busy in January as well. More weddings?"

"Not at first," I replied. "I have one toward the end of the month, and three in February. But what's keeping me busy through mid-January is a self-help retreat I'm planning for Miri Janek."

He looked impressed by that revelation. Miri Janek was a number-one *New York Times* best-selling self-help guru who hosted sold-out seminars all over the country. This was her first full-blown retreat, though, which would be held over the long Martin Luther King weekend that coming January in a compound in Malibu. That

I'd been tapped to manage the entire affair, from the floral decorations in the various retreat rooms to planning the meals and overseeing the various printed handouts the attendees would receive, was a very big deal. In fact, it was such a big deal that I was secretly worried whether Dee and I could handle it all on our own. Yes, I'd hired temporary workers to manage registration and to act as general gofers for the two of us, but even so, I didn't know whether that would still be enough.

I didn't want to confess these misgivings to Allan, though, and so I went on, "That's why I wanted to take time off after the Blankenship wedding. I knew that planning the retreat would take up a big chunk of my time. So far, though, it's all been going smoothly enough—I was lucky in that Miri's management was okay with me using my regular vendors, and the resort we're renting out is used to doing this kind of an event."

"Well, it sounds as though you have it well in hand." Allan drank some more of his chardonnay, and then glanced over at my glass, which was less than half full. "Like a refill?"

"Sure," I said, knowing I was probably being a little reckless. Still, I'd planned for contingencies, and if it turned out I was too tipsy to drive, then I was pretty sure he wouldn't have too much of a problem with me crashing at his place. In fact, I got the impression that he'd be more than happy to have me as an overnight guest…a feeling that was definitely mutual.

We both got up from the sofa, and he topped off our glasses. I looked once again at the dining room table, noting the elegant place settings…but also the complete lack of anything that looked like food preparation in the kitchen. Not that Allan really seemed like the type to whip up a gourmet meal, and yet I assumed we were going to eat *something*. Maybe he was going to order out for pizza.

He must have noticed my sidelong glance in the direction of the dining room, because his mouth quirked a little and he said, "Never fear, Belinda. A Christmas Eve feast is en route as we speak."

"Oh?"

A sip of chardonnay, and he said, "Yes, I ordered us dinner from Petit Trois, and it's being delivered by an Uber Eats driver. Have to love all these modern conveniences—especially on a rainy night such as this one."

This explanation relieved me somewhat, although I had to feel a little sorry for whoever was out there hustling take-out meals on Christmas Eve instead of relaxing somewhere with family and friends. Then again, unless I'd misread Allan completely, I had a feeling that driver was going to earn one heck of a tip.

"In the meantime," he continued, "I have a little something for you."

"'Something'?" I echoed, a small thrill of nervousness hitting me somewhere in the midsection.

"Yes," he said, then set down his glass and went over to the Christmas tree. I now saw that it had a single small package lying on the elegant cream-and-gold embroidered skirt, a package wrapped in pale gold paper and tied with white ribbons. He picked it up and handed it to me. "Just something I saw that reminded me of you."

"I didn't know we were doing presents," I told him, not quite able to keep a faint note of accusation from entering my tone. "I didn't get you anything."

My comment only made him smile. "You being here is present enough for me."

There really wasn't anything I could say in response to his remark that wouldn't sound foolish, so I looked down at the package I held and carefully slid the ribbon off the box. After it was out of the way, I ran a fingernail under the tape to undo it, and pulled out the flat velvet case the wrapping paper had hidden.

That kind of case usually hid only one sort of thing. I could feel my heart begin to speed up, even as I told myself that I shouldn't be too worried, that at least I didn't see a Tiffany's logo, or one from Van Cleef & Arpels, Bulgari, or any of the other expensive jewelry stores in Los Angeles. Still....

Hardly daring to breathe, I opened the lid. Lying inside was an absolutely exquisite large blue-green gem that I thought was an aquamarine, surrounded by a halo of diamonds, with diamonds also encrusting the round bale, which floated on a multi-strand white gold chain. It was so impressively beautiful, for a long moment I could only stand there and stare down at it, not sure how I was supposed to react.

"It reminded me of your eyes," Allan said, looking a little puzzled by my lack of reaction. "Do you like it?"

"It's beautiful," I replied at once. The last thing I wanted him to think was that I didn't appreciate how stunning the necklace was. Only.... "I just—you really shouldn't have gotten me something so...so...."

I'd been about to say "expensive," but that would have sounded crass. Honestly, I'd never had anyone make such an extravagant gesture for me before, so I had no idea how I was supposed to act.

He said, "I wanted to get you something. Don't think about 'should' or whether it's appropriate or not. Do you like it?"

"I love it," I replied. After all, he'd called me

the only honest woman in L.A. just moments before. Probably, it wouldn't have been very smart to start lying then and there.

"Well, then," he said, as if that solved everything. "Do you want to wear it? It's very handy that you didn't wear a necklace tonight."

I hadn't, mostly because I didn't have anything that really went with the outfit I was wearing. Instead, I'd put on my white gold and diamond hoop earrings, a splurge from the previous year after I'd seen that my company's income was going to push past the three-quarter-million mark.

Those earrings would look stunning with the aquamarine necklace, I knew.

Allan came over and lifted the necklace from the box, then undid the clasp. I stood quietly as he slipped it around my throat and fastened it once again. The pendant felt heavy and cool lying against the exposed skin of my chest, and I reached up to touch it, to feel the smooth metal and the faint sharpness of the prongs that held the diamonds in place.

"Perfection," he said, although he was looking at my face and not at the necklace.

"I—I don't know what to say."

"Then don't say anything."

He bent and kissed me then, and it was just as good as it had been on the pier—maybe better, because I felt slightly lightheaded already, thanks to the wine, and we were indoors someplace warm. I pressed up against him, felt his arms go around me, strong and yet gentle at the same time, tasted the chardonnay on his tongue. Welcome thrills surged through my body, and I wondered if we were even going to make it to dinner.

However, the doorbell rang just then, and he pulled away from me with a rueful smile. "You've got to love their timing. Hold that thought."

Feeling a little wicked, I winked at him and then went to retrieve my glass of wine so I could take a bracing swallow. He headed toward the front door, where I heard him have a brief convo with the delivery driver before he returned to the kitchen, large brown paper bags with carry handles in either hand.

"Do you need help with anything?" I asked as he set the bags down on the pale quartz-stone countertop. "I'm pretty good at dinner setup."

"Yes, I'd love that," he replied. "I'll admit that when I get takeout, I'm usually eating Thai food out of a carton in front of the TV."

The image was so incongruous—mostly because he seemed so flawlessly suave no matter what he was doing—that I had to chuckle. "Well, then, let's see what we've got here. I'll definitely need some serving pieces, though, and whatever serving utensils you've got."

Dinner turned out to be *coq au vin,* with garlic mashed potatoes, balsamic-grilled green beans, fresh bread, and salad…along with bread pudding with vanilla bourbon sauce for dessert. I left the bread pudding on the counter and transferred everything else to the serving pieces Allan had fetched for me, while he corked the remainder of the chardonnay and went to fetch a bottle of burgundy to go with our meal.

In not very much time at all, we were sitting at the table, amazing aromas from the food drifting upward, while votives flickered in the centerpiece and the rain fell outside, coming down hard enough that I actually could hear it clearly. That was all right, though, because the two of us were held there together in our little bubble of light and warmth, shielded from the elements.

Just as he was about to sit down, he said, "Oh, just a moment," and went over to the living room. A few seconds later, I understood the reason for the delay—he'd turned on the tabletop Bose sound system, and the sound of Mel Tormé singing "Silver Bells" began to drift over toward where I sat in the dining area.

"Can't have Christmas Eve dinner without Christmas music," I remarked with a smile as Allan returned to the table and took his seat.

"Absolutely not." He set his napkin in his lap, then said, "Thank you for coming tonight."

My hand went—almost inadvertently—to the heavy aquamarine pendant hanging at my throat. "I think I should be the one who's thanking you."

"I'm not so sure. After all, you had family you could have been with tonight, but you came over to share the holiday with me."

I wouldn't exactly have called that a sacrifice, not when I would be seeing everyone the following day, but I thought protesting would have sounded churlish, so I only lifted my shoulders. "I'm very glad to be here."

"Then we'll drink to that." He raised his glass, and I followed suit. After the customary clink of glass against glass, he said, "To being together on Christmas Eve."

I was glad he'd tacked the bit about Christmas Eve onto the end of his toast, or I might have been worried that he was hinting at something a bit more long-term. As much as I might have wished for such a thing in my heart of hearts, I knew I couldn't encourage him, couldn't do or say anything to lead him to believe this little fling of ours would last past the end of the year.

And maybe I should have protested a little more strongly the gift of the necklace, although I guessed he would have been offended if I hadn't accepted it. While I had no true idea how wealthy he actually was, I somehow had the feeling that buying me the aquamarine, while it was obviously worth a great deal, hadn't even put a dent in his discretionary budget for the month.

So I would enjoy it, and have something to remember Allan by when this was all over.

At least the curse would allow me that much.

CHAPTER ELEVEN

THE FOOD WAS FABULOUS, AS WAS THE WINE. More amazing to me, though, was how easy I found it to sit there and talk to Allan, whether discussing something as simple as whether I should add a second bathroom to my modest house—it would definitely increase the resale value, but since I didn't plan on going anywhere, I wasn't sure whether the expense and the hassle was worth it—or what we should do with our time over the next week. Christmas Day, of course, was already spoken for, but we had days and days to fill after that. A lot depended on the weather, I supposed, although I could give it a wink and a nudge to cooperate if the forecast called for storms on the day of an outdoor expedition…not that I planned to tell Allan about my convenient little gift.

"Have you ever been horseback riding?" he asked as he gave me a second helping of *coq au vin*. "I read somewhere that you can go on guided tours in Malibu."

"Once, when I was around eight or nine," I replied. "I'm not sure who was more scarred for life—the horse or me."

Allan lifted an eyebrow, mouth twitching. "That good?"

"Or bad, depending on how you look at it," I said. "I know most girls are supposed to go through their 'horse' phase at that age, but that ride convinced me I didn't want to get within ten feet of a horse ever again. So…while I appreciate the idea, I'd rather do something else."

"Noted." He drank some burgundy, expression thoughtful. "What about a helicopter ride to Catalina Island?"

That sounded like more fun, especially since I'd never ridden in a helicopter. Still, I had to ask. "Why not take the ferry?"

Looking slightly sheepish, he said, "I get seasick."

A common enough problem. And since money didn't seem to be a problem for Allan, I supposed the cost of paying to fly both of us to Catalina Island didn't even factor into the equation. "I think that's definitely an idea," I said. "What day?"

"Maybe Thursday? I'll have to check availability—I assume they'll probably be busy because of so many people being on vacation this week. Still, I should be able to work something out."

No doubt. If he could get someone over to his house to decorate it for Christmas at the last minute and have a gourmet meal delivered on Christmas Eve, and still find time to shop for expensive jewelry, then I had a feeling that coming up with a set of round-trip helicopter fares to Catalina wouldn't be a big deal, either. I'd been there once when I was a freshman in high school, but that was more than ten years ago, and I assumed I'd be looking at the place with very different eyes if I went now.

Especially if I visited the island with Allan D'Alessandro at my side.

"Thursday sounds perfect," I said, and he looked pleased.

"I'll check on that tomorrow sometime. If there isn't anything available online, then I'll call on Wednesday."

He sounded casual, almost off-hand, but his words reminded me that he'd be here all alone on Christmas Day. Obviously, he didn't have a pet, or I would have seen evidence of one before now. For some reason, the thought of him by himself without even a dog or cat to keep him company saddened me. That rush of pity was probably what prompted me to say, "Why don't you come over to my mom's with me tomorrow? We always have enough food for an army, so I know it wouldn't be a problem."

For a few seconds, he just stared at me, clearly surprised. Then he shook his head. "No, I wouldn't want to intrude on a family gathering like that." Gaze softening, he reached out with his left hand to touch my right where it had been resting on the tabletop. "I appreciate the offer, Belinda...I really do. But I'll be fine. I have things I was planning to work on, so don't worry about me."

"You're sure?" I asked, a little relieved that he'd turned down the offer. Oh, I had to admit that some part of me wanted to show him off, but I also realized that bringing him to meet my mother and Faye and my grandmother would probably open a huge can of worms. For one thing, I was fairly sure all my mother would have to do was look at me with him to realize that I wasn't playing this whole thing quite as casually as I'd intended. And while she would be on her best behavior while he was around, I knew I'd probably be subjected to some in-depth lecturing about how I should never have allowed things to get so serious. If he'd agreed to come over, I would have considered a grilling by my mother a fair exchange to avoid having him spend

Christmas Day alone, but it was probably better this way.

"I'm sure," he replied. His fingers gave mine a gentle squeeze. "If the weather clears up, I'll sit outside and enjoy the fresh air. It'll be fine."

"All right," I said. "But if you change your mind—"

"I won't," he cut in. "I'm just happy to have you here tonight."

Since I could tell he didn't want to talk about it anymore, I figured it was better to change the subject. "Why don't we go to the movies on Wednesday? It'll be something low-key and fun to do. We could go to the ArcLight—"

"No, better somewhere else," Allan said abruptly, and I stared at him for a few seconds, wondering what in the world would make him so adamant about not going to that particular theater. I liked the assigned seating and being able to bring a glass of wine with you into a showing, but I could do without those refinements if he preferred to go someplace different.

"Sure," I said. "The Chinese?"

"Better. Sorry—I just had a bad experience at the ArcLight once." He picked up his wine and sipped from it. "I'm not picky, so you can choose the movie."

I honestly had no idea what was even playing —my schedule in general didn't allow me to pick up and go to the movies whenever I felt like it—but I'd check the showtimes sometime the next day and send him a text or something.

"In fact," he went on, eyes lighting up a little, "I just thought of someplace we could go afterward for dinner. But you'll need to bring an evening dress you can change into after the movies."

That sounded mysterious. L.A. was a pretty casual place, so in general, there weren't a lot of venues that required you to dress up. However, because there were so few, I was able to guess pretty quickly exactly where he planned to take me.

"We're going to the Magic Castle?" I asked, hoping I didn't sound like a little girl who'd just found out her parents were taking her to tea at the Disneyland Hotel with the princesses for her birthday.

He looked so crestfallen, I had to prevent myself from laughing out loud. "How did you guess? I was hoping to surprise you."

I patted him on the hand and tried not to grin. "I'm an event planner, Allan. I have pretty much all the upscale venues in the greater Los Angeles area memorized. There are very few that have a strict dress code—and since the Castle is just down the hill from this house, it didn't take a rocket scientist to put two and two together."

"I suppose I should have thought of that."

Another question popped into my head. No, I wasn't going to ask how we were going to gain entry to the private club; knowing Allan, he'd bought himself an associate membership. However, even if you were a member, it wasn't the sort of place where you could simply waltz in on a whim. "How are you going to get reservations on such short notice, though? I thought that place was booked weeks in advance, but you want to go the day after tomorrow?"

A small, secretive smile played around his lips. "Oh, I have my ways."

I supposed he did. Asking about his methods probably would have been crass, so I pushed my curiosity aside as best I could, mentally inventorying what I had in my closet that would be fitting for an evening out at the Magic Castle. Yes, I had plenty of nice dresses, since they were a necessity for my work, but none of them were quite fancy enough to be categorized as cocktail attire. Well, except one, an insanely beautiful Sue Wong beaded silk dress in a dark teal shade not too different from the sweater I'd worn for this Christmas Eve date. I'd bought the gown on clearance a while back just because it was beautiful and fit me like a dream, even though I couldn't clearly formulate any true need for it.

Well, it looked like I had a need now.

"Okay," I said. "Luckily, I have something I can wear. Otherwise, I'd have to brave the department stores the day after Christmas, and that thought is too frightening to contemplate."

His eyes danced with laughter. "I'm glad I won't be inconveniencing you too much."

"Oh, I'd put up with a lot of inconvenience in exchange for dinner at the Magic Castle. But it won't be necessary."

He chuckled, and we finished our meal, then took the plates over to the kitchen. "Ready for dessert?" he asked.

As luscious as that bread pudding looked, I knew I needed a little time to let my food settle before I tried to fit anything else in there. "In a little bit," I said. "If that's okay."

"It's fine. But," he went on, "maybe a drink to bridge us?"

After sharing part of that bottle of chardonnay and an entire bottle of burgundy, I didn't know whether having anything else to drink was such a good idea. However, Allan didn't seem to notice my dubious expression—or maybe he was simply ignoring it—because he went over to the wine fridge and got out a small bottle and removed the cork, then fetched two cordial glasses from one of the cupboards.

"Late harvest malbec," he explained, pouring a small measure of the dark liquid into the glasses.

"Not as heavy as port, but just as good. Or at least, I think so."

I'd tasted a lot of wines, but I had to admit I'd never tried this particular after-dinner drink before. "'Late harvest'?" I echoed. "Does leaving the grapes on the vines concentrate the sugars, making it stronger?"

"Exactly," he said, and looked pleased. "I didn't know you studied enology."

"I didn't," I replied. "I try to read about wines and go to tastings when I can, just because it helps with my work, but at weddings, people are mostly drinking champagne after dinner, and I don't pay as much attention to what the bartender might be pouring at that point in the evening."

"I doubt most open bars would be serving this sort of thing." Allan handed one of the glasses to me and kept the other one for himself. "*Salut.*"

We touched glasses—carefully, since the tiny crystal cordial glasses looked quite fragile—and I allowed myself a small sip. Oh, yes, that was marvelous, not as syrupy as port, but still with that kind of concentrated, almost raisin-y flavor, albeit with a much lighter touch.

"That's amazing," I said.

"I thought you'd like it."

I definitely did. And I also knew it was a good thing he'd poured us such small glasses, because I could tell the concentrated liquor was pretty potent. While I wouldn't have classified myself as drunk or anything even close to it, I knew by that point in the evening, I was a little tipsy…just enough to feel elevated, to have a glowing sense of well-being, whether merited or not.

Allan took his glass and headed over to the piano, so I followed. Was he going to play? Ever since I first saw that white baby grand in the living room, I'd wondered whether he actually used it or whether it was simply a prop.

I didn't see him pick up a remote or anything, but I assumed he had, since the holiday music coming out of the Bose system stopped abruptly. A moment later, he sat down at the piano and placed his glass of late harvest malbec on one of the flat shelves to one side of the keyboard.

Then those long, strong fingers of his moved across the keys, playing the introduction to "The Christmas Song," and that seemed to answer my question. He definitely could play—maybe not at Carnegie Hall level, but certainly good enough for a nightclub or piano bar.

"You're a man of many talents, I see," I told him.

A bright flash of a smile. "Oh, compared to a lot of people in this town, I'm a hack. But I do like to play when I have a chance. It relaxes me."

I could see that. Other than choir in high school, I'd never done much with my voice, but I still liked to sing along with the radio as I was cleaning the house or watering the plants. "Music is definitely a good diversion."

"Do you play?" he asked, hands still moving over the keyboard.

"No," I said. "I took guitar in junior high and did choir in high school, but I never learned to play the piano."

He looked pleased, pausing mid-chord. "Oh, so you sing?"

"I didn't say that," I responded at once, realizing my misstep. "I said I was in choir."

"Well, you have to sing in choir, don't you?"

Technically, yes, although there were a few people in my high school choir who probably should have been told to take drama or wood shop as an elective instead. However, I'd been in the madrigal group my senior year, something you had to audition to get into, so I supposed I was probably being a bit disingenuous about my singing abilities.

"Well—" I hedged.

"Do you know the words?" he asked, retracing his steps back to the intro of the song he'd been playing.

Of course, I did—I knew the words to most Christmas songs, thanks to my mom and Faye being obsessed with the holiday, not to mention organizing more holiday parties than I probably wanted to count where that sort of stuff was always blaring away in the background. But I wasn't sure I wanted to admit such knowledge, not when it seemed as if Allan wanted me to sing along with him as he played. And that was something I really didn't want to do. Despite my currently tipsy state, a wave of self-consciousness rolled over me.

"Um—"

His blue eyes glinted up at me. "I know you do. Here, I'll get you started. *Chestnuts roasting on an open fire….*"

His voice was surprisingly good, a warm tenor that hinted it could probably dip down into the upper baritone range without any problem. And while he sang, he kept watching me, that glimmer in his eyes seeming to indicate that he would keep on singing until I joined in.

Fine. "*…Jack Frost nipping at your nose,*" I sang, joining my voice with his, and his smile broadened, although he didn't hesitate, only kept on playing.

I sang along with him until we got to the end of the song, and, as if he expected I would flee at the earliest opportunity, he rolled right into "Have Yourself a Merry Little Christmas" without even pausing.

In for a penny, I thought, and sang along with that one as well. Or rather, we sang in unison at the beginning, but partway through, he stopped so I had to continue alone, blood rising to my cheeks as he watched me in approval. When the song was over, it took all my courage to remain standing where I was instead of running to hide in the bathroom. Yes, I'd sung in front of other people before, but not for years and years. Anyway, it was one thing to do a solo in a high school auditorium with the stage lights blazing in your face so you couldn't see all that much of the audience or their reactions, and quite another to stand a few feet away from someone and have them listen to you, close enough to catch every gasped breath or strained note.

"You have a wonderful voice," Allan said, once we were done and his hands were still and quiet on the keyboard.

I started to wave a hand, and he shook his head.

"Don't try to downplay your talent," he told me, his tone a very mild rebuke. "It's your choice whether or not to do something with it, but don't try to tell me it doesn't exist."

My shoulders lifted in a shrug. "There are thousands more talented people than I am in Los Angeles."

"You might be surprised," he said, his smile returning. "There are a whole lot of people out there who think they're way more talented than they actually are."

Which I supposed was the truth, or otherwise, shows like *American Idol* wouldn't exist. I didn't really feel like arguing the point, however. "Everyone's got a dream," I replied. "Mine definitely isn't singing in front of people."

Allan seemed to get the message, because he didn't challenge me, only closed the piano lid and stood. "That's fine. It was still fun to share some Christmas music with you."

He was very close to me. For a second or two, we remained where we were, looking at one another, as if neither of us was quite sure who should make the next move. Then I reached out and tangled my fingers in his, and he pulled me close, kissing me with a thoroughness that was almost breathtaking, the dessert wine sweet on his tongue.

We stood there for several long moments, pressed up against each other as the flames in the hearth hissed gently and the rain continued to beat down outside. When Allan lifted his mouth from mine, I couldn't quite prevent a shiver from moving through me at the intensity of his gaze.

"I want to take you upstairs," he whispered, and I nodded.

"I want to go upstairs with you."

There, I'd said it. The words had slipped so

easily from my lips, I halfway wondered what I'd been so nervous about. This was the only logical place for the evening to end up, after all.

Fingers still entwined, he led me over to the stairs, and we climbed up to the second floor. The master bedroom was simply furnished, with a king-size bed on a platform that appeared to be integrated with a wall-spanning headboard and a pair of low nightstands, but the spare decor was certainly intentional so it wouldn't detract from the eye-popping panorama provided by multiple walls of windows that overlooked downtown, now an impressionistic blur of lights in the falling rain.

Of course, while the view was impressive, I didn't know if I wanted to make love to Allan in an enormous fishbowl. He must have picked up on some of my unease, because he let go of my hand and went over to a switch on the wall and touched it briefly. At once, automated shades dropped down from a hidden recess above the windows, obscuring the skyline and providing some welcome privacy.

"Better?" he asked, and I nodded.

"Yes," I replied. "It's a gorgeous view, but—"

I didn't get any further than that, because he bent and kissed me again, mouth insistent on mine. Only for a moment, though, and then he brushed my hair out of the way so he could touch his lips to the sensitive skin of my throat. A gasp escaped me, blood warming at the sensation. I'd always loved being kissed there, but so few men seemed to know how to do it properly.

Obviously, that wasn't a problem with Allan.

I didn't really recall moving, but suddenly, we were up against the bed, and his fingers pulled at the hem of my sweater so he could lift it up and over my head. The light was dim, since the only illumination came from what looked like a single under-cabinet fixture in the bathroom. Still, Allan's gaze went over me in admiration as he looked down at the swell of my breasts in the green satin bra I wore.

"You are very beautiful, Belinda," he murmured.

A protest rose to my lips, but I made myself stay silent. He'd told me the day before that I shouldn't compare myself to anyone else, and so I wouldn't tell him that I was nowhere near as beautiful as Nina Nomura, that my barely C-cup breasts could possibly compare to her lush curves. No, this moment was about the two of us, and I knew better than to allow any ghosts from our respective pasts to ruin our time together.

So I smiled, and then reached over to undo the buttons on his dress shirt, to loosen them one by one until I was able to pull it free from his trousers and remove that garment as well, to drop it on the rug next to the spot where my sweater already lay. He wore his clothes well, and so I'd assumed his body was good, but I hadn't expected it to be quite as toned as this, stomach muscles faintly defined, biceps bulging a little in the soft light that slipped into the space from the bathroom.

"You're beautiful, too," I whispered, and he grinned.

"I'm not so sure about that, but thank you."

I opened my mouth to reply, and he stopped me by kissing me again, lips hot against mine, and then we sank down onto the bed as Allan pushed the covers out of the way and then reached for the zipper of my skirt. A moment later, it was gone, followed by his trousers and socks. Now we both lay there in our underwear, his black boxer briefs molding nicely to his muscular thighs, and yet I knew we weren't going to remain in this state for much longer, not with the way the blood was racing through my body and I ached with need for him.

And yes, his fingers found the clasp of my bra and undid it, then removed the garment so his fingers could close over my bare breasts. I moaned at his touch, at the ripples of pleasure that started to move through me as he traced his fingertips over my hardening nipples.

Then his mouth was on my breast, tongue moving against the sensitive flesh, and that only made me moan louder, even as he reached down to slide his fingers under the waistband of my panties and pull them down. He touched me, stroking, and I gave a startled gasp before I let myself lie back against the pillows so I could relax into the sensation.

Not for too long, though, because he kissed his way down my stomach, mouth trailing lower and lower. Oh, dear lord, it had been a long time....

I realized, though, as he tasted me, made love to me with his tongue, that it wasn't just that it had been a long time since I'd shared this sort of intimacy with a man. No, I knew that no one had pleasured me with this sort of intensity, his entire being focused on making sure I felt as good as I possibly could. And it was working, because I could feel the orgasm building already, my body starting to thrum with an almost agonizing pleasure as my fingers curled into the sheets and I shut my eyes for a moment.

Yes, there...*there*....

And I came, crying out into the rainy darkness, as he held on to me and let me ride the wave of exquisite sensation, my entire body shaking from the intensity of the climax. Had I ever come that hard before? I didn't think so, but honestly, my brain wasn't working very well right then, was overloaded by the way my nerve endings kept tingling with the echoes of that earth-shaking orgasm.

He kissed the inside of my thigh, softly, the stubble on his chin pleasantly scratchy. Without speaking, he trailed his way back up over my hipbone and across my stomach once again. I shuddered at his touch, my body aching for him even though he'd just brought me to a screaming climax a moment earlier. And then I reached over and grabbed hold of the waistband of his briefs, pulled them down so my fingers could close on him, so I could feel how heavy and hard he was, how ready.

His breath hissed out between his lips, and his hand settled in my hair as I bent and took him into my mouth, tasted the faint saltiness of his skin, ran my tongue over his length. That touch made him moan and lean back against the pillows while I suckled him, moved so he slid in and out ever so slightly. Eventually, though, I could feel his body tensing, could tell he was probably getting close, and so I backed off, lifting my mouth from him.

He reached for me at once, bringing me close, kissing me as my breasts pressed into the smooth, hard muscles of his chest. I could feel his cock against me, pushing closer…until he paused, eyes intent on mine.

"Do you want me to get a condom?" he asked.

"I've only been with Nina recently, and I was tested, but—"

Some men might have lied about such a thing, but I somehow knew Allan was telling me the truth. I was on the pill—more to regulate my cycles than anything else—and so there wasn't much risk. And I wanted to feel him...*really* feel him.

"No, it's all right," I whispered. "I'm on birth control. I want...I want you."

He bent and kissed me, breath warm against my neck, and then I felt him shift, felt him push into me. I gasped, taking him in, letting him fill the empty spaces inside. We clung to each other as our bodies moved as one, finding our rhythm, blending perfectly, just as our voices had blended earlier while we sang those old songs together.

The rain fell, and we made love to one another, finding our way in the dark to a perfect moment where we lost ourselves in the other person's touch, where nothing seemed to matter except the way our bodies fit together. And then another orgasm flooded through me and I cried out, even as he climaxed as well, his groans blending with my gasps, until he lay on top of me, body shaking.

Neither of us spoke. We only held on to each other, both of us possibly a little stunned by the intensity of our shared experience, until at last we drifted off, lulled to a gentle slumber by the sound of the falling rain and a sense of utter, perfect peace.

In that endless moment between sleep and waking, I knew I loved him.

And I didn't know what the hell I should do about it.

CHAPTER TWELVE

WE SLEPT UNTIL A LITTLE BEFORE MIDNIGHT, and then Allan gave me a spare robe—it was supposed to be knee-length on him and so was around mid-calf on me, although the sleeves were impossibly long—and we went downstairs to snuggle in front of the fire and eat bread pudding and drink some much-needed water. The rain still fell, and that surprised me a little; storms in Southern California usually weren't quite this intense.

But it was all right, since we certainly weren't going anywhere. After we were done with our belated dessert, I retrieved my emergency overnight kit from my tote bag and took it with me when we went back upstairs again. We brushed our teeth in the marble and stainless bathroom, each of us at our own sink while we worked in companionable silence, and then we went back to bed, although not to sleep. Not at first, anyway—we made love again, slowly, almost tenderly, exploring one another's bodies, until some time later, we finally closed our eyes and snuggled up against each other, and let slumber take us.

The next morning, the sun was out, shining so brightly that it was hard to believe rain had fallen so heavily the night before. However, the telltales were obvious in the backyard...puddles everywhere, fallen leaves making sodden little clumps on the immaculate lawn. I sat up in bed and looked at the clock on the nightstand, surprised that it was already almost nine o'clock. Normally, I never slept that late, not even when I'd been out past midnight working an event.

Allan sat up next to me, hair looking adorably mussed. "What time is it?"

"A little before nine."

He scrubbed a hand over his stubbly chin and frowned a little. "Is that going to be a problem?"

"No," I replied, then leaned over and kissed him on the cheek. "I don't have to be at my mom's house until two o'clock."

"Good," he said. "Then I can make you some breakfast."

I lifted a surprised eyebrow. "You cook?"

"Well, I wouldn't call scrambling eggs and

putting bread in a toaster exactly 'cooking,' but I can manage enough to pull off breakfast."

Scrambled eggs and toast sounded great. I'd slept like the dead the night before, which I honestly hadn't been expecting. Not that I made a habit of sleeping in strange men's beds, but the few times I had stayed overnight at a date's house, I'd been restless, and ready to get up and away as soon as it was at all possible.

I wasn't quite sure how to feel about being so comfortable in Allan's bed.

Since analyzing my current emotional state seemed fraught with problems, I instead got up and retrieved the fresh pair of underwear I'd packed in my emergency kit, and then started putting on my clothes from the night before. Allan watched me, one eyebrow cocked at an inquisitive angle.

"You can take a shower here, you know."

"I know," I said, "but I'd rather shower at home. It's Christmas, so I need to wash my hair before I go over to my mother's house, and I didn't pack any of that stuff."

"All right," he said, looking resigned. He also got out of bed and put on a clean pair of underwear, although he didn't bother to get dressed, but only drew on the robe he'd worn the night before when we'd gone downstairs to have dessert.

I didn't put on my boots, but carried them

with me as I headed down to the ground floor of the house. L.A. sparkled outside the windows, looking as freshly scrubbed and shiny as a child on their first day of school. Allan followed me, and headed into the kitchen while I stood at the window and continued to gaze at the world beyond.

"Do you ever get tired of it?" I asked.

"Tired of what?" he said, putting ground coffee into a stainless-steel contraption that looked only mildly less complicated than the control panel of a rocket ship.

"This view."

"Not so far," he replied as he went over to the sink to get some water. "But then, I've only been in this house for a little over ten months. Maybe in a few years...but I somehow doubt it."

I doubted that as well. Of course, I really didn't want to think about him standing here and looking out this window years from now, because that would be imagining a future without me in it. By then, he would have moved on from me, just as he'd clearly already moved on from Nina. I'd probably be no more than a small footnote in his life, a brief amusement before he found something far more rewarding to focus on.

That melancholy thought did a pretty good job of erasing the afterglow from the night before. I made myself take a breath before I turned back around to the kitchen. The coffeemaker was going, and a warm, welcome scent had begun to fill the space.

"I hope sourdough is okay," he said, producing a loaf from inside the pantry. "That's all I have for toast."

I rarely ate bread, but when I did, sourdough was one of my favorites. "That's actually perfect."

He smiled and dropped four slices into the toaster, then went to the refrigerator and got out some eggs.

As he began to break them into a bowl, I asked, "Is there anything I can help with?"

"There's some fruit in the fridge—strawberries and blueberries. Could you cut up the strawberries? There's a knife over there."

He pointed to a wooden block that held an impressive array of cutlery. Quite the display for someone who claimed not to cook, but I had a feeling he owned the knives simply because they were what was required for a gourmet kitchen. The same thing with the heavy marine-blue Le Creuset skillet he was setting on top of the big stainless-steel six-burner stove—he'd probably only used it a handful of times, but he wanted to make sure he was working with the best equipment money could buy.

I fetched the knife he'd indicated, then got out the strawberries and blueberries, rinsed them in a colander he'd left by the side of the sink, and hulled the strawberries and put them and the blueberries in a bowl. While I was working, Allan poured the eggs into the skillet and got the toast going.

We did all this in silence, but it was a friendly, relaxed quiet, the kind you usually didn't achieve until you'd been with someone for a while and knew you didn't have to keep chattering away to prove you were having a good time. Or at least, I assumed that was how it was supposed to work; I'd never been with anyone long enough to know for sure.

The coffeemaker beeped, and Allan paused tending his eggs long enough to pour some for both of us. "There's cream in the fridge," he offered.

"Thanks," I said. I generally didn't allow myself that particular indulgence, but hey, it was Christmas. I got out the cream and poured some in my coffee, then sent him a questioning glance. "Do you want any cream?"

He shook his head. "No, I drink it black."

Which meant he must have bought the cream especially for me. I probably shouldn't have been so pleased by that small gesture, but it meant he'd been thinking about what I'd like, what he could do to make me comfortable. It also meant he'd been expecting me to stay over, although I wouldn't hold that against him. I'd been thinking the very same thing…and it was what had happened, after all.

A few minutes after that, breakfast was ready, and we both went to sit at the dining room table to have our morning meal. I could think of worse places to have breakfast, that was for sure. From where we sat, we could see all the way to downtown in one direction and out past Century City and the Westside in the other. Sunlight streamed over the wet grass, awakening diamond sparkles on each blade.

Had there ever been such a beautiful morning? I didn't see how, although I was forced to admit to myself that a lot of my current sense of well-being probably arose from my memories of that amazing, toe-curling sex of the night before. And it felt good to sit there at the table with Allan, to take in all his adorable, rumpled morning-after good looks.

A warm, welcome feeling seemed to settle somewhere in my midsection, a sensation that couldn't exactly be attributed to the coffee I'd been sipping. I found myself keeping my gaze fixed on the view because I didn't know whether I'd be able to keep my feelings to myself if I allowed my eyes to meet Allan's. Even the deep sleep I'd enjoyed hadn't been enough to remove my memory of the thoughts that had slipped across my mind right before I'd sunk into oblivion. I knew I was falling for this man, and I didn't know what in the world I was supposed to do about it.

Well, the logical escape route would have been to claim some sort of emergency had come up with a client, something pressing enough that I could effectively disappear from his life. I didn't want to do that, though. I wanted to go to the Magic Castle with him and fly in a helicopter to Catalina and do whatever other crazy things he might dream up to amuse ourselves until December thirty-first rolled around. And anyway, ghosting him wasn't really an option, because I still had his party to manage. I certainly wasn't going to bail out on him when he needed me; even if I refused to acknowledge how much space he'd already claimed in my heart, I wouldn't allow my professional reputation to suffer by pulling a disappearing act.

"How are the eggs?" he asked. I had a feeling he could tell my thoughts were churning but had decided it was wiser to focus on something more neutral, like the food.

"Great," I said, which they were—light and fluffy and buttery. Actually, everything tasted wonderful. Maybe it was just my stomach wanting something solid after all the wine I'd drunk the night before, but I thought the simple fare rivaled the brunch we'd shared at the restaurant in Malibu on Sunday morning. "This will definitely hold me until Christmas dinner."

Something in his expression shifted, but it had come and gone so quickly, I really didn't have time to figure out what it might have been. "Good. I don't want to send you home feeling hungry."

"Oh, I didn't say I wouldn't be hungry," I replied, daring myself to hold his gaze for a few seconds before I looked back down at my plate.

That response made him chuckle. "I know the feeling. But I suppose we'll just have to wait until Wednesday."

I'd wondered if he might ask me to come back here after I was done at my mother's house, but his comment seemed to answer that particular question. As much as I would have liked to see him again that soon, I didn't think driving over to Hollywood after a big Christmas meal was a very good idea, and so I knew I was a little relieved not to be forced to decline such an invitation.

"Well, some things are worth waiting for," I said, and he smiled at me, his gaze lingering on my lips.

"Yes, they are."

We finished our meal, and afterward I gathered up my things and kissed him goodbye—although not before promising to check the showtimes at the Chinese Theater so we could figure out our timing for Wednesday afternoon.

Then I was walking out to my car, which was still covered in drops from the rain the night before but otherwise no worse the wear for its stint in the driveway. I realized Allan hadn't asked me to park inside the garage but guessed he must have a second vehicle in there, even though I hadn't seen anything so far other than the Tesla.

The streets were strangely quiet for L.A., with most people already wherever they'd planned to be for the holiday. I made it home in less than twenty minutes, where Mr. Mittens let me know—loudly —that he didn't appreciate being left alone overnight.

"Sorry, kitty," I said. "I'd say it won't happen again, but I have a feeling it will."

The cat gave me the evil eye, but looked some-what mollified when I opened his favorite cat food —Blue Buffalo chicken paté—and put it in his bowl. He still had plenty of dry food, and he hadn't been in any danger of running out of water, and yet I couldn't help feeling a little bit guilty.

However, I didn't have much time for self-flagellation over abandoning my pet, because once Mr. Mittens was settled, I needed to shower and do my hair, then get dressed and head over to my mother's house. Her present—and Faye's and my grandmother's—had been purchased and wrapped weeks before, so all I had to do was retrieve the boxes from where they'd been residing on the shelf in my office closet, and then set them on the coffee table, thinking I could scoop them up as I headed out the door.

We never got too dressy for Christmas, so I put on a good pair of jeans, a winter white cashmere cardigan, and an ivory tank top. As I was fussing with my hair, my gaze fell on the aquamarine pendant Allan had given me, which lay on top of my dresser where I'd taken it off before getting in the shower.

Should I wear it? Part of me wanted to show off the exquisite piece, but I knew doing so would only raise questions I really didn't want to answer. Although Allan had made it sound as if it was no big deal, I knew that most men didn't make a habit of buying jewelry worth thousands of dollars for women they were only seeing casually. I was already anticipating some pointed questions from my mother about Allan, so I didn't think it was a very good idea to complicate matters even further.

With a sigh, I picked up the pendant and put it in the little organizer from the Container Store that I kept in my dresser drawer.

"Tomorrow," I promised it, since I already planned to wear the piece with my beaded evening gown. The colors would complement one another perfectly—and I knew it would make Allan happy to see me wearing my Christmas present.

With everything ready, I headed out the door, pausing briefly to pick up the family's Christmas gifts. Although my mother always told me not to bring anything, I also had a bottle of rosé I thought we could drink with the cheese course that preceded the holiday meal.

Faye and my mother lived less than a mile from me. In nice weather, I sometimes walked over there, but that wasn't really feasible with all the things I was bringing, even though this Christmas day had turned out to be just about picture perfect. Instead, I drove, arriving about five minutes later to see my grandmother's Subaru Outback already parked in the driveway. However, she'd left plenty of room for me to slip in next to her car, so I pulled up beside the Subaru, gathered up my holiday offerings, and got out of my SUV.

No need to knock—my mother left the door unlocked when she was expecting me, and I let myself in, calling out, "Merry Christmas!"

"Merry Christmas!" my mother said, coming up to greet me so quickly, I wondered if she'd been lurking in the entry and peering out through the narrow windows next to the front door so she could get a glimpse of the exact moment I arrived. She gave me an awkward sideways hug, doing her best to maneuver around the packages I carried.

"Christmas tree?" I asked, even though she

and Faye set it up in the same corner of the living room every year.

"Right there," my mother said, pointing, and I went over to set the presents down on the floor under the tree—an artificial one, because neither she nor Faye believed in cutting down trees just to decorate your house for a week or two out of the year.

I straightened up after I was done, and my mother beamed at me. Her hair used to be as red as mine, but she'd started to go gray when I was in high school and hadn't tried to fight the process. Now it was pure white, cut in choppy side-swept bob, a contrast to her otherwise youthful face. She'd turned fifty-five the previous spring, but she still had only a few laugh lines around her eyes and otherwise looked at least ten years younger than her actual age. More than once, I'd hoped I inherited the aging genes from her side of the family.

"You look wonderful," she said. "It looks as though taking some time off is agreeing with you."

Actually, I guessed what was really "agreeing" with me was getting spectacularly laid the night before, but I had a feeling that pointing out that particular fact probably wouldn't be very tactful. Instead, I made a noncommittal sound, then said, "Faye and Grandma?"

"In the kitchen, of course. You know your grandmother won't let anyone else make her spiced cranberry chutney."

For good reason, I thought. Faye was an amazing cook, but my grandmother could have bottled that chutney and sold it at local gourmet stores. I'd actually suggested it to her more than once, although she always laughed and said she was retired and didn't want to start a new business at this stage of the game.

"And cookies, too, right?" I asked, knowing I sounded like a hopeful twelve-year-old and not the successful twenty-something business owner I actually was.

"It wouldn't be Christmas without your grandmother's cookies," my mother reassured me. "But come and sit down—they're almost done, so no need to go in there and make the kitchen more crowded than it already is."

I couldn't really argue with her on that point —the house was bigger than mine, but not by a lot, and the kitchen really was pretty cramped, especially when you were trying to cook much more than a simple meal for two.

"I'll just get some glasses," she said, eyeing the bottle of rosé I still held. "Make yourself comfortable."

Protesting that I wanted to help wouldn't get me anywhere, so I nodded and headed over to the comfy slipcovered couch that had been a fixture in the living room ever since I could remember. From time to time, the slipcovers got replaced, but that sofa seemed as permanent as the Santa Monica Mountains.

There was already a tray with cheese and crackers sitting on the stone-topped coffee table, along with a little silver wine caddy. I set the bottle of rosé in the caddy and took a quick look around. Everything was decorated just as it had been for at least the past ten years—lighted faux pine garland on the mantel adorned with red velvet bows, cheerful poinsettias in places of honor on the side tables. The regular throw pillows that sat on the couch had been replaced by ones with embroidered holiday motifs—holly leaves on one, a wreath on the other. And there were a few new items, too—the brass votive holders with star cutouts hadn't been here the year before, and neither had the centerpiece with its red hurricane glass at the center and the faux pine boughs that surrounded it.

I didn't have time to observe more than those few details, because Faye and my grandmother emerged from the kitchen then, my grandmother with a plate of cookies and Faye holding a box of crackers, as though she feared what had been set out already wouldn't be enough. Good thing that I hadn't gotten myself a snack while I was at my own house, even though I'd started to feel hungry again as one o'clock came and went. I knew I was expected to eat at Christmas…and eat a lot. If I hadn't already been a few pounds light, thanks to all the running around I'd done for the Blankenship wedding, I might have worried about slipping into that bias-cut beaded gown I intended to wear to the Magic Castle the next day, but I thought I should be pretty safe.

After she put down the plate of cookies she held, my grandmother took the seat of honor in the armchair off to one side of the couch and eyed me critically for a moment. Like my mother, she had pure white hair and lively blue eyes, and was slim and looked far younger than her seventy-eight years. "Your mom tells me you have a new boyfriend."

I shot my mother a sideways glance. To her credit, she didn't deny spreading the news, only said, "It's not a state secret is it?"

"No," I replied. "But he's not my boyfriend. We're just…holiday dates, I guess."

That felt like a horribly off-hand way to refer to the man who'd rocked my world to its foundations the night before, and yet I knew I had to downplay the effect he had on me, had to do my best to act as if we were fuck-buddies and nothing else…although I also knew I would never dare use that kind of language in front of my family. Dee and I could get pretty raunchy when it was just the two of us—we tended to act like best friends rather than boss and employee—but my mother and grandmother expected me to curb the F-bombs except in times of extreme stress.

"He's an agent, right?" Faye asked. She'd also put down the crackers she'd brought with her, and had now settled herself next to my mother. They were only a year apart in age, but Faye's face was more lined, her dark close-cut hair still salt and pepper in tone. She had some of the kindest brown eyes I'd ever seen, although right then they were lively with curiosity.

"Yes," I said, figuring that Allan's profession was a safe enough topic of conversation. "I bumped into him at one of clients' weddings."

If we'd been a different family, either my mother or Faye might have made a comment about it being romantic to meet a man at a wedding, since all the trappings of romance were already there. However, Faye knew all about the Carson curse—it wasn't the sort of thing you could hide from someone who'd shared your life for more than thirty years—and so she also knew that any man who entered my life would only be in it for a very short amount of time. And unlike my mother, she'd never made subtle hints about seeking female companionship since I couldn't be with a man for the duration. I still didn't know all the details, but I did know that Faye had been married briefly and disastrously to a man who was her family's choice when she was in her early twenties, and therefore she understood more than most people the very real consequences of trying to make yourself be something you weren't.

"And you had a nice time last night?"

"Yes," I said. That was skirting more dangerous territory, but I figured I could provide some information without having to go into all the gory details. "He ordered in an amazing dinner, and we sat and talked in front of the fireplace for a long time. Oh, and he plays the piano really well—we did a couple of duets."

"You did?" my mother said, looking genuinely startled. She'd encouraged me to take voice lessons after high school, but I hadn't seen the point, since I was already working for Margie by then and had a pretty good idea of the direction where my life was going to head. "I'm surprised he managed to talk you into doing something like that."

But the smooth-tongued devil had managed to convince me to cast aside my embarrassment, something that still made me inwardly shake my head. I just shrugged, however, and snagged a piece of cheese and a cracker. "Well, the couple of glasses of wine I had with dinner might have had something to do with it."

Everyone chuckled, and Faye said, "Speaking of which, let's have some of the rosé Belinda brought."

The next few minutes were spent in pouring wine and diving in to the cheese and crackers—and my grandmother's amazing Christmas cookies, somehow rich and buttery and light at the same time, with her insanely good homemade buttercream frosting on top. My mother asked a few more questions about Allan, but nothing too probing, and then we opened presents. Faye and my mother had gotten me a beautiful planner, since they knew I liked to write things out longhand in addition to storing them on my laptop, and my grandmother gave me a lovely aquamarine ring set in white gold.

I stared down at it, startled. There was no way she could have possibly known that Allan had gotten me a pendant set with the same stone, but—

She tilted her head slightly and said, "I know you're not much of one for rings, but that's a family heirloom—it belonged to my mother, and it's been sitting in a box ever since she passed away. I took it to the jeweler and had it cleaned and the prongs tightened, so it should be ready for its next hundred years."

"It's beautiful," I told her, and it was. The stone wasn't as large as the one in the necklace Allan had given me, but it was also pear-cut and surrounded by small glittering diamonds, with milgrain edging that told me it had probably been created in the early years of the twentieth century, when white gold and platinum first became popular. I slid it on the fourth finger of my right hand, and it fit perfectly.

"I'm glad you can wear it," my mother put in. "I've never bothered much with rings, either, since my hands are in clay most of the time, but you attend enough fancy events where you dress up that your grandmother and I both thought the ring should go to you."

I stretched out my hand and looked down at my present, at the shimmering blue-green stone in its halo of diamonds. "It's perfect. I'll definitely wear it tomorrow night—Allan's taking me to the Magic Castle."

"He is?" Faye said, looking suitably impressed. "Is he a magician, too?"

"Not that I'm aware of," I responded, and tried not to smile. His touch was definitely magic, but I knew that wasn't what she'd meant. "You can get an associate membership in the club without auditioning as a magician. I assume that's what he did."

Her eyebrows lifted, although she only nodded and didn't comment further. Although I doubted she knew the particulars, she was probably able to guess that membership was pricey enough that it wasn't the sort of organization you joined on a whim…even though it sounded as if that was pretty much exactly what Allan had done.

I'd bought my grandmother a journal, a beautiful handcrafted one bound in faux leather and with handmade paper, since she liked to start a new journal at the beginning of each year. She ran a hand over the slightly rough artisan paper, a smile on her lips. "It's lovely, Belinda. I can only imagine what I'll be able to write in here for the coming year."

Probably all sorts of interesting things, because she might have been retired, but she still kept busy, went on day trips to museums and other local points of interest, was taking a watercolor painting class and also spent a lot of time in her garden, which was the envy of everyone on her block.

And my mother and Faye got a gift certificate to Musso and Frank's Grille from me, along with a set of tickets to *Hamilton*—nearly impossible to get, but Allan wasn't the only person who knew how to pull strings and use connections to obtain something that might otherwise have been out of reach.

"How did you do it?" my mother asked,

staring down at the tickets as if she was afraid they might disappear in a puff of smoke.

"Trade secret," I replied with a smile, and she only shook her head.

"Thank you so much," Faye said.

"I hope you enjoy the show," I told her. "I've heard great things."

And I had, but I honestly didn't have much opportunity to go to the theater, not when I had so many claims on my time. Besides, I was just happy to see how thrilled the two of them were to have the chance to go to a show that was sold out for months.

Eventually, we adjourned to the dining room, where we feasted on roast turkey and mashed potatoes and all the trimmings, and eventually found just enough room to squeeze in my grand-mother's amazing apple pie. By the time I was done, I felt as though I'd have to be rolled out the door. The whole time I was eating, though, I couldn't quite keep myself from thinking about Allan, wondering what he was having for dinner on what must have been a very lonely Christmas for him, even though he'd reassured me that he had plenty to keep himself occupied and that I shouldn't worry about him.

I didn't think anyone noticed that my thoughts were elsewhere. And when I eventually left at a little after nine o'clock, I couldn't help but feel a little relieved, just because I knew that, now Christmas was over, I didn't have any more real claims on my time, and could focus solely on Allan for the next few days.

Oh, boy...I was in a lot of trouble.

INTERLUDE

The house felt much too large with Belinda gone, although Asmodeus did his best to ignore how huge and echo-y it felt. He turned on the stereo and opened a few windows to let in some fresh air, since the day had warmed up enough that the wind was no longer chilly, but mild and friendly, like a promise of spring even though he knew that season was still months away.

Despite these measures, he ached for her, wanted her at his side, even if they ended up doing nothing more exciting than watching television. At least they would have been together. But she needed to be with her family, and although she'd invited him along, he knew it was better to keep some separation between them for now. He'd had dinner with Nina's parents several times, and although they'd been cordial enough, he'd always gotten the impression that Nina's father—a renowned plastic surgeon—hadn't thought he was good enough for his daughter.

Smirking a little, Asmodeus wondered if Dr. Nomura felt the same way about Brian Hart.

Odd how it didn't hurt at all to think of Nina with Brian. Just a few weeks earlier, the thought of her betrayal—of how quickly she'd gone to Brian when he'd made her a better offer—had made Asmodeus grind his teeth, had made him wish he could summon a wave of hellfire to wipe that miserable excuse for a man off the face of the planet. However, that sort of display would definitely have gotten the attention of upper management, and since he knew he had to be on his best behavior in order to retain God's favor and be free of Hell forever, he'd done his best to push aside thoughts of revenge and get on with his life.

Now, though...now he had Belinda, and he didn't care about any of that. He thought of the sweetness of her flesh, the tiny hint of a dimple that showed in one cheek when she smiled, the surprising throatiness of her voice as she sang those old holiday songs with him. She certainly wasn't the first woman he'd been with...but he definitely wanted her to be the last.

And he honestly didn't think things could have gone any better the evening before. They'd been easy and comfortable together at dinner, and scorching afterward in the sheets. In a way, he was almost surprised by the passion she'd displayed when he took her to bed; Nina had been fierce and inventive, but Belinda was intense in her own way, responding to his touch with the sort of heat her serenely lovely exterior did a very good job of hiding.

He put aside his laptop—he'd picked it up from the Apple store just a few hours before Belinda arrived on Christmas Eve—and went out through the sliding glass door so he could stand on the grassy area just beyond the patio and to the right of the swimming pool. From this spot, he could see past the curve of the hill beyond his own property and all the way across the Westside, could just barely glimpse a shimmer at the very edge of his vision that was the Pacific Ocean.

Belinda was out there, enjoying Christmas Day with her family. While he missed her, he knew he would see her again soon enough. Besides, it was enough for him to know that she was happy, that she'd been reluctant to leave his house, even though she understood that she needed to be with her relatives. The bond between them grew each time they saw one another, and he had no reason to believe she wouldn't respond to a declaration of love when the time came.

He'd already decided to tell her on New Year's

Eve. Some might have said that was cutting things too close, but Asmodeus knew she was his only chance of salvation. Either she would be in love with him by that time, six days hence, or she wouldn't. While possessed of a certain sunny optimism that definitely wasn't typical of a demon, he wasn't foolish enough to believe he could find another woman in the few days that remained until the turn of the year. No, he must pin all his hopes on her, no matter what happened.

The thought didn't trouble him terribly, however, because he knew he'd already seen a dawning affection in her eyes, a sort of pure emotion that he now knew he'd never been able to detect in Nina. Oh, she'd cared about him, enjoyed being with him, but it wasn't the same thing. Belinda might pretend that she was too busy for love, and yet he believed it had already found her, no matter how hard she might try to push it away.

Asmodeus himself welcomed that unfamiliar emotion, letting it fill his heart...and yes, his soul. There were some who would have liked to argue that demons had no souls, but he knew better. His might have been a small shallow thing, but it existed. It was as much a part of him as the heart that beat within his chest and the lungs that inhaled breaths of the mild, clean air as he stood there and looked down on the city.

He thought he knew love now. All he could do was hope that same love had made a home in Belinda's heart as well.

Beelzebub scowled and shut the laptop, then leaned against the upholstered headboard of his bed at the Beverly Wilshire Hotel and uttered a curse under his breath. It had seemed a simple enough thing to obtain this room so he could avail himself of the free wi-fi, to snap his fingers and summon a computer for his use so he could continue his search for the mystery woman at Asmodeus's side in the online photo.

Unfortunately, even though he'd downloaded the photo and then re-uploaded it to every image-matching site he could find, so far his efforts hadn't yielded any results. Her face was turned just enough away from the camera that the algorithms couldn't seem to work properly.

So much for human technology.

Still frowning, Beelzebub reached for the uneaten half of the turkey club sandwich that sat on a plate on the nightstand and took a bite. That was one thing he did like about coming topside—the food was much better. There was even a helping of cranberry sauce on the side as a nod to the season, although he had to inwardly smile at the note of pity in the voice of the woman who'd taken his room service order, as if she felt sorry for him at being alone on Christmas Day.

He certainly cared nothing for that. Actually, he wanted to laugh at these simple mortals, since the day they wasted so much time and energy on wasn't even His actual date of birth. They'd only co-opted it to more closely match their solstice rituals, although they couldn't even get that part right.

No matter. If the clerk wanted to feel sorry for him because he was by himself in an expensive hotel room on a made-up holiday, so be it. He certainly wouldn't waste any mental energy on her.

He had far more important matters to occupy his thoughts.

All right, since technology had apparently failed him, he needed to explore other means of discovering the woman's identity. The most obvious would be the bride and groom them-selves, since he had to assume that they would know the names of everyone who had attended their wedding. However, as the online article that contained the photo had pointed out, they were currently on their honeymoon in the Seychelles, half a world away. The distance itself wasn't an issue—Beelzebub could go wherever he liked in the blink of an eye—but he knew he would only attract attention to himself if he popped up at their resort in the Indian Ocean and then started asking pointed questions about their wedding guests. No, he would have to think of something else.

Perhaps the mother of the bride? Beelzebub closed his eyes and let his otherworldly senses range forth, seeking the woman in question. She hadn't returned home to Dallas, was enjoying an extended holiday in Los Angeles. Today, she was at the home of some friends who lived in the area, sharing the holiday with them, which meant she also would be difficult to approach. In fact, he realized he wouldn't be able to accomplish anything useful today, that anyone who might possess the information he needed would be occupied with this utterly pointless holiday.

Still, if Loretta Blankenship was in Southern California, that meant she would be easier to find. Or possibly....

Beelzebub tapped a finger against his chin and opened his laptop, then scanned the article again. It didn't mention any particulars, but he did catch a brief mention of the wedding being planned by a Los Angeles–based company. If anyone would know exactly who had been on the event's guest list, it would be the person or persons involved in organizing the wedding.

Now he had something.

He went to the search engine's home page, then typed in "Blankenship wedding planner" and the month and date. The article he'd already read occupied the top of the results, but immediately below it was a hit on a page titled "Recent Events," on a website belonging to a company called Carson Creations. He clicked on the link, and sure enough, the Blankenship/Holloway wedding occupied the top spot in the list, which was apparently in reverse chronological order.

Excellent. He could try contacting the owner of Carson Creations the next day to see if he or she would be willing to help him out…not that he had any real doubts, since he could always use some subtle demonic coercion to make sure the person in question provided the information he needed. And since he figured it was a good idea to know who he was dealing with, he navigated to the "About" page on the Carson Creations website.

There were only two bios on the page—one for a young woman named Dee Rodriguez, who had improbable dark magenta hair and elaborate makeup. The other was for a woman probably a couple of years older than Dee, delicately pretty and with lustrous red hair.

Beelzebub knew that hair—knew it all too well, since he'd been staring at a picture of it for the past several hours. A slow smile spread across his mouth.

"Hello, Belinda," he said. "I'm looking forward to meeting you."

CHAPTER THIRTEEN

THE MOVIE I CHOSE WAS AT FOUR-THIRTY—
not that I had a lot of choices, since if you wanted
to sit in the big auditorium at the Chinese
Theater, you went with whatever they were
showing—and so I met Allan at his house at a
little before four. He looked rested and relaxed,
casually handsome in jeans and a white shirt with
the sleeves rolled up, since the weather had
warmed since that rainy Christmas Eve and
temperatures were kissing the low seventies.

"Did you have a nice Christmas?" he asked as
he bent and kissed me on the cheek.

Just that brief brush of his lips against my skin
was enough to send a welcome little thrill down
my back. "Very nice," I replied. "I ate way too
much, and my grandmother sent me home with a
ton of cookies. In fact, here are some for you."

I hefted the care package I'd brought with me in one hand, and Allan smiled as I followed him into the house and to the kitchen, where he put the tin of cookies down on the counter. "I can't remember the last time I had Christmas cookies," he said. "Thank you."

"You'll love them," I told him. "My grandmother used to own a bakery, so she knows what she's doing."

"You're a family of many talents, I see."

I reflected that he had a point—my grandmother was a true pastry artist, and my mother taught ceramics and had original pieces in galleries around town, and I did well enough with my wedding planning business. A shrug, and I said, "We try."

"I'd say you do more than try."

Smiling somewhat awkwardly, I hefted the garment bag and small tote I held in my other hand. "Is there someplace where I can hang this up?"

"I'll go put it in the master bedroom for you…if that's all right."

There hadn't been a hint of suggestion in his voice, and yet I still thought I could feel my cheeks flush—probably from the memory of what we'd last done together in that bedroom.

He glanced down at the expensive watch on his wrist. "I suppose we'd better get going."

"Good idea—the traffic was a little thick today."

We headed out to the garage, where I saw Allan had a sleek black Maserati SUV in addition to the Tesla. To be honest, I hadn't even known that Maserati made an SUV, since I didn't pay a lot of attention to cars, but I supposed it made sense for him to have something practical in addition to the Tesla roadster…or at least, as "practical" as a Maserati ever could be.

The streets were crowded, but we still made good time to the theater and were able to park in the structure just down the street. Honestly, I wasn't as interested in the film itself—an action movie that was rated PG-13, so it wasn't too over the top—as simply being together with Allan, doing something as normal as going out to the movies with him. We shared a bag of popcorn and had bottled water to wash it down, and when we were done with the popcorn, we held hands, arms draped over the armrest that separated us. I loved the touch of his fingers on mine, loved the feeling of closeness even though we had that darn piece of plastic and metal preventing us from getting too cozy.

Dusk had fallen by the time we got out, but that was fine; it made a good prelude to an evening that I knew was just beginning. I went into the bathroom to fuss with my makeup, shading it a little darker for nighttime, and pulled my hair into an up-do that left a few loose waves falling around my face. Once I was done with that, I stepped into the walk-in closet and slipped out of my jeans and sweater and put on the gown, then slid into the strappy high heels I'd brought to wear with it.

Allan had left his suit lying on the bed, and so he was already dressed when I emerged. His eyes widened a little. "You look fabulous."

"So do you," I told him. Which of course he did—the guy definitely knew how to wear a suit.

"And you just had that gown hanging in your closet?"

I shrugged, and went over to where I'd left my purse so I could transfer my I.D., lipstick, and credit cards into the much smaller bag I planned to carry that evening. "Sometimes you see something on sale and know you just have to buy it, even if you don't know what you're going to use it for."

"Lucky find." His gaze went to my throat, where the aquamarine pendant he'd given me hung on its intricate chain. "I'm glad the necklace goes so well with that dress."

"It's perfect," I said. Then I extended my hand so he could see the ring that had belonged to my great-grandmother sparkling on my finger. "My grandmother gave me this for Christmas. Isn't it a perfect match?"

"It is," he agreed, bending a little so he could take a closer look. "I'd call that serendipity."

Or fate, I thought, although I didn't say anything, only smiled up at him. I knew the last thing I should be doing was thinking we were destined to be together or something. Because we weren't, and no matter what I might feel for him, this was all going to come to a crashing halt in the very near future.

However, that didn't mean I couldn't enjoy myself in the meantime.

"Shall we?" I asked, and he looped his arm in mine, blue eyes glinting a bit.

"Let's go make some magic," he said.

The Magic Castle stood on a rise above Franklin Avenue, and was a large Victorian mansion that had been built right after the turn of the twentieth century. Apparently, it had originally belonged to farmers when Hollywood was still a bunch of orange groves and not much else, but the house had been the Castle for more than fifty years by the point I finally got to visit the place as a guest. I doubted the original owners would have recognized much of it, since the club now boasted an opulent dining room, five bars, and multiple theaters in various sizes to accommodate a variety of magic acts. However, the interior was still dark and clubby and uniquely Victorian, with its carved accents and wood-paneled walls and lamps of jewel-toned glass.

They were definitely serious about their dress code at the Castle; I'd worried that I might be a little overdressed in my full-length beaded gown, but most of the women were just as dressed up as I was, and every man I saw was wearing a suit, or at least a sport jacket and dark slacks. Several of the women we passed turned and sent admiring glances at Allan as he escorted me to our table, and I felt a little inner thrill at knowing I was with someone so handsome and—corny as it sounded—dashing.

The food was amazing. Even I, inured as I was to L.A. prices, found myself a little shocked at the cost of the meal, but my companion didn't even blink at the size of our tab. If it didn't bother him, I knew I shouldn't let it bother me, either, and yet I hoped he knew I didn't expect him to be this extravagant every time we went out.

Then again, since he was planning to take me on a helicopter trip to Catalina the next day, I had the feeling he didn't plan to back off on the whole "extravagant" thing any time soon. Under different circumstances, I might have felt guilty about the amounts of money he was spending on me, but clearly, he could afford it. And also…well, it was also kind of nice to feel so pampered and taken care of, if only for a short while.

After dinner, we went to the show in the big theater first, a spectacle afforded to us because we'd eaten at the club and hadn't merely dropped in for drinks. I'd actually never seen a magic act in person, only on TV, and was a little surprised at how I found myself gaping in astonishment over and over, wondering how in the world the magician performing that night had managed to pull off those tricks without giving even a hint as to how he'd accomplished them.

"Smoke and mirrors," Allan told me as we went to get a drink after the show. "They know how to misdirect you so you're looking in exactly the place where they want you to look."

"I know that," I said. "But it's still pretty impressive. And honestly, I like not knowing how they do things. Sometimes you just want to be…transported."

His blue eyes glinted down at me. "I'll have to remember that."

Oh, you've already transported me, I thought, *just in a slightly different way.*

However, I didn't rise to the bait, only tilted an eyebrow at him. By that point, we'd reached the bar, a cozy space with a row of leatherette chairs in front of the long burnished-wood counter. It was dark and intimate, the ceiling coffered with pressed-copper tiles and more of the ubiquitous wood paneling.

A man maybe a few years older than I, his dark hair slicked back into a ponytail, stood behind the bar and sent a smile in our direction as Allan and I sat down. "Hi, Mr. D'Alessandro. The usual?"

He nodded and then looked over at me. "What would you like, Belinda?"

"Oh, just a glass of wine—pinot noir would be great."

"Coming right up," the bartender said.

As he went off to fetch our drinks, I sent a questioning glance up at Allan. "You're a regular here?"

"I guess you could put it that way," he replied. "When you think about it, the Castle is probably one of the closest bars to my house."

True, considering you had to jog past the landmark on your way up to the street where Allan's house was located. As neighborhood bars went, I supposed a person could do a lot worse.

The bartender came back with a glass of wine for me and a martini for Allan. We'd only had a single glass of wine with dinner, since he'd said we'd want to have drinks throughout the course of the night. Which was fine by me—I could handle alcohol well enough, but more than a drink or so an hour, and it would start to take its toll.

"Have anything new to show off, Jason?" he asked the bartender, who nodded. "All the bartenders here are also magicians," Allan added, probably because I knew I must have been wearing a puzzled expression.

"Yes, it's part of the job," Jason told me as he slipped a deck of cards out of his vest pocket. He shuffled them quickly and expertly, and fanned them out toward me. "Choose two cards, but don't tell me what they are."

I did as he requested and studied them. Jack of spades and queen of hearts.

"All right, put them back in the deck."

"Anywhere?" I asked.

"Anywhere you like."

I slid them back into the stack, and he shuffled it again, then turned toward Allan and said, "Your turn, Mr. D'Alessandro."

Wearing a faint smile, Allan also selected two cards, glanced at them briefly, and then replaced them in the deck. Jason shuffled it several times before setting it down on the polished wood of the bar's counter. The whole time, I kept my gaze fixed on the deck, doing my best to watch and see if he'd slipped one of the cards up his sleeve or palmed it in some other way. However, his sleeves were rolled up, leaving his forearms exposed, and so there wasn't really any place for him to hide something.

"All right," Jason said next. He looked over at me, frowned for just the barest second or two, and said, "Your cards were the queen of hearts and the jack of spades, correct?"

A dishonest person might have lied and said that was wrong, just to throw him off, but I guessed anyone good enough to be working at the Magic Castle probably had a contingency planned for that sort of behavior. Besides, doing something like that would just be mean. "Yes, those were my cards," I told him.

"Great." He glanced at Allan. "Yours were the ten of diamonds and the king of clubs, right?"

"Right again," Allan said, still smiling.

"Perfect. Now, could you both lift your cocktail napkins and tell me what's underneath?"

Now I could feel myself frowning. My drink had sat on its napkin, untouched, the entire time Jason was performing the card trick. There was no way—

I lifted the glass of pinot noir and the napkin where it had rested. Sure enough, lying there on the bar were my two cards, the jack of clubs and the queen of hearts. Next to me, Allan removed the napkin from beneath his martini to reveal two cards: the king of clubs and the ten of diamonds.

"How did you...?" I began, then realized

Jason would never tell me how he'd managed to pull off such a trick.

"Excellent," Allan said. "I didn't see that one coming."

Now wearing a grin of his own, Jason took the stack of cards and slid them across the bar toward Allan. "Your turn, Mr. D'Alessandro."

And instead of demurring, Allan picked up the deck of cards and shuffled them, almost as gracefully and efficiently as Jason had. Where he'd picked up that particular skill, I had no idea, but I was beginning to learn that he had an infinite capacity to surprise me.

Once he was done shuffling, he set down the deck. "Belinda, could you please cut the cards twice?"

I nodded, then did as he instructed, squaring the deck when I was done. After I removed my hand, he fanned the cards toward the bartender. "And Jason, if you could pick a card?"

Smiling a little, but with narrowed eyes, as if he was doing his best to keep track of Allan's every movement, Jason took out a card from the middle of the deck. "Now what?"

"Look at it, and show it to Belinda, but don't let me see it."

The bartender nodded and angled the card toward me. Three of clubs. I inclined my head slightly to show that I'd made a note of which one it was.

"Now put it back in the deck."

Jason did as he was instructed, and Allan shuffled the deck again. When he was done, he withdrew a card and showed it to me. Eight of diamonds. "Is this your card?" he asked.

"No," I replied, wondering whether he'd actually made a mistake or whether this was just part of the trick.

"Hmm." He shuffled the deck again and pulled out another one, this time holding it in Jason's direction. "Was this the card?"

The bartender shook his head. "Nope."

"Well, damn." Allan shuffled the deck again, a frown furrowing his brow. Then he gave an exasperated shrug and said, "I don't think it's here. Do you see it?"

And he fanned the deck out on the top of the bar. I scanned all the cards but didn't see the three of clubs. "No, it's not there."

"Definitely missing," Jason agreed, his smile broadening.

Allan ran a hand through his hair, mussing it ever so slightly—and making him look that much more gorgeous. "Well, it couldn't have gone far. Belinda, why don't you check in your purse?"

For a second or two, I couldn't quite understand what he was asking. My little satin evening bag had been sitting on the bar the whole time, near my left elbow and not within Allan's reach. There was no way—

Without answering him, I picked up the bag and undid the clasp. It was so small that I was able to see card immediately. I pulled it out, and he took it from me.

"Three of clubs. Is this the one?"

"Um…yes," I managed, even as Jason grinned and said,

"Nice one, Mr. D'Alessandro."

I stared at the card in Allan's hand and knew I was gaping in astonishment. The trick was just as mystifying as the one Jason had performed only a few minutes earlier, and I had no idea how it had been accomplished. The bartender chuckled at my incredulous expression, gathered up his deck of cards, and went down to the other end of the bar, where another couple had just sat down.

Allan picked up his martini and took a sip, casual as though he hadn't just managed a parlor trick worthy of one of the up-close magic rooms in this very club. I'd assumed that he'd bought an associate's membership, and that was how he'd gotten in, but maybe he'd auditioned just as all the other magician members had.

When I found my voice, I said, "So, you're a magician, too?"

"I wouldn't say that," he replied, then sipped

at his martini again. "I dabble a little. It's a fun hobby."

"I guess so," I said, and picked up my own drink and allowed myself a healthy swallow. "Any other hidden talents I should know about? Chariot racing, or maybe skydiving?"

That comment made him grin. "Not really, although I do make a mean pitcher of margaritas."

I almost told him I'd like him to make me some margaritas, although it really wasn't the season for that sort of drink. If my life had been different, I could have made a comment about looking forward to that when warmer weather rolled around, but unless we had a heat wave in the next couple of days that sent temperatures back up into the eighties, I knew I'd never get a chance to sit on that amazing patio of his and share some of those legendary margaritas.

But no, I didn't want my thoughts to head in that direction. It should have been enough for me to enjoy my time with him now, to let those perfect little moments happen so I could store them up and thumb through them later, like photographs from a summer romance that had taken place years and years earlier.

"However," he went on, apparently not noticing my distraction, "I still think you and I would have a great lounge act if the agenting and wedding planning gigs don't pan out."

"Singing and piano playing and a bit of sleight of hand on the side?" I inquired. There, I'd sounded amused and a little flip, and definitely not like someone who was mooning over the impending loss of the first man who'd made her realize everything she'd been missing for the past few years.

"Exactly." He swirled the little plastic stick with olives impaled on it through his martini in a contemplative sort of way, then took a drink. "Of course, we probably couldn't start out in the big time. We'd have to launch our careers in Laughlin, Nevada, or someplace like that."

"And then we could move up to Reno," I suggested, and he chuckled.

"Have you ever been to Reno?"

I shook my head. "No. I haven't traveled that much. Up to the Bay Area a few times, and my mom and Faye took me to Hawaii the summer between my freshman and sophomore years in high school. Otherwise, I've mostly been a homebody."

"Well, there are worse places to be stuck than Southern California," he remarked. "But actually, Reno is a beautiful town. Sierra Nevada Mountains, pine forests—it's nothing like Vegas."

It did sound appealing, although his comment made me lift an eyebrow. "I didn't take you for the outdoorsy type, Allan."

"I'm not," he said at once. "Or rather, I suppose I like it when I can enjoy the outdoors and then come back to a luxury hotel suite that night. You'll never catch me camping."

Something else we agreed on. I'd done the whole Girl Scouts thing when I was in elementary school, and my biggest takeaway from the whole experience had been if I never had to sleep in a tent again, I could count myself a happy person.

"I promise I'll never ask you to go camping," I told him, to which he raised his martini.

"I'll drink to that."

We clinked our glasses together, then finished the rest of our drinks so we could move on to the next theater, a much smaller space than the first show we'd observed, this one only seating twenty people. The tricks the magician performed there were on a more intimate scale but just as amazing, and yet, the whole time, I kept thinking of the card trick Allan had done back in the bar. I still wasn't sure exactly how he'd managed it…and I somehow doubted he would tell me his secret, even if I asked nicely.

Some hours later, we emerged from the Magic Castle. By then, it was almost midnight, and a half moon rode high above the city, casting a gentle light as we made our way over to the Tesla. From there, it was a drive of only a few minutes to get back to Allan's house.

"I want you to stay," he said after he'd pulled into the garage and parked next to his Maserati SUV.

There hadn't been much question in my mind how this evening was going to end, but it still heartened me to hear that he didn't want me to go home. "I'd love to stay," I told him. "I brought some overnight stuff with me, just in case."

"And a change of clothes?" he asked, looking hopeful. "That way, we can head straight out to San Pedro tomorrow."

Luckily, I'd been thinking ahead and had done that very thing—and let my mother know that she would probably need to come by in the morning to look after Mr. Mittens. She hadn't been exactly thrilled with me, but she hadn't said no, either. I'd made it clear that I was going to see this thing with Allan through to the end, even if that end was only a few days away.

"Two steps ahead of you," I said with a grin.

"Perfect."

We got out of the car and went inside. Almost at once, he reached for me and pulled me to him, kissing me with such fervor that I got the distinct impression that he'd been holding back all night, just waiting for the chance to be alone with me. Not that I minded, because as soon as his lips touched mine, heat flared within, making me press myself against him, loving the sensation of the crisp wool of his suit jacket brushing against my bare arms.

He slid down one beaded strap of my gown, baring my breast. At once, his mouth closed on me, suckling, and I moaned aloud, knowing how ready I was for him, a little startled by how quickly he was able to arouse me to a fever pitch.

And then we were moving, stumbling out of the kitchen and going toward the living room, where we collapsed on the rug in front of the fireplace, his hands pushing up the skirt of my gown, even as I tugged at his jacket, fingers working next on the buttons of his shirt. All in silence, the only sound our panting breaths, a sure sign of the need that drove us.

Eventually, we were both naked, bare flesh pressed against bare flesh, as he stroked me for a few moments, then pushed inside. I gasped and wrapped my legs around him, pulling him farther in, savoring the feel of him filling up my very core. Strange how perfect our coupling was in that moment, even hurried and urgent as it felt. I clung to him, wanting to feel every inch of his body pressed against mine, every hard muscle and expanse of smooth, slightly damp skin.

I came, crying out as I drove him deeper inside me, and just a few seconds later, he climaxed as well, breaths coming in short, hoarse pants. And then we both collapsed against the rug, still holding on to one another, still saying nothing. The house was dark, the only illumination the faint glow of the city lights coming in through the expansive windows. Probably a good thing; if any of the interior lamps had been turned on, we would have given the neighborhood quite a show.

Eventually, he kissed me and offered a lopsided little smile. "I really did mean to get you up to the bedroom," he said.

"It's all right," I replied. "At least this isn't a scratchy rug."

He chuckled, and then slowly slid out of me. I sighed, just a little, and then got up so I could retrieve my gown—luckily, no worse the wear for the rough handling it had just suffered—and pick up my shoes, which I didn't even remember kicking off. Allan did the same with his own clothing, and we both climbed the stairs, still in darkness so no one would be able to see us.

I was relieved to see that the blinds in the master bedroom were still shut from when we'd changed before heading out to the Magic Castle. Padding across the wood floor in my bare feet, I went over to the closet and hung up my gown, and set my shoes down immediately below it. A brief pause to grab a pair of panties and a tank top from the little bag I'd packed, and then I headed over to the bed, where Allan had already climbed in. As soon as I slipped under the covers, he reached over and pulled me against him so I could snuggle up next to his body, could feel the heat of his flesh as I pillowed my head on his chest.

Once upon a time, I would have said it was impossible for me to fall asleep in such a position. That night, though, I realized how safe I felt right then, how comfortable and at ease…how at home I was in his arms.

If I hadn't been so tired, that thought might have scared me shitless.

As it was, I went promptly to sleep.

INTERLUDE

Beelzebub hated phones, which was why he decided to drive over to the offices of Carson Creations the morning after Christmas so he could speak with Belinda Carson in person. Besides, he thought his was the sort of news better delivered face to face.

Hello, Ms. Carson. I just wanted to let you know that the man you're currently dating just happens to be a demon.

Yes, he thought that should go over very well.

However, after he'd parked his rental car at the curb in front of her office on Montana Avenue, he found an entirely unwelcome note—nicely laser-printed in an attractive font—taped to the reverse side of the glass door.

Carson Creations is closed until after the first

of the year. Please leave a message at (310) 555-8316 if this is an emergency.

Typical human laziness. A single day off apparently wasn't enough for Ms. Carson. No, she had to take the next week away from work as well.

Scowling, he fished his phone out of his inside breast pocket and entered the number on the sign. While he hated cell phones, Beelzebub had to acknowledge that they were a necessary evil while operating topside, although he certainly didn't bother with getting some extravagant "smart" phone that did far more than he ever needed it to. No, he had a no-frills feature phone that still had too many bells and whistles but was infinitely less complicated.

A cheerful woman's voice sounded in his ear, making him frown that much more. "Hello. This is Belinda from Carson Creations. Please leave your name, number, and a brief message, and I'll get back to you as soon as I can. Have a wonderful day!"

No, he was not having a wonderful day, and having Belinda Carson admonish him to do so was definitely not improving his mood any.

However, he knew he needed to leave a message, and he had to think of something that would encourage her to call him back even if she was ostensibly on vacation. "Hello, Belinda," he said, doing his best to sound slightly harried but not so crazy that she'd hesitate to return the call. "My name is Benjamin Blake, and I was given your name by a friend. You see, the company I hired to organize my New Year's party has skipped town with my deposit, and I'm really in a bind. I was hoping you could come to the rescue. Please call me when you have a chance—I'm at 310-555-0188. Thank you."

He ended the call there and shoved the phone back in his pocket. With any luck, she'd be checking her messages soon and would return his call. After all, he'd certainly sounded properly piteous. Surely she couldn't ignore someone who was so obviously in need...could she?

Unfortunately, he didn't know for sure. He knew next to nothing about the young woman in question, except that she organized weddings and other events...and that she was foolish enough to have fallen for Asmodeus's cheap charms. Surely she couldn't be terribly discriminating, or she would never have been taken in by him in the first place.

However, he didn't really care one way or another how bad her taste might be. The important thing was for her to answer his call and arrange a meeting. Once they were sitting face to face, he would have a few unpleasant truths he couldn't wait to deliver.

After all, what woman would want to stay

with a demon once she knew the truth about his identity?

CHAPTER FOURTEEN

WHILE ALLAN WAS IN THE SHOWER—WE'D had a leisurely morning, getting up at a little after nine and sharing coffee and breakfast afterward— I thought I'd better check my messages. Yes, I was technically on vacation until January second, but unexpected matters that needed to be handled in a timely manner could pop up at any time. Anything that seemed too important could be shuffled off to Dee to manage, since she'd already told me she was willing to run interference so I truly could enjoy my time off.

I hadn't missed anything from the day before, which I'd halfway expected. A lot of people were sort of slow to come online, so to speak, after a major holiday. This morning, I had a message from my mother saying that she'd been by the house to feed Mr. Mittens and spend some time with him, and that she'd be back in the early evening to do the same thing, since she knew I would be gone in Catalina all day. Hers was the only voicemail on my private phone, and so I turned on my work phone, which I'd brought with me but had left off the day before, to see what I'd missed.

Not much—Loretta Blankenship left a plaintive message about when she could hope to see proofs from the photographer, even though I'd patiently explained to her that it would be at least the first week in January before anything would be ready. I'd have Dee call her; while I didn't like fobbing Loretta off on my assistant, better for her to get a call sooner rather than later, if for no other reason than at least that way she'd know we weren't purposely trying to ignore her. A voicemail from the resort in Malibu where the retreat would be held in late January, wanting to reiterate that they needed a final head count of attendees no later than the thirty-first. I'd already been in touch with Miri Janek's assistants to let them know they needed to forward the information, but I made a mental note to have Dee follow up on that matter as well.

And then a message from someone named Benjamin Blake, saying he urgently needed my help for a New Year's Eve party. While I could sympathize with his plight—getting ghosted by an event organizer was certainly no fun—I already had my hands full with Allan's little soirée, and so there was no way I could help him out. Unless....

I went to my contacts list and pressed the entry for Dee's cell phone. It rang a couple of times, and I wondered if she'd made herself scarce as well. After all, technically she was off for the rest of the week, too, although I'd told her she didn't have to use up any of her vacation time, just in case there were any fires she needed to jump in and put out.

But then she answered, sounding cheerful enough. "Hi, Belinda. How was Christmas?"

"Great," I replied. "How was yours?"

"Good. I think I ate enough for three people." She paused before adding, "Please tell me you have something you need me to do. My mother keeps bugging me to come back over and hang out with the family, and I know that will drive me absolutely *loco*. Family togetherness is great and all that, but no need to overdose."

I laughed. "Actually, as a matter of fact, I do have a few things I'd like you to handle." I mentioned Loretta Blankenship's worries about the wedding photographs and the matter of the list of attendees for the retreat in January, then said, "I got a semi-frantic phone call from someone who needs help with a New Year's party. I'm swamped, obviously, but if this guy's party is a one-person kind of project, then maybe it's something you might be interested in."

"I would love an excuse to be busy on New Year's," Dee replied. "My ex keeps bugging me to get back together, and now he's making noises about New Year's. Being safely occupied somewhere else sounds like the perfect solution."

While I wished for the umpteenth time that my love life could be as uncomplicated as my assistant's, I had to admit having a pushy ex around probably wasn't a lot of fun, either. "Perfect," I told her, then gave her Benjamin Blake's contact info. "I guess just call and see what he's looking for. If it sounds like too big a project, then tell him it's not feasible, since I'm already promised to another event, but it could be an easy way to make some extra money. If you decide to organize the party, the commission is all yours."

"You don't have to do that—" she began, but I overrode her.

"Yes, I do," I said firmly. "If I'm not doing any of the work, why should I get a cut?"

"Well, because he wouldn't have even heard of me if it weren't for Carson Creations," Dee pointed out.

That might have been true, but I still didn't expect to get any of her commission. "It's fine. Fly, be free. See whether it's going to work out or not."

She laughed. "All right, all right." A slight

hesitation, and then she said. "You sound like you've been having a lot of fun."

I definitely was, but I didn't intend to give her all the gory details. My assistant and I shared far more about our personal lives than most bosses and their employees probably did, and yet there were still a few lines I wouldn't cross. She could draw her own conclusions; it didn't mean I was going to tell her that I'd been wined and dined like a queen or that Allan was the best lay in the history of, well, ever.

"I have," I said lightly. "And the fun is continuing, because we're just about to head out to Catalina for the day. I have no idea what the cell service is like over there, but if you need anything, just leave me a voicemail."

There was a hint of jealousy in her voice as she remarked, "Lucky," but that might also have been a bit of teasing. "Anyway," she went on, "enjoy your day, and I'll call Benjamin Blake and see what's up with him."

"Have a good one," I said, and ended the call. As I was turning the phone back off so I could put it in my tote bag, Allan emerged from the bathroom. His hair was still a little damp and he hadn't bothered to shave off his stubble, which only made him look that much sexier in my eyes. There was something extra attractive about a guy who was just a little bit scruffy.

"Everything all right?" he asked, rummaging in a dresser drawer for a T-shirt. He pulled out one in a dark burgundy shade. The color looked great on him, although I was a little disappointed that he'd covered up all those wonderful muscles. Then again, he couldn't exactly remain shirtless for our outing to Catalina.

"Just fine," I replied. "I had a few calls to return, that's all. But I'm done for the day, so you don't have to worry about me being stuck on my cell phone the whole time."

His mouth lifted in a half-grin. "Good, because otherwise I would have been tempted to throw your phone in the ocean."

"You wouldn't," I said, although I had a feeling he just might do such a thing if properly provoked...and then promptly buy me an upgraded replacement the very next day.

"Let's hope you'll never find out."

I chuckled and shook my head, and he finished getting dressed, in jeans and casual lace-ups and a long-sleeved army green shirt to go over the tee he'd already put on. My own outfit was similarly low-key, a long-sleeved T-shirt and jeans and a close-fitting dark blue leather jacket in case it got chilly.

"Ready?" he asked.

"Absolutely."

The drive from Hollywood to San Pedro was

remarkably free of drama, probably because so many people had the week between Christmas and New Year's off from work. We got to the tour company's helipad with fifteen minutes to spare, and were glad to see that the flight wouldn't be too crowded, and included only the two of us and another couple in their forties, who turned out to be from Des Moines and were visiting family in Los Angeles.

Obviously, they'd never been up in a helicopter before, and neither had I, so we could all be novices together. I guessed that this wasn't Allan's first ride, judging by the way he easily slid into his seat and put on the headphones we were supposed to wear, but I didn't really have a chance to ask him where else he'd been in a helicopter.

Not long after that, we were winging our way across the Pacific Ocean, a deep, inky blue beneath us, the whitecaps small foamy dots against its vast surface. I'd put a thought out into the universe that the day should be a perfect one, and so of course it was, sky blue and unbroken by a single cloud, the air cool but not cold, with a fresh breeze that carried with it the scent of salt and the promise of all sorts of adventures.

I'd told Allan that this would have to be a day trip, since I'd already spent a night away from home and my cat, and didn't want to be absent two days in a row. He took the news in stride, although I could tell he was a little disappointed that he couldn't whisk me off to some island resort for more fun and games. Even so, we had a very full day planned—an expedition on a glass-bottomed boat, a tour of the historic ballroom perched at one end of the deep harbor that made Catalina such a destination for those who liked to brave the twenty-six-mile trip from L.A.'s coastline to the island, a tour inland to see the wild bison and the bald eagles.

In between, we had a marvelous lunch at a restaurant that overlooked the bay, and drank white wine and ate scallops and grilled mahi-mahi. All the running around from place to place had made me more tired than I thought, and I actually nodded off in the helicopter ride back to San Pedro—no small feat, considering how noisy the cabin was.

When Allan drove me home, he parked in front of the house and walked me to the front porch. Once we were there, he said, "I understand why you wanted to stay home tonight...but there's no reason why I can't stay here with you, is there?"

For a second or two, I just stared at him, the words not quite penetrating...probably because I'd also slept a little on the drive from San Pedro to Santa Monica and was feeling a bit foggy. Then I said, "Um, sure. But let me open the garage so you can park inside. This is a nice neighborhood, but...."

I didn't finish the sentence, and I really didn't have to. Yes, my area was pretty nice, but any beach town attracted some questionable elements, and although Allan had driven his Maserati SUV and not the uber-rare Tesla roadster, the Maserati was still a pretty tempting target.

"That's a good idea," he agreed, and headed back to his car so he could move it.

Since I didn't have the garage remote with me, I had to go inside the house and retrieve it. Mr. Mittens wasn't all that happy to see me immediately go back outside, but once Allan had parked his SUV next to my much smaller Mercedes and we were safely back in the living room, the cat went right up to Allan and rubbed against his legs again.

"Looks like he missed me," he said with that lively twinkle in his blue eyes that I loved so much.

That I liked so much. *Liked.* I wasn't in love with Allan, or loved anything about him. He was just...someone to spend some time with.

Right. And if I could make myself believe that, I could also conjure that week's winning lottery numbers out of thin air, and maybe come up with a solution for world peace while I was at it.

"Oh, he's just glad to have people around," I said lightly. "I suppose I've been pretty neglectful lately. Not sure whose fault that is."

Allan only chuckled and squatted down so he could pet the cat, strong fingers finding the exact spot behind Mr. Mittens' ears where he liked to be scratched. "*Mea culpa*," he said. "Well, we're here now. Should we order in something? I know the timing of our trip didn't exactly line up with dinner."

No, it hadn't, because we'd caught the last flight out just as the sun was setting, and between the journey from Catalina back to the mainland, and then the drive from San Pedro to my house, it was now past eight o'clock at night. I supposed we could have gone out for a late dinner, but ordering delivery sounded like a great idea. We could kick back, turn on the TV, relax.

"That sounds great," I replied. "Anything in particular you're in the mood for?"

Allan shook his head. "Probably not seafood, since we had that for lunch, but otherwise— surprise me."

I was glad he'd said that, because I'd been craving Chinese food the past couple of days. Not that I hadn't enjoyed the meals we'd shared together, but sometimes you just wanted some egg rolls.

"I'm on it," I said, and got out my phone. My

favorite Chinese restaurant had online ordering, so I was able to get everything I wanted—egg rolls and egg fried rice and orange chicken and pepper beef—with a minimum of fuss. Once I was done, I set the phone on the coffee table and grinned up at Allan. "Hope you like Chinese food."

"I adore it," he replied. "Do you need to feed the cat?"

Mr. Mittens was now meowing loudly, his way of letting me know that while I might have provided him with plenty of dry food and water to keep him covered in my absence, his abandonment issues now needed to be assuaged by a real meal of Blue Buffalo chicken paté.

"'Need' probably isn't the right word," I said. "But I'll go take care of him. Make yourself comfortable."

I headed off to the kitchen, where I got out a can of food and emptied it into the cat's bowl, and then refreshed his water even though he still had plenty left. And, figuring Allan was probably thirsty as well, I poured us both glasses of water and brought them out to the living room. He'd apparently taken my instructions to get comfortable at face value, because he'd taken off his shoes and was now crouched in front of the fireplace in his sock feet, stuffing some crumpled newspaper under the logs there.

He looked up as I set the glasses of water on a

couple of coasters. "I hope a fire is okay. I saw that you already had some logs in the grate, and I thought it would be fun. It's kind of a damp evening."

Which was only the truth. Our day in Catalina had been all blue skies and bright sun, except for the very end. Clouds had begun to steal in, blocking some of the sunset, and by the time we'd gotten to Santa Monica, the area was pretty well socked in, the air cool and moist, telling me the fog and clouds had settled in for the night.

"I think it's a great idea," I told him, which was the truth. I'd put the logs in the grate more than a week earlier, vaguely thinking it might be fun to have a fire around the holidays. Of course, I'd been so busy I'd never gotten around to it, but the logs would only have seasoned that much more by sitting out all that time, so I figured no harm, no foul.

Obviously, Allan was good at that sort of thing, since the fire blazed up right away, crackling cheerily and warming up the room nicely. I tended to leave my thermostat set fairly low most of the time—I was gone so much and Mr. Mittens liked things on the cool side—and the fire definitely took the edge off.

My companion sent a sideways glance at the glasses of water. "That's all you have?" he asked with an arched eyebrow.

As a matter of fact, I had a second bottle of the rosé I'd taken over to my mother's house on Christmas Day chilling in the fridge. However, I didn't immediately provide Allan with that particular piece of information, only set my hands on my hips and said, "You know, most experts agree that it's a good idea to hydrate from time to time."

"I suppose so," he responded, his tone dubious. "But it's not very much fun. I can always run out to the store—"

"Relax," I cut in with a chuckle. "I have some rosé for when the food gets here."

He gave an exaggerated sigh of relief. "Good. I was starting to worry about you."

About all I could do was shake my head. Allan came over and took me in his arms and kissed me —not hard, but thoroughly enough that all the weariness I'd felt earlier disappeared. Now I was alert, nerve endings tingling...and also very glad that I'd swapped out the sheets on my bed earlier that week. Not that they'd gotten any action recently, but clean sheets were in general a good idea.

Mr. Mittens came into the living room and sent Allan a sidelong, yellow-eyed glare, as if reevaluating his opinion of the interloper in light of this strange new behavior. Allan let go of me and gazed down at the cat. "I think he's giving me the stink-eye."

"Oh, he's definitely doing that. I suppose he's not sure what to make of you kissing me."

My casual comment made Allan frown slightly. "What, he's never seen someone kiss you before?"

"No," I replied, since it was only the truth. It had always been my habit to see the guys I was dating at neutral locations—restaurants and movie theaters and bars—and only go to their places on those rare occasions when things got intimate. I figured it was safer for them not to know where I lived. "You're actually the first guy I've ever had come over here."

Obviously, Allan hadn't been expecting that particular reply. Looking a little startled, he said, "Well, I guess I should be honored."

"I suppose you should," I said with a grin.

As he was mulling that over, the doorbell rang, and I went over to answer it. Out on the front porch was Mike Kang, the oldest son of the couple who owned my go-to Chinese restaurant. He sometimes ran deliveries for them when he was home from school; I knew he was going to college up at Stanford.

"Hey, Mike," I said as I took the bags of food from him. Since I'd paid online with my credit card—including the tip—I didn't have to worry about handing over any cash now. "How's school going?"

"Great," he replied. "I'll be heading back the middle of next week."

"Don't let your parents work you too hard while you're down here," I told him, and he grinned.

"Doing my best. Have a good one."

He headed back to his car, and I shut the door to see Allan watching me with a smile. "You must order from them a lot if you're on a first-name basis with the delivery driver."

"It's very good Chinese food," I said primly on my way to the kitchen. My first thought had been to set the bags of food down on the coffee table, but that probably would have been ruinous to the wood finish, so I thought I'd better dish it up on some plates to be safe.

Allan followed me, and watched as I got out a couple of dishes and some bowls, and transferred everything over. Then he seemed to realize we were forgetting something important. "Wine?"

"In the fridge. And the glasses are in the cupboard next to the sink."

Without replying, he went over to the refrigerator and retrieved the bottle of rosé, and then got the wine glasses from the cupboard I'd indicated. It took a little juggling, but we were able to transport everything to the living room without too much fuss. Mr. Mittens watched all this activity from a safe spot near the hearth, just close enough to soak up some of the warmth from the fire, but not so close that he had to worry about a random spark flying out and singeing his fur.

Allan and I put down the food and drink we were carrying, then settled ourselves on the sofa. He eyed the bottle and said, "A twist cap?"

"Don't be a snob," I told him. "It's very good wine. Lots of wineries are switching to twist caps to avoid spoilage."

His eyes danced, but he didn't bother to contradict me, only said, "Of course. My bad."

He poured some wine for both of us, and we didn't even bother with a toast, only had a sip and then plowed into the food. I'd put a little bit of everything on each of our plates, then sealed up the take-out containers and left them on the kitchen counter in case we wanted seconds.

"This is good," he commented—after demolishing an egg roll and most of the pepper beef and fried rice on his plate. "Now I'm wondering why I don't have Chinese food more often."

"It's my comfort food," I said. "Well, that and Faye's mac and cheese. She uses three different kinds of cheese, and it's sublime."

Since he'd been working on a mouthful of orange chicken as I spoke, he had to wait until he was done chewing before he could reply. "That does sound good."

He looked a little wistful, and I found myself

wondering if he regretted not coming over for Christmas dinner two days earlier. Not that we'd had macaroni and cheese for our holiday meal, but still. And although we still had some time left before the thirty-first rolled around, I didn't think it was a good idea to have him over at my mother's for dinner. I knew that Faye and my mom would be glad to see him and would feed him well…but I also knew I might be raising his expectations if I did something like that, might make him think there was a possibility this little romance of ours could extend past the first of the year. No, better to keep him as separate from the rest of my life as possible. That way, there wouldn't be any dangling threads to make our inevitable breakup even harder than I knew it was going to be.

If you could even call a mutually agreed-upon separation a breakup. I was in uncharted territory here, trying to feel my way through without making a total hash of things.

Unfortunately, I had a feeling I was already well beyond that point.

"But since Faye doesn't do takeout," I said, knowing how falsely cheerful I sounded, "I figured Chinese from Kang's was the next best thing."

Allan made an affirmative sound, his mouth full again, and I could tell we'd safely gotten past that one awkward moment. After he'd sipped some more wine, he asked if I wanted to turn on the television, to which I said yes. That seemed the safest thing—we could eat and watch, and most likely we'd make love once we got to the bedroom.

All I had to do was make sure this pattern continued for the next couple of days. Then we'd have arrived at New Year's and the party, and we could go our lonely ways after that. Don't talk about anything too personal, avoid as much contact with family as possible.

Easy.

Yeah, right.

INTERLUDE

Doing his best to curb the urge to hurl his phone out the window of his hotel room, Beelzebub instead tossed it onto the bed in disgust and went to stare out the window. It overlooked a busy street crowded with overpriced vehicles—he was in Beverly Hills, after all—and the sight only made him scowl that much more fiercely.

How dare she fob him off on a mere underling?

Because that was exactly what Belinda Carson had done. No, she couldn't even be bothered to return the call personally to let him know she was simply too busy to manage his fictional party. Instead, she'd had her assistant, someone with the improbable name of Dee Rodriguez, contact him and let him know that Ms. Carson was already booked on New Year's managing a catered cocktail party for an important client, but if he was really in a bind, then Dee would be more than happy to help him out.

Which of course was out of the question. There was no party, after all; his only reason for making up that story was so he could speak to Belinda Carson in person and let her know exactly who it was she'd been spending time with this past week. If she wouldn't even see him, then there was no reason to continue this charade.

He'd told Dee Rodriguez that he wanted Belinda or no one, and then ended the call. Not for the first time, he wished he had the same vast powers at his command that his former overlord had possessed, but even though Beelzebub was now the de facto Lord of Hell, he was still only a demon. Well, all right, *a* devil, if not *the* Devil, simply because he and Asmodeus had been among the highest order of angels before the Fall, and so were far more powerful than the demons who guarded those unfortunate souls whose earthly crimes had barred them from ever attaining the Kingdom of Heaven. Even so, he couldn't simply command his phone to call Belinda's private cell, and he couldn't read her thoughts or the thoughts of those close to her without physically possessing them. Since he'd already crossed off that possible avenue as far too risky, he appeared to be running out of options.

If he could just come up with some way to get her alone....

Unfortunately, even though he'd been racking his brains, he simply seemed unable to devise a plan that wouldn't raise her suspicions...or worse, those of Asmodeus himself. It was extremely inconvenient that demons were able to sense when they were near another of their kind, or else Beelzebub would have arranged a chance meeting —while carefully disguised, of course—and approached her when she was out with his erstwhile companion.

However, since Asmodeus would sniff him out if he got within fifteen feet of her, that sort of plan wouldn't work at all. And since it also seemed as though the two were currently joined at the hip, Beelzebub honestly didn't know if he would get any kind of viable chance to speak to her in private. Every moment that ticked by seemed a grinding agony, because it brought the world closer and closer to the time when that foolish human female would decide she actually was in love with Asmodeus. And since he was obviously all too willing to be in love with her, probably all she'd need to do was declare her love to him out loud, and it would all be over. Then Beelzebub would be left to rule Hell alone.

Not that he minded ruling Hell...far from it. What he minded was having his capable lieutenant taken from him in order to live a life of sloth and excess here in Los Angeles. If Asmodeus somehow succeeded and managed to stay in this world and live out his life as a mortal man, then Beelzebub would have to get someone else to take over his position. Belial, probably, although that lesser demon was not someone he had any desire to work with. For all his faults, Asmodeus was at least capable if he put his mind to something. Belial, on the other hand, was a demon who would need constant minding. He never seemed to take anything seriously.

A grinding sound came to Beelzebub's ears, and he realized it was coming from himself, from his teeth grating together as he clenched his jaw. He relaxed it as best he could, then scowled again as he caught a glimpse of himself in the mirror that hung on the wall across from the bed. Why he'd been saddled with such an unprepossessing human appearance, he had no idea. A little joke from the Man Upstairs, he supposed. While he guessed some mortals might have found this visage attractive, Beelzebub thought it was entirely lacking in character. About the only advantage it afforded him was that he looked exceedingly unthreatening, a quality which did come in handy from time to time.

However, that baby face certainly wasn't going to do him any good if he never had an opportunity to use it on its intended target, i.e., Belinda Carson.

The question now was whether to go back to Hell and see if familiar surroundings might allow him to formulate a workable plan, or whether returning to the underworld would only be an admission of defeat. Beelzebub contemplated that conundrum for a moment before deciding it was probably better to stay where he was for the time being. If he left now, he might miss an opportunity, should one present itself. And while he had his doubts about Belial, for the moment, the other demon seemed to be managing adequately, probably because no crises had yet arisen to tax his limited skills.

That matter settled, Beelzebub sat down on the bed and reached for the phone. If he was going to be stuck here, he might as well order another one of those delicious sandwiches....

CHAPTER FIFTEEN

ALLAN AND I ENDED UP COCOONING ALL DAY Friday, making languorous love in the morning, then rising to whip up an elaborate breakfast. Well, actually, since I didn't keep many breakfast fixings on hand, I sent Allan off to the grocery store while I showered, and then we spent nearly an hour making pancakes and eggs and bacon, all from organic ingredients he'd gotten at the local Whole Foods. And after we'd eaten our fill, we cleaned up the kitchen and watched a little TV, then headed out to the backyard to get some sun, since the fog and clouds had burned off and the day was mild and sunny again. We talked about what we should do the next day, and decided to wander around Venice, since he'd never been there. And either LACMA or the big Getty Museum on Sunday, although we thought we'd wait to choose which one on the day of our expedition, depending on how we were feeling.

Through all of this, I kept wondering when the other shoe was going to drop, so to speak. Whether we'd get tired of each other's company or get bored, or find our attention wandering to something else. The strange thing was, none of those things happened. It was so easy simply to be with him, to spend time talking or being quiet, to listen to the sound of his voice and that throaty chuckle of his, or to see all the shifting colors in his blue-gray eyes and watch the sun pick out glints of gold in his dark blond hair. For the first time in my life, I understood how good it was to simply be with a person, to understand that the important thing was to enjoy everything about them without analyzing it too much or trying to find something to criticize.

True, I'd looked for faults in the previous men in my life because I knew I had no future with them, and so it had seemed better to come up with all the reasons I shouldn't be with them beforehand in order to save myself some time.

The problem with Allan was that I really couldn't find any faults in him. Or rather, the imperfections I was able to detect only made him that much more lovable to me. And that particular realization seemed to indicate I was in even worse trouble than I'd already thought I was.

However, I tried to convince myself that it didn't matter, that I could allow myself to feel these things for him because they weren't reciprocated. Of course, he appeared to enjoy being with me, but I could also feel reassured in the knowledge that he'd bounced back pretty damn quickly from Nina Nomura dumping him, and so he was probably the sort of person whose feelings didn't run all that deep. Yes, he was having a good time with me now…and he'd have an equally good time with someone else once this fling of ours—or whatever you wanted to call it—had run its course. But he wouldn't be scarred by having me walk away because he'd simply never been that involved in the first place.

I did get him to agree that I wouldn't stay at his place the night before New Year's Eve day, just because I had last-minute business I needed to handle with both the caterer and the florist, and it was better for him to be home by himself anyway, since he was having his cleaning crew come in specially that day to make sure everything was perfect for the party. Even that small separation didn't sound like much fun to me, although I did my best to tell myself that I needed to get used to it, since I wouldn't be able to see him after New Year's anyway.

But that was more than seventy-two hours from this particular Friday, and I pushed my worries aside as best I could, choosing to focus on the here and now. Already it felt completely normal to fall asleep next to him, to hear him watching television in the living room while I put on makeup in a bathroom that felt awfully cramped compared to the luxurious marble-walled *en suite* space at Allan's house. However, he seemed happy enough here, despite these much more modest surroundings, and I had to admit I felt better about not leaving Mr. Mittens alone for so long. And, to be honest, the Santa Monica house was a better home base for the weekend outings we had planned, rather than having to drive all the way from Hollywood.

That was how I rationalized things to myself, and I noticed Allan hadn't mentioned anything about the way Monday kept looming closer and closer, almost as though he thought if he just ignored it, our arbitrary little deadline might magically disappear.

Well, there were a few slightly useful things I could do with the magic I'd inherited, but stopping time definitely wasn't one of them.

Still, over the years I'd gotten pretty good about compartmentalizing so I wouldn't become completely depressed over the curse that ruled my life, and so I felt as though I was in a generally upbeat mood as Allan and I left the house on Saturday morning and drove over to Venice. We'd made love again when we woke up, and had even squeezed into my shower together to extend our fun, although once again, I thought how those activities probably would have been a little easier to manage in the large glass-encased shower stall in the Hollywood Hills house.

It wasn't quite as brightly sunny as the day we'd gone to Catalina, but there was still more sun than clouds, which was probably about the most you could hope for in late December, even in Southern California. Thanks to Allan's excellent parking karma, we were able to get a decent spot in the public lot as someone was just backing out, and then it was time to start exploring.

Although we'd gone to the Santa Monica pier together and walked a little along Ocean Boulevard there, Venice was a completely different experience. Although he didn't comment, I could see his eyes widen occasionally as he took in a particularly funky specimen of humanity, like the guy in board shorts and no shirt, rainbow dreadlocks, and an enormous top hat, or the woman who walked barefoot in head-to-toe tie dye as she strummed a ukulele to herself. I'd been here enough times that none of this fazed me too much, but even for someone who spent a good amount of time in Hollywood, this was probably more wackiness than Allan was used to.

At least now that cannabis had been legalized

in California, I no longer had to worry about all the people who used to range up and down the boardwalk and would try to get you to come into their dispensaries with promises of medical marijuana cards so you could get your fix without getting busted. Oh, sure, the dispensaries were still there, and you could definitely smell the faint haze of marijuana smoke in the air, but it wasn't quite as in your face as it used to be.

Allan looked around at the crowds and shook his head. "It feels as if the whole world is here."

"Well, we definitely get people from all over the world," I said. "And even in as crazy a place as Los Angeles, Venice is the place to come and let your freak flag fly."

"It's hard to believe Beverly Hills is only five miles away," he commented.

Yes, that pricey enclave did feel as if it existed in an entirely different world. We were both dressed casually enough, but it still seemed as though Allan and I stood out—most people could probably tell we weren't tourists, but we also weren't grungy or spacey enough to be true locals. I might have lived in Santa Monica, but the two beach cities were worlds apart when it came to style. My hometown had its share of surfers and hippies and artists, and yet it was still nowhere close to Venice when it came to the true free spirits.

We walked along the beach, watched people flying kites in a multitude of shapes and sizes, saw plenty of people surfing even though the water temperatures had to be in the mid-fifties at best. At some point as we walked, Allan's hand stole into mine, and I marveled at how good just that simple touch felt, to have our fingers entwined while we gazed at the sights and pointed out various points of interest. Never before in my life had I felt so completely at home with someone, and even as I smiled and chuckled at his quips, I also sensed a quiet, dull ache, a hurt that I knew would only be so much worse a few days from now.

I didn't think he noticed anything, though. My job required me to be very good at wearing a public face no matter what else might be going on in my life, and so I made myself do the same thing that afternoon in Venice. I told myself that we had so little time left, it would be foolish to mar these last few days by bemoaning a fate I couldn't change. And anyway, I needed to keep things light and fun, if for no other reason than knowing I had to make sure Allan didn't suspect I'd begun to care for him much more deeply than I'd ever thought possible. The only way he'd be able to get away unscathed was if he thought I had no more involvement in this relationship than he did.

We ate at a burger place and had a beer, and after we'd gone back out to the boardwalk to work off our meal, he said, "So far, I have a hundred and ten confirmations for the New Year's party. I didn't know if you needed to pass that information along to the caterer."

I'd been doing my best not to think about the party, even though I usually would have been stewing about an event only two days off, playing out various scenarios in my head so I could think of everything that might go wrong in advance. That way, I'd have my contingencies lined up, just in case. However, I realized that I would need to knuckle down soon enough, although at this point, most of the true work was in Marcelle and Tori's hands.

"I'll let Marcelle know," I said. "In general, she always incorporates a little overage when she caters a party, just because she knows some people are terrible about RSVPing and show up anyway."

"It does seem to be a custom that's fallen by the wayside," Allan agreed. "I've been sending follow-up emails for the past two days, but I'm sure there'll still be some stragglers. Gone are the days when not responding to an invitation meant you were shut out, period."

True enough. Not that I was old enough to have been around when manners and deportment were a big deal, but I'd been raised to always

RSVP, to always send thank-you notes and do all the little things that so many people seemed to consider a waste of time these days.

Thinking about my family made me wonder about Allan's. He'd mentioned an estranged brother, but otherwise, he'd told me practically nothing about his past, except that he'd come here from New York.

"Was your family traditional about those sorts of things?" I asked as we paused near a large open area next to the beach where a reggae band was playing an actually quite good cover of "One Love."

"'My family'?" Allan repeated, looking a little blank. But then he gave me one of his quick, flashing smiles, the kind that tended to make my knees go slightly weak. That day, though, I felt hyper-aware, too on edge, and I got the feeling there was something false about that smile, as though he'd put it on exactly because he knew it would disarm me. "Oh, I suppose you could say we were traditional. Big brownstone, family in finance. Summers in the Hamptons, that kind of thing."

"Ah," I said. Well, that explained it. Obviously, he came from money...a lot of money. That didn't mean he wasn't committed to making his new agency a success, only that it wouldn't be the end of the world if he crashed and burned and decided to return to the East Coast after all.

In a way, maybe that would be better. Maybe it wouldn't hurt so much once this was all over if I knew he was three thousand miles away from me instead of barely ten.

"Thank-you notes on engraved paper," I added, since he was watching me closely, as though I'd allowed some kind of betraying expression to show on my face.

He chuckled. "Exactly that sort of thing. It could be a little stifling. That's why I prefer being out here. In L.A., you can become whoever you want to be."

That was the story, anyway. I supposed for some people, it might even be true. Come to a new place, start over, reinvent yourself, create a new narrative. My problem was that it didn't really matter where I went—the curse would always follow me. Maybe that was why my grandmother had decided to settle in Santa Monica so many years ago. If her life was going to be ruled by some kind of supernatural hex from beyond the grave, better to do it in a place with an amazing climate and the ocean only a few blocks away. In a setting like that, you could almost pretend that everything was fine and that you didn't care whether there was a man in your life or not.

"You seem very quiet," Allan said, and I inwardly cursed myself for letting my thoughts run away from me.

"Oh, I guess it's the salt air," I lied. "After a while, it starts to tire me out."

"Do you want to go home?"

I didn't, not really, because if we were out and doing something, I had a better chance of pretending that everything was fine and that I didn't have only about forty-eight hours to go before I had to say goodbye to him forever. On the other hand, there was only so much wandering up and down the Venice boardwalk that a person could do.

"Sure," I said. "It might be nice to put my feet up for a while."

Allan shot me a look of concern, but he only nodded and turned so we were heading back to the public lot where we'd left his SUV. Once again, he took my hand, and I made myself focus on the sensation of his fingers entwined with mine, how strong and warm they were, how our fingers seemed to fit together perfectly, even though my hand was so much smaller than his. I needed to do that, if only to engrave the memory in my mind, so I could go back and revisit it whenever I was feeling tired and alone.

Actually, going home made me feel a little better, just because I'd purposely done my best to ensure my house was as cozy and welcoming as I was able to make it, a sanctuary where I could pretend my life wasn't ruled by forces I couldn't control. Allan and I curled up next to each other on the couch and watched TV, with Mr. Mittens purring loudly by the hearth, and I made myself focus on only that one perfect moment, on this quiet time of peace. Maybe I would never be able to experience anything like it again, but I had this time now and intended to enjoy it.

Anything else seemed like a betrayal of my feelings for Allan.

The next day, I actually felt a little more cheerful. By rights, I shouldn't have been, since it was only that much closer to the time when we would have to say goodbye to one another, but it was almost as though I'd needed to experience the funk of the day before in order to come out on the other side and steel myself for what was coming next. Since we still had breakfast fixings left over, we made a big brunch before we headed out to the Getty— the newer museum by the freeway in Westwood, not the one we'd already visited in Malibu.

It was a cold, gray day, with fitful spurts of moisture that couldn't decide whether or not it wanted to be drizzle or actual rain. I supposed I could have done something to clear it out if I'd really wanted to, but I thought it better to save my energy for the next day, to make sure Allan's New Year's party wasn't interrupted by bad weather. Although all those guests probably could have fit inside his house if necessary, the plan was to have them spill out onto the large patio and the even larger pavilion that would be set up on the lawn, and a rainy night would definitely put a damper on those preparations.

Anyway, although the Getty certainly had some beautiful outdoor spaces, it was what was inside the galleries that mattered the most, and better to wander those on a gloomy afternoon instead of missing out on some sunshine. To my surprise, Allan appeared to know a good bit about art, certainly more than I'd guessed he did. Possibly that was because his summers-in-the-Hamptons family back east collected art, or maybe he'd decided to study it in case he wanted to start collecting pieces for his home. I'd noticed that, while the downstairs area in his house displayed a couple of very good originals, everything I'd glimpsed in the master bedroom and the upstairs hallway appeared to have been prints— nicely framed, but nothing terribly valuable.

I asked him about collecting art as we took a break and had some coffee and croissants in one of the museum's cafés, and he shrugged.

"I've thought about it," he said, "but it seems like kind of a quagmire. I mean, you get so much conflicting information about what things are worth that it's hard to know if you're doing the right thing or not."

"My mother says you shouldn't think about how much something is worth," I told him as I broke off a piece of croissant. After I ate the morsel, I added, "It's more about how something makes you feel."

He seemed to consider my comment for a moment, his head tilted slightly to one side. "She's an artist, isn't she?"

"Ceramicist," I replied. "She teaches at the community college, but she's also had some shows of her own and has a lot of pieces in local galleries and stores. Anyway, she says if a piece of art doesn't touch some part of your soul, then it doesn't matter how much it's supposed to be worth."

His eyes narrowed slightly, but then he nodded. "I suppose I can see her point...although I think some of the fine art galleries and auction houses might want to argue it with her."

Yes, I doubted they'd want to hear someone say they didn't care about a five-million-dollar Chagall or Picasso because it didn't "touch their soul." I grinned and said, "Well, true. But since I'm never going to be in a position to be buying something from Sotheby's or Christie's, it's advice I think I'll try to live by when it comes to collecting art."

For some reason, Allan didn't answer my smile. Looking thoughtful, he said, "You don't know that for sure, though. It seems as if your business is very successful. Or something could change in your life that would get you to a place where you might be buying fine art."

His eyes met mine then, and a strange little shiver went through me. No, he hadn't said anything outright, and maybe I was fooling myself, but I couldn't help thinking that there had been a subtext to his words, that he'd imagined a future for us where maybe I would live with him in that sleek, modern house in the Hollywood Hills, where maybe I might help him choose new pieces to adorn the master bedroom we shared.

That wasn't possible, though. I picked up my coffee and made myself take a sip, using that as an excuse to pull my gaze from him. No, I was imagining things that weren't there. I had to be, since he hadn't said one thing, uttered one word to make me think he'd imagined any future for us beyond these few days we were sharing.

And thank God for that. He needed to be amusing himself and nothing more. I desperately needed him not to care.

You can't fall in love with me, I thought. *I won't let you. We're so close. Don't screw this up.*

I gave a little laugh that probably sounded even more false to him than it did to me and said, "Well, I've learned to never say never, so I suppose it's remotely possible. I'm not going to hold my breath, though."

For a second or two, I thought he was going to argue with me. But then he gave a philosophical shrug and returned to his neglected croissant, and I allowed myself an inner sigh of relief.

I needed to make sure we didn't have a repeat of that moment.

And it seemed I had my wish, because the rest of the afternoon passed without incident, and we had an intimate but uneventful dinner that night at Tar & Roses. I knew Allan had taken me there because he wanted to make sure our last meal out together would be a memorable one, and I did my best to pay attention to the marvelous food we were sharing, the way his blue eyes warmed almost to green in the golden candlelight, the sound of his voice and all the thousand other details I needed to memorize so I could tuck them away with all my other memories of him. After all, a little more than twenty-four hours from that lovely dinner, he'd be out of my life forever.

We made love afterward, slowly, carefully, as though each of us was unwrapping a gift we knew we'd never receive again. As he shuddered to a climax inside me, I found myself wondering whether I should have stopped taking my birth control pills. After all, even if I couldn't have him, maybe I could have had a child of his.

That was when I knew what a claim he'd made on my heart. I'd told myself I didn't want children, didn't want to subject anyone else to the harsh dictates that had ruled the lives of Carson witches for generations…but I wished I could have had Allan's child. At least that way, I would have been able to hold on to a piece of him, wouldn't have thought my love for him would be lost forever.

After he fell asleep, I wept into my pillow, silently, making sure I didn't move or utter a single betraying sound. I didn't want him to wake up and find me crying, because right then, I was feeling weak enough that I feared I might tell him the truth, might tell him why I could never be with him. And that was something I knew I couldn't do.

I looked at the clock on my nightstand and saw it was a couple of minutes after midnight. Twenty-four hours to go. Twenty-four hours until this was over.

I love you, I thought. *I always will.*

Too bad it didn't matter.

CHAPTER SIXTEEN

I MADE SURE I WAS ALL SMILES WHEN I SENT Allan home the next morning. He didn't seem nearly so chipper, and all my worries of the day before came flooding back. However, I pretended to misunderstand the somewhat grim air he wore, and said, "Everything is totally under control. I'll be seeing Marcelle and Tori later today, and then I'll be over around four to help with all the last-minute stuff. The party is going to be a raging success."

He perked up a little at those words. "I think so. Of course, I can't wait to see everything set up —that's when it will all come together."

"It's going to be spectacular," I assured him. "Now, go on. I've got a bunch of stuff to do, but I'll see you later."

His hand brushed a lock of hair away from my

face, even as he bent and kissed me. A tender, sweet kiss, nothing too over the top, but it awoke an ache of longing within me far more than a truly passionate embrace might have. Still, I managed to smile as he picked up his duffle bag and walked down the front steps so he could head over to the garage and get into his Maserati SUV. And I remained there as he backed out of the driveway, then pointed the remote at the garage to shut the door. Once I knew he was truly gone, I closed the front door.

I hadn't been lying to him when I said I had a lot to do that day. However, I knew there was one errand I needed to run here in Santa Monica before I headed out to meet with the caterer and the florist.

I needed to go visit my grandmother.

When I'd awoken that morning with my heart still aching, I knew there was only one person I could talk to. My mother would be sympathetic, but she wouldn't understand. Not really. She was with the person she cared about—they were lucky enough to be able to grow old together.

My grandmother hadn't been that lucky. She knew what it was like to be forced to walk away.

I'd let Mr. Mittens out in the backyard for his morning potty break, and he was well stocked with food and water, and so I knew he'd be fine until I returned late that night. My tote bag was packed with my shoes and makeup kit, and the cocktail dress I planned to wear to the party was already hanging from the hook in the back seat of my little Mercedes SUV. Everything was ready, and so I knew there was no reason to delay... none, except worry over what my grandmother might say to me.

However, I knew I needed to hear those home truths, no matter how much they might hurt.

My grandmother's house was much closer to the beach than my place or the house my mother and Faye shared; she'd bought it back in the mid-1960s, when a single secretary could actually afford a house of her own. The home was still the same little one-story cottage it had always been, but was now worth millions because of its location; she was approached by realtors at least once a week, doing their best to convince her that selling the place and moving to a more low-maintenance condo was in her best interests. However, I'd heard her say more than once that she wasn't leaving until she was carried out on a stretcher, so I knew those realtors were wasting their time.

The sun was shining brightly that day, illuminating the riot of roses in her front yard. A lot of people had trouble growing roses so close to the beach because of the damp salt air, but the flowers in my grandmother's garden looked like something out of *The Secret Garden*. For all I knew, she used a little Carson magic to get the roses to bloom so well nearly all year 'round—the only time the yard was at all bare was in late winter, when she pruned the bushes to ensure a bumper crop of blooms the next spring and summer and fall.

I hadn't called to say I needed to come over, figuring I would leave things up to fate. If my grandmother wasn't home when I got there, well, I'd call that the universe at work and go on to my meetings. However, she was out in the garden when I parked at the curb out front, her hands busy as she methodically went about deadheading the blooms that were past their peak.

She looked up in some surprise as I opened the garden gate and let myself in, but then she appeared to nod to herself, as if she was somehow able to guess at the reason for my visit.

"Belinda," she said, then set her clippers down inside the basket she had looped over her left arm. "This is a pleasant surprise."

"Hi, Grandma," I replied, glad that I sounded steady and relatively normal. Since I'd examined my face critically in the bathroom earlier that morning, I knew I didn't bear any traces of my weeping from the night before, no red eyes or puffy lids. Possibly, I'd looked a little tired, but some concealer and blush and lip gloss had hidden any signs of weariness. "Can I talk to you for a minute?"

Her eyes, shielded by the brim of the straw sun hat she wore, studied me for a few seconds. "Of course, sweetie," she said. "Let's go inside. You look like you could use a cup of tea."

Only if you pour a little whiskey into it, I thought, but I simply nodded and followed her inside. Honestly, I didn't even drink spirits, since I disliked the taste—it just seemed as though I would need something a lot stronger than plain old tea to make me feel better about life.

Inside, the house was just as homey and somehow beachy as it had ever been, with its pale oak floors and oak furniture, the overstuffed dark blue couch and the watercolors of seascapes and shells on the walls. I'd always liked coming here, since the home was only a block away from the ocean and on days when my grandmother had the windows open, as she did today, you could hear the faint roar of the surf and smell the salt on the air.

She went into the kitchen and put the kettle on the big six-burner stove, then got down a couple of cups and matching saucers. I went and sat down at the round dining room table, knowing that there was no point in offering to help, since she'd only tell me she had everything under control. In a way, it felt good to sit there, to let myself breathe in the ocean air and watch as a rectangle of sunlight came in through the wood-framed window and gleamed on the polished floor.

Eventually, the tea was ready, and my grandmother brought it over and put a cup and saucer in front of me, then set the other one down in front of the empty chair next to the one where I sat. Since she knew I didn't take any cream or sugar—and because she drank it the same way—she hadn't bothered to bring any over.

"Don't you have a party you're running tonight?" she asked as she lifted her cup to her lips so she could blow on it gently.

I nodded. "Yes. I'm meeting with the caterer and the florist after this. But…."

"But?" she probed, her blue eyes filled with understanding…and compassion.

"But I don't know how I'm supposed to do it."

"Because this is your last night with Allan."

Tears stung my eyes, and I made myself pull in a breath before lifting the cup to my mouth so I could take a sip of tea. It was far too hot, burning my tongue, but I willed the pain away, knowing I could use a small bit of my magic to heal the hurt I'd just given myself if necessary. "Yes," I said at last. "I thought I was being smart, that I could let myself have this bit of fun with him and then walk away, but…."

She didn't say anything, only sat there and waited, as though she knew I needed to work my way through this myself in order to find any peace.

"But I love him," I said simply. It hurt to say the words, and yet, at the same time I felt a certain relief. I'd allowed the thought to pass through my mind, but I'd never said the words aloud. Now they seemed far more real…and at the same time, their very reality somehow made them easier to manage.

"There's nothing wrong with loving him," my grandmother told me, her gaze fixed on me and filled with a terrible understanding. "It's only a problem when he loves you back."

I knew that as well as she did. "How do you keep it from hurting?"

Her mouth quirked a little, and the lines around her eyes deepened as she smiled. "Oh, sweetheart, you can't keep it from hurting. You don't want it not to hurt. That hurt tells you it's real."

"Did you love him?" I blurted out. "My grandfather, I mean."

The smile faded, and she took a measured sip from the porcelain cup she held. "Of course, I did. Times were very different back then—I wouldn't have allowed myself to be with a man I didn't love. I knew I wanted to have a child, and I wanted that child to have come from love…even if that love was one-sided."

"Because he was married."

"Separated, but yes." Another swallow of tea, and my grandmother set her cup back down on its saucer. A pause, and then she went on, "Love is never a waste of your time, Belinda. You need to remember that, even though this hurts now."

"How do you go on, though?" I asked. The pain of losing Allan was a hard knot in my chest, in my belly. No, he wasn't gone yet, but he might as well have been. Less than twelve hours from this very moment, he would be out of my life forever. "It's like—it's like he filled a space in my heart, and there won't be anything else to fill it after he's gone."

She reached out and placed her hand on mine. Her fingers were thin but strong, still warm from working in the garden under the sun. "You have to fill it yourself, sweetie. No one else has the power to make you happy. Your happiness comes from yourself. You were happy before Allan came along, and you'll be happy again after he's gone."

I wanted to believe her. But had I been happy…*really* happy? If asked, I would have said I was content in my work and my life, that I certainly didn't need anything—or anyone—to complete me. Now, though, after spending the past eight days with Allan, I understood what I'd been missing all that time. All right, I could be a perfectly functional adult without a companion. Whether I was actually *happy* was a completely different question.

Probably because I was taking so long to answer her, my grandmother let out a gentle sigh and went on, "I know that's hard to believe right now. You've let him into your life this week, and even after so short an amount of time, you're having a hard time remembering what it was like before he came along. But you'll go back to that life—you'll get busy and have your work to occupy you, and after some time has passed, it won't hurt as much."

"I should have let him knock me up," I said bitterly, and she laughed and reached for her tea.

"That's not always the optimal solution," she replied. "Oh, I'm very glad I had your mother, but you should decide to have a child because you truly want one, and not because you're hoping that child will be a keepsake to remind you of a person who's not in your life anymore."

Since I wasn't sure what else to do, I picked up my own tea and took a large swallow. It had cooled enough that I didn't have to worry about burning my tongue this time, and so I drank some more as I sat there with the fragile little cup cradled in my hands. "You seem to have an answer for everything."

Her eyes crinkled with amusement. "I'd like to think so, after kicking around on this planet for seventy-eight years, but that's not really true. It's more that…I've been where you are now. I know it hurts. But it passes. That's the thing about life. These things always pass."

"They do?" Right then, I didn't know if I could even imagine a future where it wouldn't hurt to think about Allan D'Alessandro. I wanted to believe my grandmother was right, that she was only telling me the truth, hard as it might be to listen to right then.

"Yes." She set down her teacup and gave me a very direct look. In her face, I could see an echo of the glamorous young woman who'd attracted the attention of the hotshot lawyer who was my biological grandfather, although I doubted the starry-eyed secretary who'd come to Los Angeles on her own in 1960 had ever worn quite such a knowing, yet earnest expression. "And you need to know something else, Belinda. Love is never wasted. You might think that it is, since you can never be with the person you care for, but…that energy is still out there. Love is strong. Love will bring good to your life, even if not exactly in the way you might have thought. Trust in love."

Once again, she reached over and patted my hand. This time, though, I allowed myself to take some comfort from her touch, to understand that she wasn't making a careless gesture. It reminded me of the blood that connected us all, the strength that had allowed generations of Carson women to continue even when they knew the curse would prevent them from ever having a so-called normal life.

Well, normal was highly overrated. And I reminded myself of what she'd told me just a moment earlier.

Love was never wasted. I loved Allan...and that was all right.

I just needed to make sure he would never know.

INTERLUDE

Asmodeus stood at the window that looked out on the backyard and smiled, even as he made sure to keep a safe distance from the glass, since his cleaning crew had just departed and the enormous sliding glass window—like everything else in the house—was so clean it sparkled. The entire place was ready for the party tonight. Or at least, the final stages of the preparations could now begin, since the party rental truck had just pulled up at the curb and the crew was already busy pulling out the poles and canvas for the pavilion that would be erected in the yard. Nothing too large, but enough to hold fifty guests or so, thus keeping the interior of the house from getting too crowded.

And, just as Belinda had promised, the weather was perfect. The clouds and rain from the day before had disappeared as if they'd never existed, and the sky was cheerfully blue, even as the sun began to slide toward the horizon, toward the last sunset of the year.

His last sunset as a demon, if all went well.

Because he now knew beyond a shadow of a doubt that Belinda cared for him. Although she'd tried so hard to be quiet, to avoid doing anything that might wake him up, he'd still heard her weeping the night before, had known that she cried silently and hopelessly into her pillow.

She'd been crying over him, he was sure. She thought he was about to disappear from her life forever.

Well, he had a little surprise planned for her. This would be the night when he declared his love and told her there was absolutely no reason for them to be apart. He would be able to stay here and have Belinda at his side.

For just the briefest moment, he thought of Beelzebub, of his veiled threats, but it seemed the other demon must have given up the entire enterprise as hopeless, since Asmodeus hadn't detected the slightest hint of his erstwhile partner-in-crime's presence. No, he'd probably realized there was no use interfering in a venture that Asmodeus and God Himself had embarked on together, and so was probably back down in Hell, sulking that —once again—things hadn't gone his way.

He could sulk all he liked. All the pouting in this world or the next wouldn't change what Asmodeus knew to be an incontrovertible truth, which was that he and Belinda Carson were meant to be together.

Absolutely nothing could change that.

Nothing.

Beelzebub sat in his rented car and reflected bitterly that it was clear the English language didn't contain enough curse words, since he'd already run through all of them and still hadn't sufficiently vented his ire. After biding his time for the past several days, waiting until Asmodeus and Belinda Carson at last weren't together for five minutes, she got in her small SUV and drove away. He'd followed her, only to see her go to a small, neat, cottage-style house a block from the ocean. The grandmother's house, he realized, since he'd made a note of where all her relatives lived, just in case an opportunity to accost her at any of those places presented itself.

She was inside for quite a while, more than half an hour. When she emerged at last, he was annoyed to see that she had her grandmother with her. The two women embraced, and then Belinda immediately got in her car and drove off, heading east.

All he could do was follow her, making sure to keep enough distance and other vehicles between them that she wouldn't notice the white Camry a few car lengths back. This maneuvering wasn't as easy as he'd hoped, given the volume of vehicles on the road, but he managed to tail her into West Hollywood, where she went into a florist's shop first. Again, since she wasn't alone, he couldn't go up and accost her, tell her whose bed she'd been sharing for the past week.

And although she walked the block from the florist's to a discreet storefront whose sign read "Aux Delices" in curly script, he again was denied any chance to approach her, since she was on her phone the entire time. All right, he supposed he could have gone up to her and taken the phone from her hand, but if Asmodeus had been on the other end of that call, he might have heard his fellow demon's voice or been able to still sense his presence somehow, and then the game would have been over.

Beelzebub hoped he might be able to go up to her once she was done at Aux Delices, but again, the universe intervened. She walked out of the storefront and had a companion with her this time, a slight woman in her early forties with short-cropped dark hair and the most enthusiastic hand gestures he'd seen on this side of the Atlantic. They talked all the way back to Belinda's Mercedes SUV, at which point the dark-haired woman made a few more gestures, laughed, and then headed back to her shop.

The only thing Beelzebub could do at that point was follow Belinda again, and pray that she might be a little more approachable wherever her next stop might be. However, as she continued into Hollywood and then began to wind her way up into the hills, he realized she could be heading to only one place.

Asmodeus's house.

Scowling ferociously, he took his foot off the gas and let his rental car slowly drop away so he could turn down a side street and pretend it had been his destination all along. Once she'd disappeared from sight, he cast a jaundiced eye at the digital clock on the dashboard. Four fifteen. A little less than eight hours to put a stop to this thing once and for all.

As he sat there, parked at the curb in front of an ostentatious edifice of glass and concrete, his frown slowly morphed into a smile. He had one more chance to get this right.

Good thing that Asmodeus had already invited him to his party….

CHAPTER SEVENTEEN

ALL WAS ORGANIZED CHAOS AT ALLAN'S house. Or rather, everything seemed to be going exactly the way it should, but between the crew from the party rental place setting up the pavilion in the backyard and Tori's assistant Evangeline supervising her own crew in getting all the floral arrangements set out exactly where they were supposed to be, things seemed a lot more out of control than they actually were.

Allan gave me a kiss on the cheek as he let me in, and I did my best to smile up at him. I had to pretend everything was fine, that my heart wasn't breaking a little every time I looked in his direction. Like me, he was still in casual clothing—jeans and a dark long-sleeved T-shirt—but I had no doubt that he had some custom-tailored piece of perfection hanging in his closet, just waiting for the moment when he could debut it at the party.

"Sorry I'm a little late," I said. "Traffic was heavier than I expected. It looks like everyone in L.A. is heading somewhere this afternoon."

"It's fine," he replied. "Since you showed me Tori's notes on the photos you sent her of the house, I basically knew where everything needed to go. Not that either crew really needed much input from me—they all seem to know what they're doing."

Which was exactly why I'd hired this particular caterer and florist for Allan's party. I knew they would get the job done in a spectacular fashion and with a minimum of fuss. "And you didn't have a problem getting your cleaning crew to come in, even though it wasn't their regular day?"

He shook his head. "None at all. I'm not saying there weren't any bribes involved, but they were done around three." His hand rested on my arm. "It's all going to be great."

Intellectually, I knew that, but I was restless, probably because I was all too aware of time passing and would rather have been busy supervising the workers. At least that way, I could put off any awkward conversations with Allan.

If there even were going to be any. He looked completely relaxed and at ease, as if he had already envisioned how all this was going to go, as though he knew he'd just have to give me a casual goodbye and "best of luck" at the end of the night, possibly with a small kiss on the cheek as a way of saying thank you for the fun times we'd had together.

His expression seemed to indicate that he hadn't suffered any misgivings about our impending separation. No, breakup. Might as well call it what it was. A separation implied there was a chance the parties involved had a possibility of getting back together, while I knew there was no hope of a reconciliation for Allan and me. There couldn't be.

"Well, I'm going to head outside and take a look at everything, just in case," I told him.

He opened his mouth, as though he planned to tell me that really wasn't necessary. However, his phone rang just then, and he frowned briefly as he retrieved it from his pocket. After glancing at the screen, he said, "I should probably take this."

"Please do," I replied. "I've got work to do anyway."

Thankful for the reprieve, I headed out through the sliding glass doors and went to inspect the pavilion. It wasn't overly large, but elegant, with its built-in clear plastic windows and scalloped trim. Because the night promised to be mild, it was being kept mostly open. Already several members of the crew from the party rental company were putting out the tables and chairs Allan had ordered, while two others were beginning the process of stringing the gilded star-shaped paper lanterns—each holding a battery-powered votive—that would hang from the ceiling.

There was still a long way to go before the pavilion was completely ready, but I could see things taking shape and knew it would all come together in just the way we'd imagined. Even so, I stood off to the side for a long while, pretending to scrutinize their work, although I knew the real reason I remained outside was so I could avoid talking to Allan. As much as I wanted to be around him, doing so was painful as well, since I could only think of how I'd never get to hear the sound of his voice after this evening, would never get to see that wicked glint in his blue eyes or watch the casually graceful way he entered a room and somehow took command of it.

I did my best to tell myself that I was probably being melodramatic. Yes, we couldn't stay romantically involved. Still, in some ways, Los Angeles wasn't that big a town, and there was probably a decent chance that our paths would cross again at some point, whether because of a party I was planning, or because we simply happened to be invited to the same events.

Just please, God, I thought as I showed the foreman of the setup crew where the closest outdoor outlet was located so they could plug in the lights, *please, if he gets engaged to someone, don't have her hire me as a wedding planner. I don't think I could take that.*

Of course, if something so improbable were to actually occur, I'd find a way to gently suggest that it was probably a good idea if they found a different event coordinator.

There was a minor moment of drama when the box that contained the floating lights which were supposed to drift gracefully across the swimming pool went missing, but that turned out to be a false alarm, since they turned up eventually, hidden behind the box that had held the tablecloths for the bar-height tables in the pavilion. I went this way and that, directing traffic, making sure everything ended up in its intended place, until at last Allan emerged from the house.

"It's nearly seven o'clock," he said. "You should probably get changed."

I realized he had traded his jeans and black T-shirt for an exquisitely cut steel gray suit with the faintest blue pinstripe, a color scheme echoed in the gray and black and blue tie he wore. As I'd thought, he looked amazing, and as I allowed myself to admire his appearance, I couldn't be sure whether I was simply lusting after him or just immensely saddened that I'd never get to wake up next to him again, would never be able to watch him bend down and scratch my cat behind the ears.

Funny how someone could become such an integral part of your life after such a short amount of time.

"Right," I said, hoping he hadn't noticed the way I was staring at him. "I'll just run upstairs and get myself put together."

"And I'll hold down the fort," he replied, then added after a brief glance around the patio, "although it looks as though all the work has been done."

He was right—the pavilion glowed from within like some luminous shell, and more lights sailed on the calm, blue-green waters of the swimming pool. Bistro-style lights hung above the patio, and candles flickered from within the heavy blown glass vases of the flower arrangements Tori and her team had set out on the tables. Inside the house itself, all was in readiness as well, the recessed lights dimmed to a level that brought out the flames in the hearth and the votives in the floral decorations that graced the tables and several dim corners. Honestly, the place looked breathtaking, and I allowed myself a moment of professional pride at what we'd accomplished in such a short planning period, even while I had to almost physically push back the sadness that wanted to overwhelm me.

"Fifteen minutes," I promised, and then went upstairs. I'd put my things in one of the secondary bathrooms on that level, rather than in the master bath; I figured that was a subtle way of indicating I didn't have a place in Allan's bedroom any longer. He'd probably noticed but hadn't commented, which seemed to tell me he understood and had no reason to argue with the gesture.

I shut the bathroom door and got out of my jeans and long-sleeved T-shirt, then retrieved my makeup bag from my purse and methodically went about giving myself a proper evening look, with liner and heavier mascara and a darker lipstick than I normally wore. Since I was wearing a cocktail dress and not a real evening gown like I had worn to the Magic Castle, I'd already decided to leave my hair down, although I plugged in my big-barrel curling iron and touched up the waves I'd set early in the morning.

My dress was a dead-simple black sheath with a low V-cut neck—no frills, no ornamentation at all. I'd bought it to wear to those weddings where the bride preferred her guests to wear dark colors, figuring it was so plain that it couldn't possibly allow me to stand out from the crowd. However, I had to admit I wasn't quite as unobtrusive as I would have liked, partly because my red hair tended to attract attention anyway, and partly because I'd placed the aquamarine pendant Allan had bought me around my neck, and it sparkled like crazy against all that black.

Maybe I shouldn't have worn it. But the necklace was definitely the nicest piece of jewelry I owned, and I knew I wanted to show him that I appreciated the gift and would continue to wear it whenever I had a chance. I had to hope he wouldn't read anything more into the gesture than what I'd intended.

A glance at my watch told me it was now almost seven-thirty. The party was supposed to start at eight, but sad experience had told me there were always those few who liked to show up early, possibly because they miscalculated...or possibly because they wanted to see if they could catch their host off guard.

Well, no chance of that happening at this particular party. As I'd come upstairs to change, Marcelle and her assistant had been putting the final finishing touches on the hors d'oeuvres laid out on the dining room table—now pushed up against one wall to facilitate flow— but otherwise, the food was ready to go, and so was the bar, set up to the right of the dining room table. The waiters had arrived, and everything was decorated just so. No one was going to catch me with my pants down.

When I descended the stairs, I saw that Allan was standing next to the bar, chatting with the bartender as he mixed up a martini. However, he turned as soon as I entered the dining room and sent me an admiring smile.

"You look wonderful."

I smiled and murmured a thank-you, even though I didn't really believe him. My reflection in the bathroom mirror had looked a little pale and tired, despite my careful application of makeup. "So do you," I said.

"Would you like a drink, ma'am?" the bartender asked.

Ma'am. Please—the guy couldn't have been more than a year or two younger than I was, if even that. But I knew he was only doing his job, and so I let it slide. "Just a club soda and lime, please."

Allan looked actually offended by my choice of drink. "It's New Year's Eve, you know."

"Yes, I do know," I replied, then took the club soda from the bartender. "And it's early. I'm not saying I won't have a drink later in the evening, but I have to watch it, since I'm driving home after this."

As soon as those words left my mouth, Allan's brows drew together in a frown. Was he somehow surprised by that particular revelation? Hadn't he stopped to think about the evening's logical conclusion?

It seemed that he hadn't, because he said, "You don't need to run off like that."

"Yes, I do," I responded, trying not to sound too upset about that eventuality. "The clock will strike midnight, and we'll all turn into pumpkins, remember?"

"It doesn't have to be that way," he said in an undertone, and placed one hand on my elbow so he could guide me away from the bartender, who'd been watching our exchange with a half-curious expression on his face. "We could—"

Whatever he'd been about to say, it was interrupted by the sound of the doorbell. "I'll get that," I said at once, thankful for whichever early bird had prevented Allan from telling me something I really didn't want to hear. If he was having second thoughts about our little arrangement, then I definitely needed to make sure I did whatever I could to stay out of his orbit during the course of the evening.

A cowardly part of me thought that the logical thing to do would be to slip out quietly long before midnight rolled around, but I knew I wouldn't do that to him. All he had was me and the waiters and bartenders to keep things going, since Marcelle and her assistant had packed their things and left while I was primping in the bathroom. What if an emergency came up? Professional pride dictated that I stay here to make sure everything went smoothly, even if I now had to do my best to dodge Allan so he wouldn't utter some truths that could very well put him in danger.

The new arrivals turned out to be an actress I vaguely recognized from a now-canceled sitcom, along with her husband and a couple of hangers-on who might have been friends or simply her personal assistants. I was so relieved to see them that I was probably a little more effusive in my welcomes than the actress had expected; she sent me a curious sidelong look, but then perked up as soon as she saw Allan—and the bartender. She kissed Allan on the cheek and told him how amazing the house looked, and then she and her group started requesting drinks, and it seemed we were off to the races.

Not long after that, more people arrived, and more...and more. By the time eight-thirty rolled around, the house was full, and people had begun to spill out onto the patio and fill up the pavilion as well. I moved from one spot to the other, checking to make sure that trays of hors d'oeuvres were replenished, that both the bartender indoors and the one stationed out in the pavilion didn't run out of anything they needed. Technically, that was the job of the hired waiters, but flitting around kept me occupied and well away from Allan, which was of course the reason for my activity in the first place.

A little before eleven, a newcomer appeared, apparently someone Allan knew well, because he spoke to the man— who was good-looking in a sort of pretty-boy, frat-guy way, although he wore an improbable blue plaid suit and a bow tie—for a few minutes before the stranger made his way over to the bar. I'd been in the process of setting more bamboo skewers in the silver cup to the right of one of the hors d'oeuvres trays, and when I looked up, the strange man was staring at me with an odd intensity in his hazel eyes.

For some reason, a strange little shiver ran down my back. I didn't like the guy, whoever he was. However, since Allan obviously knew him, I offered him a smile before I hurried out to the patio, squeezing through the people crowded around the fire table before I made my way to the pavilion.

I didn't see anyone I knew out there, which was exactly how I wanted it. Just as I'd done at least a hundred times so far that evening, I checked my watch. Eleven forty. Twenty minutes before all this was over, although I knew I'd stay here past midnight, if for no other reason than to help supervise the clean-up after the party-goers headed for home. Already I'd noticed that things had begun to thin out, probably because many of the attendees had other parties to go to. In fact, I was surprised to see that the pavilion was already deserted.

Well, it was starting to get cold, despite the gas heaters that had been set up everywhere. They could only do so much, after all, especially if you were wearing a flimsy cocktail gown like the dress I had on.

I glanced over at the bartender, who looked a little awkward, as if he wasn't quite sure what to do with himself. "It looks like the party's moved inside, Luis," I said. "Why don't you go and help Curt? I'm sure he could use some assistance with getting all the champagne ready for the midnight toast."

"Sure, Ms. Carson," Luis said, and hurried out, clearly glad to be sent back inside where it was far warmer and more comfortable.

And I needed to do exactly the same thing, even though I privately thought it was a shame that no one would be out in this lovely tent to toast the new year. As I turned to go, however, I saw that someone was blocking my way.

Allan.

"I was hoping I'd get a chance to talk to you alone," he said, moving closer.

Damn it. I hadn't checked to see what he was

doing when I'd come out here, and now I was fairly trapped.

"I don't know what we have to talk about," I replied, in what I hoped was a brisk, no-nonsense voice. "I mean, we both knew how this evening was going to end."

Now he stood very close. If this had been any other evening, I would have welcomed his near-ness, would have closed the gap between us so I could feel his arms go around me. This time, however, I just wanted to get away before he said something he would regret—if he was even given the chance to regret it.

"What if I don't want it to end like that?" he asked softly.

I pressed my lips together. They felt dry and cold, despite the lipstick I'd applied earlier that evening. Maybe it had eventually worn off as the hours crept along. "It needs to end like this," I told him, my tone firm. Or rather, I wanted to sound firm, but even I could hear the faint quaver in my voice. Despite that audible sign of weak-ness, I took a breath and continued. "Life is going to be crazy for both of us next year. We don't have time for this."

A frown touched his brow, but then his mouth lifted in a faint smile. "You don't have time for love?"

No. He couldn't say that word—couldn't even

think it. "This isn't love," I said, feeling my heart wrench as I uttered the lie. "It's just…infatuation."

His hands reached for mine, but I pulled them away. Mouth thinning, he said, "You don't really believe that, do you?"

"It doesn't matter what I believe," I told him. "I just know—I know that you don't want to be with me, Allan. It's dangerous."

"'Dangerous'?" he repeated, eyebrows lifting. "Darling, how could you ever be dangerous?"

"I can't tell you that," I responded. Oh, how stupid that sounded! But he could never know the truth. I'd already said too much. "Just—let me go. Find someone else. It's safer."

Before he could reply, I'd pushed past him and had begun to run across the grass, the spike heels of the strappy sandals I wore sinking into the soft ground. I stumbled but regained my balance, and hurried inside. My purse was upstairs, and I had to retrieve it, but I hoped that Allan would realize this was a lost cause and would let me go, wouldn't want to make a scene in front of his guests.

I slowed to a more decorous pace once I was inside, although I still hurried upstairs as quickly as I could and went to the bathroom, where I'd stowed my clothes and my purse in the vanity under the dual sinks. Once they were in my shaking hands, I turned and prepared to flee down the hallway.

Except that my escape route was blocked. It wasn't Allan standing there, however, but the stranger in the blue plaid suit. He smiled, although there was nothing pleasant about that smile, and then said, "Hi, Belinda. I was hoping I would have a chance to talk to you."

INTERLUDE

In moments like this, mortals would often say, "There is a God!" However, since Beelzebub was already aware of God's existence, he could only an utter silent thank-you to the universe for putting Belinda Carson in his path.

She stared at him, wild-eyed. Most of the lip color she'd been wearing had worn off, and she looked pale and not at all like the polished woman in the photograph on her website. "Who are you?" she said. "How do you know who I am?"

"That's not important," he replied. "However, if you need a name, it's Ben. Benjamin Blake."

"The man who wanted help with his New Year's party," she said slowly as she apparently made the connection in her mind. "Only I have a feeling there was no party at all."

"Very good, Belinda," he said. "No, there

wasn't a party. I just needed a chance to talk to you."

Her fingers tightened around the handle of the large black bag she carried. He could see the edge of some folded blue jeans peeking out past the zipper, and so he guessed she'd been retrieving her belongings so she could get out of here. Had she and Asmodeus quarreled? Maybe it would be better to simply allow her to go on her way.

But no—he couldn't risk a future reconciliation. He had to make sure she would never, ever want to have anything to do with Allan D'Alessandro again.

"This really isn't a good time—" she began, but he only smiled and stood his ground.

"What I have to say will only take a moment. You're involved with Allan, right?"

Her blue-green eyes—almost the same color as the glittering pendant she wore—narrowed. "I don't see how that's any concern of yours."

"Oh, but it is," Beelzebub said. "You see, he and I are…business associates. We've known each other a long time…a *very* long time."

"And?"

Clearly, she wasn't terribly impressed by that piece of information. "And it might interest you to know that he isn't who he claims to be."

She planted her free hand on her hip, but something about her seemed almost wary, as if she'd somehow guessed at what he planned to tell her. Which couldn't be correct. There was no way she could have guessed at Asmodeus's true identity. "What, he's not an entertainment agent after all?"

"Not precisely," Beelzebub replied, even as he realized she'd only been thinking about the simple lies he'd told about his occupation and nothing more. "No, I meant that he's not human."

Both of her well-arched brows lifted, and she shot him the sort of look usually reserved for the sorts of people who started babbling conspiracy theories about chemtrails and 5G wireless. "Oh, really? So, what is he?"

"A demon," Beelzebub said. "His true name is Asmodeus. You might have heard of him."

"Asmodeus," she repeated, her tone flat. "Right. And I suppose you're Beelzebub?"

For a human, she had a quicker mind than he'd expected. "Actually, yes. So, you see, he can't enter into a long-term relationship with a human. He's needed back in Hell."

"Got it." Belinda smiled at him then, although even he could recognize the falseness of that smile. "Well, you're in luck, because we just broke up. You can take him back to Hell or wherever it is you come from. Happy New Year."

She sidestepped him and headed toward the stairs. Beelzebub saw no reason to stop her, not when she'd just delivered the happy news that she and Asmodeus were no longer together. And since she clearly hadn't believed a single word he'd said, he saw no reason to remove any memory of him from her mind. She'd dismiss him as another L.A. whack job, and that would be the end of it.

Unfortunately, she didn't get very far, because a few feet away from the head of the stairs, she came to an abrupt halt. Asmodeus stood there, eyes glittering with anger as he looked past her to see his erstwhile friend standing farther down the hallway.

"What did he say to you?" he thundered.

As soon as Belinda fled, Asmodeus knew he needed to give pursuit. However, he'd only just stepped inside the house when he was accosted by Terrence O'Neill, the basketball player he was hoping to sign. Terry had obviously had more than enough to drink by that point, and had seized his arm with one oversized hand and waxed rhapsodic about the party, the booze, the women who'd been invited. Although he didn't much care whether he alienated the man or not, Asmodeus knew a display of demonic strength in getting rid of the mortal wasn't a very good idea, and he'd had to waste several precious minutes before he could disentangle himself and continue his search for his missing love.

She must have gone upstairs. It only made sense, since he knew she'd secreted her belongings in the second guest bathroom on that floor. Actually, that was a good thing, because up there, he'd have the opportunity to speak to her in private. Yes, there was always the chance that one of his guests might venture up there looking for a bathroom, but by that point in the evening, there weren't too many partygoers who were probably capable of navigating the staircase.

As he emerged in the upstairs hall, he saw at once that Belinda wasn't alone. No, Beelzebub had cornered her just outside the bathroom. Her expression was simultaneously annoyed, puzzled, and amused...which probably meant only one thing.

Beelzebub had told her the truth about him... and now Asmodeus would have to do his best to salvage the situation.

If that was even possible.

Her gaze went past the other demon and met his. If she was surprised by the anger in his voice as he'd asked the question, she didn't show it. Sounding amused, she said, "Your 'friend' just tried to tell me you were a demon. I think you'd better get him an Uber—he's obviously had way too much to drink."

"I haven't drunk anything at all," Beelzebub retorted. "And he *is* a demon—well, technically, one of the princes of Hell. But he's definitely not human."

"He looks human," she said, her tone calm— too calm, really. It was the sort of voice used on hysterical children or mental patients in order to get them to quiet down.

"He's not," Beelzebub said. "And neither am I."

His hands moved, and gouts of fire jetted forth from his fingertips. Without thinking, Asmodeus raised his hands as well, blocking the fire—and also making sure it didn't touch the pristine white walls or polished bamboo floor of the hallway.

However, the other demon's motivation hadn't been destruction. No, he'd only wanted to make sure Asmodeus was forced to use his powers, to make a physical demonstration that proved he absolutely was not human.

"You see?" Beelzebub said triumphantly. "Could a human do that?"

For a long moment, Belinda only stood there, her face pale, eyes wide. Unbelieving? He couldn't tell for sure. Then she said, "No, I suppose not." Another pause, and her gaze met his. "Allan, was he telling me the truth? You're…you're not human?"

He could attempt to lie, but that exchange of fire was clearly something no human could have managed—at least, not without a Hollywood pyrotechnics team, and that was one of the few things he hadn't arranged for this party. "No," he said sadly. "I'm not human. But that doesn't mean I don't love you."

She didn't respond right away, which he had to take as a very bad sign. Fighting the sinking feeling in his stomach, he turned to glare at the demon who used to be his best friend, his brother. "You didn't need to do this," he said, hands knotting into fists.

"Yes, I did," Beelzebub said. "This isn't your place, Asmodeus, and you know it."

Asmodeus' gaze moved back to Belinda, who stood there, white-faced and silent. Not afraid, exactly…almost curious? He didn't want to misread her expression, not when so much was riding on this. "And you don't know what you're talking about, Beelzebub."

"Neither do you," Beelzebub sneered. "You've lost, Asmodeus. See you in Hell."

And then he disappeared.

Belinda blinked at the place where the demon had been standing only the second before. Again, she was silent, as though doing her best to absorb what she'd just seen. She took a step forward, then another.

Asmodeus stared at her, not sure what she intended. Surely if she was afraid, she would be retreating from him, not coming closer and closer.

But....

Now only a few inches separated them. She reached out and touched him, ran a hand over the shoulder of his suit. "You feel human." Another blink, and she gazed up into his face. "You look human."

"This is the guise I wear in this world," he told her, figuring that, since all was lost anyway, he might as well not hold anything back.

"So, you don't really look like this?"

"It's more complicated than that." He hesitated, then went on, "This is what I look like as a human. I can't really look like anyone else except this. But when I'm in Hell...when I need to frighten the prisoners...then I look like this."

For just the briefest moment, he allowed himself to change, to let his human appearance slip away so she could see him for the fallen angel he was, scaly of skin, with horns and a tail and enormous black bat wings. She gasped and took a step back—but she didn't flee, didn't faint or scream or react in any of the other ways that might have been expected of someone confronted by such a nightmarish apparition.

No, to his astonishment, she began to laugh.

He stared at her, wondering if being shown his

true self had somehow broken her mind. But then she put a hand to her mouth and shook her head, and gasped, "Oh, I know it isn't funny...only it is."

Resuming his human appearance, he said, "You'll have to let me in on the joke, then."

Her lips were still quirked, but she nodded.

"I think you'd better sit down."

CHAPTER EIGHTEEN

W E WENT IN A LLAN'S ROOM AND CLOSED THE door. My gaze went briefly to the clock on the nightstand. Eleven fifty-five. Strange how my entire world—entire universe, really—had just been set on its head and spun around a few thousand times.

He wasn't human. He was a demon. Which meant....

"*You and all the daughters of your line will never know the love of a man,*" I said then, and he stared at me in confusion. No doubt he was thinking that I'd completely lost it.

"Come again?"

"It's a curse," I explained. "A curse that was placed on the Carson family three hundred years ago. My great-to-the-umpteenth-power grand-mother was knocking boots with a married man, and the man's wife—who just happened to be a witch—put a curse on her. That was why I had to break up with you—if you loved me, something terrible would happen to you. Leaving was the only way I could keep you safe."

He scrubbed a hand through his heavy hair, obviously doing his best to put the pieces together. Looking at him, I could only be astonished at how human he appeared, how human he acted.

But he wasn't. And, I realized as an improbable joy began to spread through me, his inhuman nature might be the one thing that would save us.

He asked something I wasn't expecting. "Your great-whatever grandmother was also a witch?"

"Yes. How did you know?"

"Because a witch can only hex another witch. Just part of the rules." His eyes glinted. "So, I suppose you're a witch, too?"

"A very minor one," I said modestly. "How else do you think I manage to always have perfect weather for the events I plan?"

He chuckled. "Ah, that makes sense now." A pause, and he went on, "And the curse hasn't struck me down—even though I love you—because I'm not human."

"Exactly," I said. Maybe it was strange to be happy that the man I loved had turned out to be demon from Hell, but honestly, it was the only way to make this whole thing work. The curse had been designed to make sure no Carson witch was ever beloved by a mortal man, but it sure as hell had never said anything about demons.

Allan stepped closer and took my hands in his. How warm his fingers were, how welcome... how human. I'd seen just about every inch of him, and he looked perfectly human to me. Only on the surface, it seemed, but that was good enough for me.

Voice very quiet, he asked, "And you—do you love me?"

I shut my eyes for a moment. All my instincts were saying I shouldn't tell him the truth, but I knew that was only years of conditioning talking. Allan wasn't at risk from the curse; it couldn't touch him.

"Yes, Allan," I said softly. "I do love you. I love you like I never thought I would ever love anyone."

He pulled me to him and we kissed, mouths hungry. The earth seemed to shake ever so slightly under my feet, and I startled, wondering if we were experiencing an earthquake, albeit a minor one.

"Not an earthquake," he said after we'd pulled apart. "That was just me becoming mortal."

I stared at him, not quite comprehending

what he'd just said. "Wait...you're not a demon anymore?"

"No," he replied with a smile. "It was a little bargain I had with Someone very important."

Oh, no. Had I just ruined everything by declaring my love for him? "But if you're human, the curse will strike you down!" I cried, fear flooding through my body.

"No, it won't," came a new voice, and I turned to see an elderly gentleman in a brown tweed coat standing over by the window.

I blinked in shock at this new apparition. We'd closed the door and locked it behind us, and the sliding doors were still firmly shut as well. Had the old man been hiding in here the whole time?

Somehow, though, I knew the reality of the situation wasn't quite that simple.

"You see," He went on, apparently using my stupefaction as an invitation to continue, "the curse was broken as soon as Asmodeus here declared his love for you. A Carson witch was beloved by a demon, not a man, and that destroyed the hex's hold over you and your family. Once that happened, it didn't matter whether he remained a demon or became a mortal."

Allan took my hand in his and faced the stranger. "And it's done, then? I can stay here?"

The old man smiled. "Yes, my boy. This world

is now yours. Enjoy it—and be glad of what you did this evening by ridding this young woman and her family of the curse that has plagued them for generations." A pause, and he added, "It's a minute until midnight—just enough time to get yourselves some champagne. Happy New Year."

He blinked out of existence just as the demon Beelzebub had not five minutes earlier. I stared at the spot where the old man had been standing and stammered, "Was—was he a demon, too?"

"Oh, no," Allan replied. Face solemn, he pointed upward with his free hand. "His is a much higher authority."

My brain took a minute to process that particular piece of information. Was he saying…?

"Yes, that's who He is." Allan's fingers tightened on mine. "And He gave us some very good advice."

"He did?"

"To go downstairs and get some champagne."

I managed to nod, head still swimming. Good thing I'd been drinking club soda religiously all evening, or I would have been even more of a mess than I was.

Still holding my hand, Allan led me downstairs. The waiters were going around with trays of champagne, and he snagged two flutes and handed one to me, keeping the other for himself. Someone had gone into the living room to turn on the television mounted to the wall above the fireplace, and the screen showed the glittering ball in Times Square.

"Ten!" one of the partygoers shouted out, and everyone chimed in.

"Nine...eight...seven...six...five...four... three...two...one! Happy New Year!"

We all raised our glasses and drank. My heart was pounding, and I knew it was going to take me a while to process everything that happened during those past few minutes, but I did know one thing. I had Allan—Asmodeus—at my side, and that was never going to change.

"A new year...and a new life," he whispered, and bent to kiss me, his mouth tart with champagne. I pressed myself against him, even as I heard everyone around us cheer. Well, I supposed it probably was sort of a spectacle for them to see their host passionately embracing the event planner.

We pulled apart, and I looked around at everyone, my cheeks flushed with excitement... and maybe a little embarrassment. That didn't matter, though. I knew I was in the place where I was meant to be.

"Stay with me tonight?" he whispered in my ear, and I nodded. But he wasn't done. "Stay with me forever?" he asked.

"Forever and always," I told him...my

charming demon, the one who had changed my world and broken the curse that had ruled my life.

Forever was no longer something to be feared. We would make forever our own, Allan and I.

The Devil You Know series continues with Beelzebub's story in *A Wing and a Prayer*.

ALSO BY CHRISTINE POPE

PROJECT DEMON HUNTERS

(Paranormal Romance)

Unquiet Souls

Unbound Spirits

Unholy Ground

Unseen Voices

Unmarked Graves

Unbroken Vows

THE DEVIL YOU KNOW

(Paranormal Romance)

Sympathy for the Devil

Charmed, I'm Sure

A Wing and a Prayer

THE WITCHES OF CANYON ROAD*

(Paranormal Romance)

Hidden Gifts

Darker Paths

Mysterious Ways

A Canyon Road Christmas

Demon Born

An Ill Wind

Higher Ground

Haunted Hearts

THE WITCHES OF CLEOPATRA HILL*

(Paranormal Romance)

Darkangel

Darknight

Darkmoon

Sympathetic Magic

Protector

Spellbound

A Cleopatra Hill Christmas

Impractical Magic

Strange Magic

The Arrangement

Defender

Bad Blood

Deep Magic

Darktide

THE DJINN WARS*

(Paranormal Romance)

Chosen

Taken

Fallen

Broken

Forsaken

Forbidden

Awoken

Illuminated

Stolen

Forgotten

Driven

Unspoken

THE WATCHERS TRILOGY*

(Paranormal Romance)

Falling Dark

Dead of Night

Rising Dawn

THE SEDONA FILES*

(Paranormal Romance)

Bad Vibrations

Desert Hearts

Angel Fire

Star Crossed

Falling Angels

Enemy Mine

TALES OF THE LATTER KINGDOMS*

(Fantasy Romance)

All Fall Down

Dragon Rose

Binding Spell

Ashes of Roses

One Thousand Nights

Threads of Gold

The Wolf of Harrow Hall

Moon Dance

The Song of the Thrush

THE GAIAN CONSORTIUM SERIES*

(Science Fiction Romance)

Beast (free prequel novella)

Blood Will Tell

Breath of Life

The Gaia Gambit

The Mandala Maneuver

The Titan Trap

The Zhore Deception

The Refugee Ruse

STANDALONE TITLES

Hearts on Fire

Taking Dictation

Night Music

Golden Heart

* Indicates a completed series

ABOUT THE AUTHOR

USA Today bestselling author Christine Pope has been writing stories ever since she commandeered her family's Smith-Corona typewriter back in grade school. Her work includes paranormal romance, fantasy romance, and science fiction/space opera romance. She makes her home in Arizona.

Christine Pope on the Web:
www.christinepope.com

facebook.com/ChristinePopeAuthor

twitter.com/ChristineJPope

pinterest.com/ChristineJPope